AN IMPROPER ENCOUNTER

He stretched his arm along the back of the sofa and leaned even closer. "Don't worry. I remember the things that are important, Miss Arabella Swann."

Good heavens! A rush of heat surged through her.

"Speaking of important things," he continued, "who is Raphael?"

Raphael? She blinked at him.

He shrugged as if it were of no importance, but the line of his strong jaw tightened. "Raphael. Your aunt mentioned him when we sat down. She hoped you would think I was as good as he."

Arabella resisted a fleeting urge to invent a fictitious beau to insert between herself and the Duke of St. Fell, the way one would throw a hunk of meat at a tiger to distract it, so one could escape out the door. "He is the duke in Aunt Ophelia's Minerva Press romance," she said.

"And am I as good as Raphael?" the duke asked in a voice that was as close to a purr as a man could get.

His hand was barely twelve inches away from her shoulder. Ten, if she swayed toward him. It was quite improper.

BOOK YOUR PLACE ON OUR WEBSITE AND MAKE THE READING CONNECTION!

We've created a customized website just for our very special readers, where you can get the inside scoop on everything that's going on with Zebra, Pinnacle and Kensington books.

When you come online, you'll have the exciting opportunity to:

- View covers of upcoming books

- Read sample chapters

- Learn about our future publishing schedule (listed by publication month *and author*)

- Find out when your favorite authors will be visiting a city near you

- Search for and order backlist books from our online catalog

- Check out author bios and background information

- Send e-mail to your favorite authors

- Meet the Kensington staff online

- Join us in weekly chats with authors, readers and other guests

- Get writing guidelines

- AND MUCH MORE!

**Visit our website at
http://www.kensingtonbooks.com**

COURTING TROUBLE

Nonnie St. George

ZEBRA BOOKS
KENSINGTON PUBLISHING CORP.
http://www.kensingtonbooks.com

ZEBRA BOOKS are published by

Kensington Publishing Corp.
850 Third Avenue
New York, NY 10022

All Kensington titles, imprints and distributed lines are available at special quantity discounts for bulk purchases for sales
promotion, premiums, fund-raising, educational or institutional
use.

Special book excerpts or customized printings can also be created to fit specific needs. For details, write or phone the office
of the Kensington Special Sales Manager: Kensington Publishing Corp., 850 Third Avenue, New York, NY 10022. Attn.
Special Sales Department. Phone: 1-800-221-2647.

Zebra and the Z logo Reg. U.S. Pat. & TM Off.

First Printing: May 2004
10 9 8 7 6 5 4 3 2 1

Printed in the United States of America

I would like to thank Kate Duffy, my clever, kind, nice, and good editor, for not giving into temptation and beating me to death with a stick. I'm not admitting she would have been justified. I'm just saying thank you. My deepest thanks as well to my family, and my fellow writers Claire Huffaker and Candice Vetter, all of whom also showed great stick restraint. I would also like to thank my friends on the Patricia Veryan list for their encouragement and my fellow members of The Beau Monde for their help in matters Regency. All errors are mine, of course. Some of them on purpose.

I would like to dedicate this book to my mother, May, who always made a point of letting me read whatever I wanted when I was growing up, except The Betsy, and she was absolutely right about that. Here they are, Mom. Not quite Nick and Nora, but at least no one got beaten with a stick.

Chapter 1

"It isn't that I do not appreciate all of the wonders of London we have seen since we have arrived." Arabella Swann licked the last of her strawberry ice from her spoon and decided that Gunter's confectionary was indisputably the top London wonder to date. She leaned back against the carriage squabs with a satisfied sigh. "But we will never find husbands if Papa keeps declining our invitations. The party at the Carrs' tomorrow would have been perfect. Aunt Ophelia says that Mrs. Carr has invited thirteen eligible gentlemen." She didn't care if she sounded sulky. She was sulky! Papa was being completely unreasonable. As usual. She wedged her empty bowl and spoon on top of Diana's and handed them through the window to the waiting footman.

"Oh, you know Papa," Diana said. "He is not suddenly going to stop being smothering just because he has finally agreed to let us come to London. He still needs time to adjust to the fact that we are determined to get ourselves married."

Arabella steadied the tower of packages on the seat between them as the carriage lurched to a start. She turned five-and-twenty in a week. If Papa took much longer adjusting, she would be obliged to adjust herself to being on the shelf.

She looked out the window. There were gentlemen all

over Berkeley Square—gentlemen strolling along the sidewalks, gentlemen chatting in the center green, gentlemen driving in carriages. London was teeming with gentlemen, yet after a fortnight in town, Papa had not let her and Diana do anything the least bit interesting. They may as well have stayed in Little Darking.

"In any event, we have met one eligible gentleman," Diana said. "Lord Belcraven."

For heaven's sake. Arabella stifled a groan. Not Lord Belcraven again. Papa had introduced them to the landlord of their Soho residence yesterday, and ever since her sister had managed to work the earl's name into every conversation. "I mean eligible gentlemen who are not fortune hunters picked out by Papa," she said.

"I know." Diana gave a small embarrassed smile. "It is just that Lord Belcraven is the first man I have ever met with whom I have felt such instantaneous affinity."

"He is the first man you have ever met who has not been a Swann," Arabella pointed out. Again.

"But he is so charming!"

Charming? Arabella snorted. The man's wit consisted of staring at Diana's shoes and turning as carrot red as his hair.

"You must at least agree he is handsome," Diana said.

"He is very handsome," Arabella agreed. If one were looking at him with the eyes of henwitted infatuation. Otherwise, Lord Belcraven was a tall red-headed scarecrow with ears that jutted out like sugar bowl handles.

Diana burst into laughter. "I know exactly what you are thinking, Arabella! You may as well shout it out loud."

Arabella turned to watch Diana, who was leaning back in her corner of the carriage and still chuckling, one golden curl peeping out from under the brim of her chip straw bonnet, a blush of pink on her round cheeks, and her eyes sparkling golden brown. Arabella's heart softened. Her little sister had not looked so radiant since Mama had died five years ago. Sweet Diana, so kind-hearted and pretty, fully deserved to be in love and happy in marriage.

Of course, in the matter of Lord Belcraven, she was completely deluded.

Arabella reached over the packages to put her hand on her sister's arm. "Diana"—she spoke slowly but firmly—"I am sure once you circulate in society and meet other gentlemen, you will realize what you feel for Lord Belcraven is nothing more than infatuation."

"I am not sure I want to meet other gentlemen," Diana said.

Arabella squeezed her sister's arm ever so slightly. "But dearest, it defeats the purpose of coming to London if you are just going to marry a man that Papa has chosen."

"Aunt Ophelia likes him."

Arabella snatched her hand back. "Aunt Ophelia likes everyone!" Aunt Ophelia liked everyone so much, they could no longer bring her out shopping. She was beginning to make the sales assistants look over their shoulders.

"I do not care!" Diana thrust out her chin in the way that meant she had made up her mind. "I want to marry Lord Belcraven!"

Arabella stared at her sister. Marriage was the most important decision a woman could make. One's entire existence was ruled by one's husband. It was hardly something to be decided on the spur of the moment, especially since it had taken them forever to convince Papa to bring them to London to choose their own husbands. It was as if meeting her very first peer had sucked her sister's wits clean out of her head. Because as a husband, the Earl of Belcraven was completely ridiculous. The only reason to marry him was so that Papa could acquire himself an earl in the family.

She took a deep breath and tried again. "You know perfectly well the only reason a penniless earl would marry a girl from a merchant family is for—"

"For my fortune, I know!" Diana bent her head and stared at her hands on her lap. "But I cannot help it. I cannot stop thinking about him, the look in his eyes, the way he smiles. He is so sweet and amiable." She lowered her voice to a whisper and shrugged, a helpless look on her face. "I think I have fallen in love with Lord Belcraven."

Hell.

"My goodness, Arabella! It isn't that bad, is it?" Diana gave her a tremulous smile.

Yes, it was. Arabella snatched the box of Gunter's bonbons from the top of the stack of packages, untied the ribbon, pried off the lid, and scoured through the confections until she found a nougat. Nothing was more soothing than nougat. She popped it into her mouth and chewed. It was an apricot nougat and it melted most satisfyingly on her tongue.

Diana cleared her throat and looked pointedly at Arabella's lap, where the bonbons were cradled.

"The nougats are mine," Arabella said, and passed over the box. She leaned back and savored the last of her bonbon. Poor Diana. Imagining herself in love at first sight with the first fortune hunter dragged home by Papa. It would be pathetic were it not so ridiculous. But still. Arabella held out her hand for the box. Things could be worse. At least Papa wasn't trying to foist a fortune hunter off on her.

August Warburton, the seventh Duke of St. Fell, took another sip of his brandy and considered the cards in his hand very carefully before pulling out the jack of clubs and tossing it onto the table. He watched with satisfaction as it beat Alward's last trump and brought home the rest of the tricks in the hand.

Alward peered down at the scorecard, and his porcine face screwed into a scowl. "You've won again."

Of course he had won again. St. Fell tossed back the rest of his brandy and signaled the waiter to bring another. No point in playing if you weren't going to win.

"There you are, St. Fell! Dash it, we have been looking everywhere for you!"

Damn. St. Fell caught his glass and righted it from where his arm had knocked it over. It was Belcraven, of course, that pestilential idiot, bellowing across White's card room, startling every man at the tables. Damned if St. Fell knew how Belcraven had ever gotten membership in White's. Clunch gambled badly. Rotten drinker, too, despite his eight years in the army—fumes alone were enough to cast him away.

But it wasn't just Belcraven jittering in the doorway, but Toby as well, tricked out in his new captain's uniform. They darted across the room to loom over the table.

Alward grabbed the deck and started shuffling. "Sit down then. Now we have enough to play whist."

Whist. St. Fell smiled. He never lost at whist.

"My brother doesn't have time to play cards," Toby said. "He has to go fetch himself a rich wife. Come on." He reached down and grabbed St. Fell's arm. "Let's pour you into the carriage."

St. Fell shook him off. He didn't need help getting in his own carriage. His brother was just being an idiot, as always.

Belcraven's eyes bulged in horror. "He isn't foxed, is he?" he squealed like a damned Methodist spinster.

Toby shrugged. "You know St. Fell."

"Shut up, Toby," St. Fell said. "Of course, I am not foxed." Not excessively. He straightened. "A man with six brothers develops a heightened capacity for the consumption of alcohol."

"Listen to him!" Belcraven wailed. "He is foxed!"

"What the devil difference does it make if I am?" St. Fell demanded.

"You cannot meet Miss Swann for the first time foxed!" Belcraven howled, his chicken-thin face growing as red as his confounded hair.

Damn. The idiot's carrying on had every man in the card room goggling at them. St. Fell pulled Belcraven down into a chair at the table.

"What the devil is wrong with him?" he asked his brother. Belcraven was his damned friend, after all.

Toby took a seat next to Belcraven. "I think he is nervous about meeting Miss Swann."

"He has already met her," St. Fell said, and a sudden chill chased up his spine as he uttered the words. He grabbed Belcraven's arm. "Good God, man! Are they that bad? You and Swann swore they were diamonds. I mean, I can keep mine up at Fairfield, but sooner or later I'll be obliged to—"

"I think Belcraven *likes* his Miss Swann." Toby laughed and shook his head.

Belcraven, incredibly, turned an even brighter shade of red and offered a weak smile.

For God's sake. St. Fell dropped Belcraven's arm and gripped the edge of the table to keep from driving his fist through the idiot's face. The dolt imagined he was in love with a woman he was marrying because her father had money. It would be pitiable if it weren't so damned annoying.

"I say," Alward said, "do you mean you and Belcraven are meeting the Swann sisters?"

St. Fell nodded.

"The daughters of Joseph Swann of Swann's Fine China?" Alward leaned forward like a pig smelling truffles. "Joseph Swann, the second wealthiest man in England?"

"He has rented Belcraven's Soho house. We met him this morning at Gabriel Carr's." St. Fell tried not to grin too triumphantly. No point rubbing Alward's nose in the fact that he was going to marry one of the richest heiresses in England. Otherwise the idiot would never pay up all the money he owed him.

"That's capital!" Alward said. "Everyone knows they have come to town to find husbands, but Swann has kept them locked up tighter than the liquor cabinet on the butler's night off."

St. Fell shrugged. Who could blame Swann? A man would be dicked in the nob to let dowries like that scamper free, not when that kind of blunt would buy him a duke for a grandson.

"So?" Alward prodded Belcraven. "What are they like?"

"Miss Diana is an angel!" Belcraven buried his head in his hands. "What if I can't think of anything clever to say? She will think I am an idiot."

"You are an idiot," St. Fell pointed out helpfully. He handed him the glass of brandy. Belcraven downed it in one gulp and put his head back in his hands. The waiter left the bottle on the table.

Alward leaned back in his chair and assumed the world-weary demeanor of the experienced ladies' man the poor dolt desperately wished he was. "I see fair Cupid has drawn his bow and unleashed his arrow to strike—"

"I'll tell you where Cupid's arrow has struck him," St. Fell said. "Right in his fat—"

"I knew you would be cynical about it," Belcraven moaned.

St. Fell gritted his teeth. "Perhaps that is because I am not a thirteen-year-old girl."

"Now, St. Fell," Toby said, "you cannot mock poor Belcraven because he has tender feelings for the woman he wants to marry."

"Not unless you were completely insensitive," Alward said. He shrugged. "Which some people might think that you were."

Toby shuffled the cards. "Only those who don't think you're an arrogant bast—"

"Shut up, Toby." St. Fell refilled the glasses.

"Perhaps you're only cynical about love because you haven't met the woman you want to marry," Belcraven said.

"Of course I haven't met the woman I want to marry," St. Fell said. "Nor am I going to until you stop blubbering enough for us to go to Swann's."

Belcraven bristled indignantly. "Dash it, you have obviously never been in love!"

"I beg your pardon?" St. Fell looked down his nose at the clod. "I have been in love more times than I can remember."

"Yes, but not *in love!*" Belcraven's voice rose to a squeak, and his face fired up like tomato again. "You know, in love with a woman that you want to marry." A cloying expression coated his face, and he gusted a sigh. "After all, falling in love with the woman you want to marry transforms a man."

For God's sake. St. Fell pinched the bridge of his nose and forced himself to take a deep breath.

"I forbid you to read any more of those damned Minerva Press novels," he said.

* * *

"I wish Papa had not thought we needed a London butler," Diana whispered.

Arabella nodded. As soon as the carriage had rolled up the front drive, Deakin had marched down the front steps of Belcraven House to supervise the unloading of the carriage by the footmen, his shoulders rigid and his mouth thinned in a disdainful expression. It almost put a damper on the pleasure of returning from shopping with a carriage full of parcels.

"Your father and your aunt await you in the south drawing room," he intoned in his usual glacial tones when they followed him into the foyer.

"I wonder why it is called the south drawing room when it is actually in the east wing of the house?" Diana said.

"The nomenclature was established by the earls of Belcraven." Deakin's tone implied that Diana had just suggested they install a pottery wheel in the middle of the foyer and dance naked around it, for heaven's sake. Which was even more ridiculous given that he himself had only been at Belcraven House for a fortnight. Arabella shot her sister an exasperated glance. This had gone on quite long enough.

"You know, Deakin," she said, "I appreciate that you would prefer to be working for quality instead of an unspeakably rich merchant family, but were we not so unspeakably rich, you would not be so grossly overpaid."

His jaw dropped.

"Have a bonbon." She held out the box.

"Certainly not, miss!" He snapped his mouth shut so hard his eyes bulged.

"Oh, come now. You know you want one." She waved the box under his nose. "You have already put one foot on the path to hell by coming to work for us in the first place. What difference is one little bonbon going to make?"

He looked at the box, then back at her, and a ghost of a smile crossed his thin lips.

She waggled the box again. "If you pick a sugared almond, I will let you put it back."

"No one ought to be obliged to eat sugared almonds," Diana said. "I do not know why they put them in. No one actually likes them. They are so dull." She smiled up at him. "You are not one of those people who actually likes them, are you?"

"Certainly not." He reached into the box and picked out a pineapple nougat. He popped it into his mouth and his spine seemed to thaw.

"You two had better go on to the south draw—east drawing room, then," he said, as soon as he could work his mouth around the bonbon. "We are having visitors and your aunt and your father are waiting to tell you about it." He smiled. "Gentlemen."

"It is Lord Belcraven, I know it;" Diana said as they climbed the staircase. "Papa was visiting Gabriel Carr this morning and everyone knows that Mr. Carr is in love with Lord Belcraven's sister. It is perfectly possible that Papa met Lord Belcraven there and invited him to call on us today, do you not think, Arabella?"

Arabella thought that Diana was giving far too much thought to Lord Belcraven. It was far more likely the gentlemen were merely elderly business acquaintances of Papa's. Except for Mr. Carr, all of Papa's business acquaintances were elderly.

"Girls!" Aunt Ophelia dropped the book she was reading and leapt to her feet as soon as they entered the drawing room. "You will never guess who is coming to call on us this afternoon!"

"Lord Belcraven?" Diana asked breathlessly.

"The very same!" Papa pushed himself off from where he had been leaning against the mantel and strutted into the center of the room and planted himself in the middle of the Turkey carpet.

"I knew it! Did I not say so, Arabella?" Diana darted across the room to wrap her arms around Papa's neck, and his chest puffed with pride to the size of his stomach.

Oh, for heaven's sake. Not boring Lord Belcraven. Arabella dropped the box of bonbons on the table and threw herself down on the sofa next to her aunt. She picked up the book. *Love's Heartsick Longing*, the latest Minerva Press romance Aunt Ophelia had brought home from the Leadenhall Street bookstore. Arabella sniffed. She had no idea why her aunt insisted on reading them, they were such rubbish. Arabella would be mortified to be seen with one herself. In any event, she had already read this one yesterday whilst Aunt Ophelia was having a dress fitting.

It was dreadfully dull. The hero and the heroine didn't even meet until page thirty-four and the whole story ought to have ended in the second chapter, were it not for the sad fact that Raphael, the Duke of Montenero, was a complete cabbagehead. Not that sweet Lady Delfinia was much better, pretending to be the unwed mother of her niece, little Ruby, because of a promise she had made to her sister, who had died in a carriage accident. And frankly, it was obvious that neither Lady Delfinia nor Raphael cared a fig for little Ruby. They were only using the child as an excuse to moon at each other. And there were too many carriage accidents. Nobody ever sat down and had an honest conversation.

"Well?" Aunt Ophelia reached over and nudged her arm. "Isn't it exciting?" She smiled brightly.

"No," Arabella said. "Raphael ought to have fallen to his knees and kissed the ground Lady Delfinia walked on the instant he clapped eyes on her. Even if he thought she was a jade, he should have realized no one else would ever put up with him. The story was a complete waste of time."

"What?" Diana cried. "What about the part where Raphael is in the carriage accident and has amnesia and Lady Delfinia bathes his fevered brow?"

Aunt Ophelia nodded. "In the inn? In the candle-light?" She sighed. "I am reading that part now." Her cheeks pinkened. "Still."

A little flutter went through Arabella's stomach. Well, perhaps that part wasn't entirely stupid.

Aunt Ophelia shook herself. "In any event, we were not speaking of the book! Were you not listening to us? The Earl of Belcraven is not our only visitor. The Duke of St. Fell is also coming to call."

The hair on Arabella's neck prickled at her aunt's expectant smile. "What do you mean?" she asked slowly.

"Duke of St. Fell!" Diana cried. "He just bought Lord Belcraven's captaincy in the Guards for his brother. Lord Belcraven is staying at his house. Papa has invited him to call this afternoon, along with Lord Belcraven."

Arabella looked over at Papa.

"I say!" He lunged at the box of bonbons. "Sugared almonds!" He popped three in his mouth at once.

Hell!

"Arabella!" Aunt Ophelia squealed.

"Well, honestly!" Arabella rounded on her aunt. "You know perfectly well he is trying to arrange a marriage for me!"

"Certainly not!" Papa bent his head over the bonbon box. "I happened to be at Carr's house and I happened to make the acquaintance of his friend the Duke of St. Fell and Lord Belcraven and I happened to invite them to call on us." He stuffed another almond in his mouth. "Delicious! Can't get this kind of quality at home, eh?"

Aunt Ophelia snatched the box away from him. "For goodness sake, Joseph! Just tell her the truth. This is not some Minerva Press romance where the poor girl is not going to notice you want her to marry the duke!" She held the box to her chest and picked out a candied violet. "I loathe those stories that have the matchmaking relatives. There is always some ridiculous meddling spinster aunt. It is most insulting. I would never interfere! I am here as a chaperone, only. Not that I have ever had anything to chaperone, these poor girls' lives have been so dull."

"There is nothing wrong with dull," Papa said. "It is just another word for steady."

No, it was another word for tedious and boring. "Thank you, Aunt Ophelia," Arabella said. At least some-one in her family understood her position. "You see, Papa, I will not marry your duke. I want to go out to so-cial events and meet my own eligible gentlemen."

Aunt Ophelia gasped. "My stars, Arabella! The man is a duke! How could you possibly not want to marry him? Whatever is the matter with you? Are you ill?" She reached over to put her hand on Arabella's forehead.

Arabella batted away her aunt's hand. "We agreed I was coming to London to choose my own husband!"

"Of course you shall!" Aunt Ophelia said. "Your papa and I are merely suggesting that you choose the Duke of St. Fell."

Papa wolfed down another almond. "Just as Diana is choosing her own husband."

"Lord Belcraven," Diana announced, as if everyone did not already know she had taken leave of her senses.

Arabella jutted out her chin. "If this duke is a friend of Mr. Carr's, why do we not go to Mrs. Carr's party tomor-row afternoon and I shall make his acquaintance there?" Along with that of all the other eligible gentlemen.

"No need to go gallivanting all over London looking

for trouble," Papa muttered. "Not when there's a perfectly serviceable duke coming to call." He looked down at the carpet, then shrugged. "In any event, the duke has to leave town the day after tomorrow to visit his home seat in Surrey. We"—he looked up with an anxious chuckle—"I mean you, of course, might want to settle the matter before then."

That did it. Arabella gave him her sternest look. "You swore on Mama's grave I could pick my own husband." Mama's grave always made him turn red and perspire and give in.

He turned red and beads of moisture sprang up on his forehead. But he pulled his handkerchief from his waistcoat pocket and wiped his face. "Your mother would have wanted you to marry the duke," he said pleadingly. "He is perfect for you!"

Perfect? Arabella clenched her fists in frustration. He thought Lord Belcraven was suitable! Honestly, Papa would put a wedding suit on a hedgehog if he thought it would get himself a duke for a grandson. He wasn't the second wealthiest man in England because he was afraid to grasp an opportunity when he saw it. He had come within sniffing distance of a duke and he had crumbled. If Mama were alive, she would have kicked him.

"I thought you'd be pleased!" He mopped the top of his head. "Dukes don't grow on trees. They're as scarce as hen's teeth."

Aunt Ophelia nodded. "He is right, even though you would not credit it, since they are in every second Minerva Press romance. But in actual fact they are extremely rare, Arabella. Especially ones with all their own teeth." She leaned back against the sofa cushions and sighed. "You could become a duchess, think of it! A Swann as a duchess. You cannot get higher than that."

"You would outrank me and I am going to be a countess." Diana flushed. "I mean, should I happen to marry Lord Belcraven."

Arabella put her hands on her hips and took a deep breath. She was over the age of majority. No one could force her to marry someone she did not want to. "I want to marry for love," she said, willing her voice not to quaver. "I have waited all this time for a husband. I am going to marry for love."

St. Fell jabbed his finger under Belcraven's nose. "I keep trying to explain to you that it doesn't matter what Isabella Swann thinks of me—"

"Arabella," Belcraven said.

The waiter took away the old bottle and brought them another, along with the ale St. Fell had requested. He didn't want to have a thick head, after all. That would give Joseph Swann the advantage. Which reminded St. Fell of the point he was trying to drum into Belcraven's thick head.

"The only thing that matters is the impression you make on Joseph Swann!" He banged his glass down on the table.

"Are you marrying the papa now, St. Fell?" Toby didn't bother to look up from the game of patience he had dealt out on the table, so St. Fell didn't bother telling him to shut up.

"Yes, St. Fell, I don't see why you keep going on about Joseph Swann," Alward mumbled.

No wonder these idiots didn't have a hope of ever getting themselves married. St. Fell jabbed his finger in Belcraven's chest. "What is the most important thing about Miss Swann?"

"Whether or not she loves me?"

St. Fell grit his teeth. "No."

Belcraven's brow furrowed. "Her character?"

St. Fell slugged back the rest of his drink. This was going to take forever. "No, you idiot," he said. "Her fortune."

Predictably, Belcraven instantly flamed red. "Miss Diana's fortune means nothing to me!" he sputtered. "I have not thought about her family's money at all!"

"Well you had damned well better start," St. Fell said. "You are not living at my house for the rest of your life."

"He has a point," Toby told Belcraven. "You've had to let both your residences and the money for your army commission barely covered your father and your uncles' debts."

Alward nodded. "A man in your restricted circumstances can't afford to marry a girl unless she's got money."

Belcraven's shoulders sagged. "I suppose you are right."

"There you are, then." St. Fell reached over and patted him on the back. "And who will determine the size of Miss Swann's fortune?"

"Her papa?" Belcraven offered with slightly more confidence.

"Exactly." St. Fell leaned back in his seat and crossed his arms behind his head. A point so obvious that even Belcraven could grasp it.

"So are you saying it doesn't matter what Miss Swann thinks of you as long as her papa likes you?" Toby asked.

"I am saying that regardless of Miss Swann's opinion, the matter will be decided between her father and me. It's the way of the world, gentlemen. Men determine the fate of women." St. Fell swept his hand to encompass their table, the card room, and all of White's. "That is why men stick together."

"That seems almost sad," Toby said. "And yet . . ."

"Pleasant," Belcraven said.

"Perfect." Alward nodded.

* * *

Arabella cradled the box of bonbons and rooted for another nougat. There had to be a way to convince them. "I want my husband to be in love with me. The only reason a duke would be interested in me is for my fortune."

"You are too hard on yourself, dearest." Aunt Ophelia patted her arm. "You have many good qualities."

"That's right," Papa said. "Just because you have a bit of a temper—"

"And opinions," Diana said.

"About everything," Aunt Ophelia added. "It does not mean that the duke won't fall head over heels in love with you."

Her idiot family thought they were all very amusing. "I am still not marrying a fortune hunter." Arabella folded her arms across her chest.

"I am sure he has other qualities," Aunt Ophelia said soothingly. She turned to Papa. "Why do you not tell Arabella something about the Duke of St. Fell?"

Papa tucked his thumbs in his waistcoat pockets and rocked back on his heels. "He's nine-and-twenty, got two hundred acres and a home seat in Surrey, a London house in Grosvenor Square, no mortgages but the six younger brothers are a considerable drain on his income and he wants money to build houses on the south side of the Thames because he thinks there will be a boom when the Vauxhall bridge is completed—"

"No, Joseph! Tell her something she actually wants to know. Is he handsome?"

"Handsome?" Papa flushed. "How should I know if he is handsome?"

"Well, what does he look like?" Aunt Ophelia prodded.

"Two eyes. Two ears . . . a nose." Papa's face grew redder

with each word. "Boots! He's got those tall shiny boots young men in London favor now. Lord Belcraven had them."

"Hessians!" Diana cried. "They are all the crack."

Arabella threw her hands in the air. "The Duke of St. Fell has shiny boots? Why did you not mention it before, Papa? Of course I will marry him."

"There is no need to make sarcastic comments, Arabella," Aunt Ophelia said. "It's bad enough we all know you are thinking them. Your father is merely trying to tell you if the duke is handsome."

"I do not care if he is handsome!" What did handsome have to do with love?

Aunt Ophelia frowned. "But it must be important. Otherwise why would all the Minerva Press heroes be handsome?"

Diana foraged in the bonbon box. "You know, Papa," she said, "I am surprised you did not mention the thing about the Duke of St. Fell that Arabella might actually find interesting." She shot Arabella a sly look from under her lashes. "Lord Belcraven told me the Duke of St. Fell is a rake."

Arabella flushed. Her sister was being ridiculous. "That does not make the duke any more attractive." It merely made him less pathetic than Lord Belcraven.

"A rake!" Aunt Ophelia clasped her hands together. "Isn't that perfectly wonderful!"

For heaven's sake! Arabella glared at her aunt. "Is there anything about any man you would not find perfectly wonderful?"

"My stars, Arabella! The man has a pulse and your father is encouraging his attentions. How could I possibly not find him wonderful?" She sniffed. "You do not want to end up a middle-aged spinster chaperoning your nieces whose father lets them do nothing, do you?"

Arabella shot her father a glare and patted her aunt's shoulder. Papa's smothering had taken its toll on everyone.

Aunt Ophelia dabbed at her eyes with her handkerchief. "In any event, everyone knows rakes make the best of husbands. Just ask your papa. He used to be a rake."

Which was one of the reasons he was so skittish about gentlemen callers. It was completely unfair.

Papa shrugged. "Times were different then. Used to mean something to be a rake. Nowadays every man who can waltz thinks he's a rake."

"There you are, Arabella," Aunt Ophelia said. "Perhaps the Duke of St. Fell is merely a rogue."

"Lord Belcraven is not a rake," Diana said.

Arabella rolled her eyes. Lord Belcraven was not even a rascal. She scooped up the box of bonbons and walked to the door. "I am going to my room. I shall come down when the duke has departed." Just because her fortune hunter wasn't as hopeless as Diana's didn't mean that Papa was going to win. He would have to accept that she was going to pick her own husband and that she was going to marry for love. After all, they could well afford it.

"The thing of it is, Arabella . . ."

The tone of Papa's voice made her stop in the doorway. She looked over her shoulder. Papa shifted his gaze to the carpet. The single strand of hair that grew on the left side of his head had unhooked from his right ear and flopped down in front of his nose from all of his head mopping.

"The thing of it is, Arabella," he repeated, his voice on the surface hesitant, yet showing the steel underneath that made him his fortune, "the size of your dowry may very well depend on the quality of your husband."

Hell! Arabella spun round to face him. "You wouldn't!"

Aunt Ophelia nodded sadly. "I am afraid he would,

dearest. My father was exactly the same way. That is why I never married. Men like to think of their money as theirs, even when they are giving it away."

"Just meet him!" Papa pleaded. "I am sure you will take one look at each other and fall head over heels in love."

"And if we do not?" Arabella demanded.

Papa mopped his head again. "Why worry about things that aren't likely to happen."

"If we do not?" she insisted.

He looked down again and shrugged. "If you do not, then you do not have to marry him."

"And?" she persisted.

He sighed. "And we will discuss your meeting other eligible gentlemen."

Arabella stalked back to the sofa and flung herself down. She narrowed her eyes as she foraged in the box for a nougat.

There were only sugared almonds left.

St. Fell poured the last of the bottle into his glass. "Don't waste your breath feeling sorry for Annabelle—"

"Arabella," Belcraven said.

As if the girl's name mattered. "Miss Swann has just arrived from the provinces for her very first visit to London and I am a duke. A young, handsome, and charming duke." St. Fell raised his glass in a toast. "Trust me, Miss Swann will be perfectly happy to go along with whatever her papa and I arrange. The minute she meets me, the girl is going to fall head over heels in love. She will be panting to marry me."

Alward elbowed Belcraven. "And even if she isn't, twenty minutes in a dark corner ought to persuade her."

"Ten," Toby said.

St. Fell snorted. Amateurs. "Five."

Toby rolled his eyes.

Alward rubbed his hands together. "Gentlemen, I think we are ready to fetch the betting book and begin picking our dates for the weddings of the Miss Swanns."

Toby shook his head. "I'm not betting against my own brother marrying a rich heiress."

"I'm not taking it either," Belcraven said. "Miss Diana is the youngest. They want her sister settled first. I need St. Fell to marry her, the sooner the better."

St. Fell frowned at Alward when the idiot's glance fell on him. "Certainly not. Nothing oversets a woman more than being the object of a bet." Even though you'd think they'd be flattered that a man cared enough to put money on it. He drained the last of his brandy and got to his feet. The other men followed suit.

"It's a shame you can't put money on it, St. Fell," Toby said as they entered the hallway. "I saw Compton's latest bill in your post this morning."

"How is your brother doing?" Alward asked.

"Five hundred pounds for one night in a brothel in Brussels," Toby announced as proudly as if he had done it himself.

"Really?" Belcraven frowned in puzzlement. "What could he possibly have done in a brothel in Brussels that cost five hundred pounds for one night?"

Toby took a deep breath. "Well, it depends on the number of—"

"Shut up, Toby," St. Fell said. They didn't have all day. He told the porter to fetch his carriage. "In any event, I cannot possibly wager. I won't know if I want to marry—Isab—her until I know the size of her dowry."

"I wager it's at least twenty-five thousand," Alward said, a wistful note in his voice.

"Chicken stakes." St. Fell waved his hand dismissively.

"That's what Coutts gave his daughter twenty years ago, and Swann is far richer. I am thinking at least fifty thousand."

Belcraven's eyes glazed over. "Fifty thousand pounds?" he squeaked.

St. Fell took him by the arm and led him to the carriage. There was hope for the idiot yet.

Diana sat down beside Arabella on the sofa and patted her hand. "He is bluffing," she whispered. "Probably."

Arabella glared at Papa. Yes, he was. Probably.

"I think we will receive them in the north reception room," Papa said in a jolly voice, as if he didn't know he was completely annoying.

Aunt Ophelia paced the length of the sofa. "First, we will have refreshments, then perhaps we will go for a lovely walk outside in the fall sunshine. The thing about a walk is that a couple can have a private conversation whilst being fully chaperoned. I know, because I have given the matter a great deal of thought. By the way, make sure you call the duke 'Your Grace,' not 'my lord.'" She looked up abruptly. "And I think, only a slight curtsy. I don't trust these London fashions."

Arabella looked down at the neckline of her new Latour dress. It was considerably lower than the dresses she had had made in Little Darking.

"On second thought," Aunt Ophelia said, the speculative look in her eyes making Arabella flush, "perhaps a deep curtsy wouldn't be amiss, just this once."

"Ophelia!" Papa barked.

"Well, make up your mind, Joseph!" she said. "A Swann is not afraid to display her plumage." She smiled at Arabella. "And Arabella has excellent plumage."

Diana cleared her throat.

"As does Diana," Aunt Ophelia said.

Arabella folded her arms across her chest. Why should she waste her plumage on someone who wanted to marry her for her fortune?

Papa declared that they should go downstairs, as their guests were expected at any moment and Arabella followed Diana and her aunt out the door.

Aunt Ophelia clutched *Love's Heartsick Longing* to her chest and sighed hopefully as they descended the staircase. "Perhaps the Duke of St. Fell will be as wonderful as Raphael!"

Arabella bared her teeth. "I am certain he will be." A complete cabbagehead.

Aunt Ophelia put her arm around her shoulder. "Do not be so pessimistic, dearest. Just be yourself and it will all go marvelously. And remember, whatever you do, try not to let him know what you are thinking."

Chapter 2

"What if she hates my aunts?" Belcraven asked.

"Everyone hates your aunts," St. Fell said wearily. It didn't take long to drive from St. James's to Belcraven's ancestral barn on Dean Street, but it was long enough to take a nap in the carriage. Or at least, it would have been long enough if Belcraven would stop gabbling about Daphne and how he adored her from the very first moment he set eyes on her and how it was his fondest hope that she would feel the same way about him and how convinced he was that she would not know the depth of his feeling, because whenever he was in her presence he was tongue-tied.

It was a shame the idiot wasn't tongue-tied when he was not in her presence.

"She could have any man," Belcraven moaned. "London is full of eligible men. War heroes. Rakes. Men who can make pretty conversation with women. Some even write poetry." He leaned forward and wrung his hands together. "I've been in the army since I was eighteen. I don't know the first thing about courting."

St. Fell sighed. "Listen, there is no great secret to dealing with women," he said. "They like compliments."

Belcraven nodded, glassy-eyed like a rabbit. "Compliments."

"Exactly." St. Fell leaned back into the corner of the

carriage squabs. "Tell her she looks nice or she smells nice, women love that sort of thing." He folded his arms across his chest and closed his eyes.

"When?"

St. Fell opened his eyes. "When what?"

"When do I give her the compliment?" Belcraven asked. "Should I say something directly when we are introduced or—"

"Good God! No! Not when you are introduced and her father is standing right there. Were you not listening to anything I said? Do not say anything in front of Swann that might vex him. He is overprotective. Extremely overprotective." Rabidly overprotective. "Wait until there is a quiet moment, then say something nice to the girl. And try to make it particular to her, you know, not something that would apply to any woman. For example, if she has blond hair—" St. Fell stopped talking. Belcraven was nodding, but his nostrils were flaring and his eyes had a glitter of panic. "Never mind," St. Fell said soothingly. "You only have to remember one thing—do not vex Swann."

Belcraven nodded. "Do not vex Swann."

"Yes, do not vex Swann." St. Fell closed his eyes again. Thank God he had the older sister. Courting would drag on forever if they all had to wait for Belcraven to impress Swann. Or the girl.

St. Fell awakened when the carriage pulled up into the circular drive of Belcraven House. It was no wonder poor Belcraven couldn't afford to pay the window tax on it. The place was a hundred-year-old hulking gray stone monstrosity. Heating alone must cost a fortune. A pretentious butler, whom Belcraven immediately denied had ever been his, didn't bother to pretend that they weren't expected and solemnly led them to what he called the north reception room.

"I don't know why we call it the north reception room," Belcraven whispered as they waited for the butler to announce their arrival. He was shaking so hard his watch fob and chain were rattling. "It is in the west wing of the house. It's odd, don't you think?"

St. Fell thought about slapping Belcraven topside the head.

The butler returned to open the door to a sixty-foot-wide room dripping in gilt moldings and portraits of what were likely by-gone Belcravens. It had to be the most pretentious room in the entire house. Excellent. St. Fell smiled. Swann meant business.

He pushed Belcraven forward and marched him to where Swann stood waiting in front of an overwrought Adams fireplace, his thumbs tucked into the pockets of his waistcoat, and a spider-welcoming-the-fly-into-his-parlor smile lighting up his round face. On his right, the two daughters, one blond, one brunette, both Swann short but slender. On his left, an older woman with salt-and-pepper hair, the same vintage and round shape as Swann. Standard issue interfering aunty, he'd bet.

As Swann presented the aunty, St. Fell assessed the Miss Swanns out of the corner of his eye. The blond one was obviously the subject of Belcraven's infatuation. By some miraculous stroke of luck she was actually gazing at the idiot with an expression of admiration on her face. Belcraven, of course, was already beet red and staring at her shoes. Poor Miss Blond Swann, stuck with the most backward suitor in London. Nice figure, though. And not afraid of letting it show.

Which meant that the brunette was his. St. Fell turned to smile at her, but Little Miss Brunette Swann wasn't even looking at him. Her attention was fixed on her father, and if the damned Belcraven House north reception room were not as frigid as the Thames in January, the glare Miss

Brunette Swann was firing at her Papa would have set him alight. Little Miss Brunette Swann was clearly a woman of opinion.

St. Fell rocked back on his heels in contemplation. Was it possible that Little Miss Brunette Swann imagined she didn't want to be married to him? Perhaps she was one of those women who objected to marriage on principle. A bluestocking who wanted her own independent life, or one of those women who had always imagined herself a spinster. He shrugged. Whatever her reasons, it wouldn't take much to persuade a green girl from the provinces of the merits of marrying a duke. In any event, Swann wanted her married to him, so there was no point worrying about it. She'd marry him. If he and Swann came to satisfying terms.

He took a better look at her. She also had a decent figure. Also not afraid of letting it show. Better than decent, actually. He let his gaze travel up from the tips of her little slippers peeping out from beneath the hem of her gown, to her slender waist and her generous bosom. In fact, given that she was barely five feet tall and her dress was cut in the latest fashion, if she gave a halfway decent curtsy when she was introduced to him, the meeting would be off to an excellent start. As for her face, she had a kissable mouth, a little snub nose, soft pink cheeks growing pinker as he watched . . .

Oh.

He met her eyes. Her brandy brown eyes. Which were now glaring back at him, sparks of outrage in their depths. It seemed Miss Brunette Swann had noticed his appreciation of her figure, and had not appreciated the appreciation. Tragic, really, since she had such a fine figure. He offered her a smile.

Miss Brunette Swann knit her eyebrows in a fierce scowl, pursed her lips, and dropped her eyes to the floor.

Then deliberately, very deliberately, she dragged her gaze slowly upward, starting at his boots, up the length of his legs, his torso, his chest, until she finally met his eyes again. She tilted her chin up in challenge and curved her lips in a small, superior smile. Which lasted approximately two seconds. Then her eyes widened in horror, and her face turned completely red.

Good God! St. Fell jammed his hands in his pockets to keep from yanking at his cravat. The damned room was an oven. And she might very well have just arrived from the provinces, but Miss Brunette Swann was no whey-faced hick. She was a woman of action.

"And these are my daughters," Swann said, thankfully oblivious. "Arabella is my eldest."

Miss Arabella Swann curtsied. Barely, damn her, with her eyes locked on his, so she would catch it if his eyes strayed downward. Not that he would stray, not with Swann watching him. He didn't need to anyway. Miss Arabella Swann was so short and the gathered neckline on her dress so low that all he had to do was take one step toward her—

Belcraven jabbed him in the ribs. Belatedly, St. Fell bowed to the other Miss Swann. Deirdre. Or Daphne, possibly. Not that it mattered, the girl hadn't noticed his lapse in manners; she only had eyes for Belcraven. Who glanced at her once, turned even redder, and stumbled back against a small wooden table which held a small china figurine. The figurine tumbled. Belcraven dove and caught it before it hit the floor.

St. Fell smothered his laughter. Well, at least from the carpet Belcraven had a better view of Miss Blond Swann's shoes. In any event, Miss Blond Swann was beaming down at the idiot as if he had just performed some astonishing feat of bravery.

Miss Arabella Swann, however, was also looking at

Belcraven as he rose to his feet, and from the exasperated twitch of her shoulders and her barely concealed snort of annoyance it was clear that Arabella Swann was an intelligent woman.

"That is the Golden Shepherdess," the aunty said proudly, pointing at the figurine still cradled in Belcraven's paws. "We made it to celebrate the success of our London store. It is one of the rarest Swanns in existence."

"Dash it!" Belcraven quickly put it back on the table.

"Oh, you will not break it," the aunty said. "Swanns are made to be touched."

St. Fell shot Arabella Swann a sideways look. Two pink spots bloomed high on her cheeks, but she didn't look down. Instead, her lips curved in the hint of smile.

"Really?" St. Fell picked up the figurine. "So one may touch a Swann any way one wants?"

Arabella Swann rolled her eyes.

"Oh yes!" The aunty nodded. "They look very delicate, but they stand up well to vigorous handling."

Arabella Swann was obliged to have a coughing fit. St. Fell grinned in triumph.

The aunty announced it was time to be seated and she and Swann installed themselves in the matching armchairs that faced the fireplace. Belcraven bolted to the large sofa on the right side, and his Miss Blond Swann casually ambled over and sat down at the other end of it. Belcraven began to study his knees.

Which left the smaller sofa on the left side of the fireplace completely empty. St. Fell watched Arabella Swann's gaze waver between it and the space between her sister and Belcraven, her dilemma playing itself out with a furrowed brow and a nibbling of her lush lower lip. Finally, she squared her shoulders and perched down on the empty sofa, although as close to the edge as possible on the left.

He sat down on the right.

Something sharp jabbed his back. He reached behind the cushion and pulled out a mottled leather book. *Love's Heartsick Longing.* A Minerva Press novel. How delicious. The aunty's, he'd wager, or the sister's.

He pasted an innocent expression on his face and held out the book to Arabella Swann. "Yours, I presume?"

Her face flamed redder than Belcraven's hair. She made a small choking sound as she snatched the book from his hand. St. Fell made a show of flinching. She didn't throw it at him, though. Miss Arabella Swann was a good girl. But she did heft it in her hand a few times before slapping it down on the hassock in front of her.

"Now, Your Grace!" The aunty shook her head. "You know perfectly well you ought not to tease Arabella. She is barely hanging on to her temper as it is."

Arabella Swann gasped as if she couldn't believe her own ears, and she narrowed her eyes, and her lips twitched. Almost as if she were cursing.

"Arabella!" the aunty squeaked. She gave St. Fell an apologetic smile and then looked back at Arabella. "In any event, there is no reason to fuss. All young women have a temper while courting. I'm sure His Grace merely takes it as a promising sign of your passionate nature." She sighed. "Because any woman would see that he is even better than Raphael."

Arabella Swann's lips twitched again, and her hands bunched into fists on her lap.

Joseph Swann leaned back in his chair and linked his hands over his stomach. "I think we are off to an excellent start," he said.

St. Fell settled himself more comfortably on the sofa.

Arabella Swann had the most expressive face of anyone
he had ever encountered. It revealed her every thought.
And if the first fifteen minutes of their acquaintance
were any indication, the revelation of Miss Swann
promised to be a very agreeable experience indeed.

  It was the most utterly wretched experience. Arabella
knew perfectly well that the Duke of St. Fell was laughing at her. Laughing at all of them, actually. Not that her
family didn't deserve to be laughed at. Or throttled.
Papa and Aunt Ophelia were being completely ridiculous. They would be more subtle had they hung a price
card around her neck and stuck her in the window of
Swann's Fine China Emporium.
  Of course, she hadn't helped matters either. Leering
right back at him like a complete idiot as if she had
never met a handsome rake of a duke before. Which she
hadn't! But it was no excuse. She had so frequently
thought about coming to London and meeting handsome men that she ought to have been prepared when
she saw one. Because except for the smirk, the Duke of
St. Fell was handsome. He had thick, straight, golden
brown hair which fell down on one side over his forehead and a strong jaw and clear gray eyes, and he was tall
and slender and had long legs that tapered up to lean
hips and strong shoulders.
  She flushed. Yes, the Duke of St. Fell was extremely
handsome. And he knew it. She flushed again, her face
burning even hotter. And from the way he was smiling,
he knew that she knew it as well.
  And as if that wasn't ridiculous enough, he had managed to insinuate his long frame into the corner of the
sofa and angle himself so that he could watch her at
leisure while she was two cushions down, obliged to sit in

proper ladylike fashion, her back straight, head facing forward, clutching her hands in her lap and willing herself not to fiddle with the muslin of her skirt because he was watching her and he would laugh.

She knew he was watching and laughing at her because every time she chanced a glance in his direction from the corner of her eye, he was watching her as if he was waiting for her to look at him, his dark gray eyes glinting nearly black. And when their eyes caught, he'd give her the tiniest half smile and he'd quirk his eyebrows and tilt his head ever so slightly, as if to say he found the whole thing very amusing, and Arabella's pulse would hammer so fiercely that she would have to look away to get her breath back.

And it would all happen so quickly that Papa and Aunt Ophelia didn't even notice. They carried on their interrogation of Lord Belcraven about his family as if the Duke of St. Fell were not sitting ten feet away from them, smirking at her like a cat who had found a wingless canary. Sitting in a cream pot. Holding a trout.

She chanced another glance at him. He was waiting for her again. He tilted his head back, and his shoulders shifted that same way they had when he had been standing. Her stomach quivered. She should never have eaten so many bonbons. She had obviously made herself ill. In fact, she might very well be feverish. Her head was muddled and she had quite lost the thread of the conversation. Papa and Aunt Ophelia and Diana and Lord Belcraven were getting to their feet. But all she seemed to be able to think about was not looking at the Duke of St. Fell, who obviously was not feeling the same way because he wouldn't stop looking at her.

"Well, Arabella?" Aunt Ophelia looked down at her with an expectant expression.

Arabella's heart froze. Aunt Ophelia wasn't going to

mention that she had been looking overmuch at the duke, was she? In front of him? She glanced at Diana for help, but her sister was preoccupied with the wonder of not being looked at by Lord Belcraven.

Aunt Ophelia pointed to the far wall, the forty-foot length of which was covered from floor to ceiling with paintings of illustrious Belcravens. "Lord Belcraven is going to explain his family portraits."

Good heavens. Arabella couldn't imagine anything more boring. But she fixed a polite smile on her face and stood up.

"Oh, no, dear," Aunt Ophelia said. "Your papa and I thought perhaps you and the duke would like to stay here and have a nice conversation."

"Where we can see you," Papa added, not taking his eyes off the duke who had remained on the sofa.

Honestly. What she ought to do was announce that she had other pressing business and march out of the drawing room to make the point to Papa and the duke that she had a mind of her own.

She glanced at the duke out of the corner of her eye, and he smiled and tilted his head back and half lowered his eyes, and he gave that little hitch to his shoulders, as if he were realigning his spine, and Arabella sat back down. On the other hand, she had come to London to meet gentlemen, and the Duke of St. Fell was a gentleman. And she knew perfectly well he was a rake and a fortune hunter. She wasn't going to give up her lifetime ambition to marry for love just because he made eyes at her. Even if they were excellent eyes.

Without further delay, Aunt Ophelia and Papa and Diana and Lord Belcraven walked across the room to begin their tour. Forty feet away. Completely out of earshot. Arabella's heart began to hammer. She was going to have her first private conversation with a gentleman! And heaven only knew the kind of conversation a fortune hunting rake would get up to. Not that he would admit that he was a fortune hunter or a rake, of course. No, she had no doubt that he would try to convince her that he was truly interested in her for herself. That he had finally met the woman that he wanted to marry, and it was simply the most astonishing of coincidences that she happened to have the largest dowry of any marriageable girl in England. Except for Diana.

As soon as her family reached the far wall, the Duke of St. Fell leaned across the sofa toward her. His lips curved into a smile and he looked deeply into her eyes.

Arabella held her breath.

"What the devil is your aunt's name?" he asked.

Hell. A wave of disappointment washed over her. The Duke of St. Fell was stupid! He hadn't looked stupid, but it wasn't as though she had a wide experience of men from which to make her assessment. She fixed a polite smile on her face and told him.

"And your sister's?" he said.

Very stupid. Arabella tried not to let her smile falter. It was hard enough to forget a name like Ophelia, but her sister was the youngest and therefore she was called Miss Diana. Furthermore, from the way he was mooning over her, Lord Belcraven must have mentioned Diana's name. Constantly. Arabella gave her sister's name and braced herself. Obviously the duke would ask what hers was next.

But the duke's smile deepened into a smirk. "I gather from the look of horror on your face that I have failed some kind of test for suitors?"

"Of course not," she said politely. She wanted to marry an idiot.

He stretched his arm along the back of the sofa and

leaned even closer. "Don't worry. I remember the things that are important, Miss Arabella Swann."

Good heavens! A rush of heat surged through her.

"Speaking of important things," he continued, "who is Raphael?"

Raphael? She blinked at him.

He shrugged as if it were of no importance, but the line of his strong jaw tightened. "Raphael. Your aunt mentioned him when we sat down. She hoped you would think I was as good as he."

Arabella resisted a fleeting urge to invent a fictitious beau to insert between herself and the Duke of St. Fell, the way one would throw a hunk of meat at a tiger to distract it, so one could escape out the door. "He is the duke in Aunt Ophelia's Minerva Press romance," she said.

"And am I as good as Raphael?" the duke asked in a voice that was as close to a purr as a man could get. He was a rake!

"I would not know, Your Grace. I do not read Minerva Press romances." Reading them when Aunt Ophelia left them lying about the house didn't count.

"Neither do I." He stretched his hand a little closer along the back of the sofa.

His hand was barely twelve inches away from her shoulder. Ten, if she swayed toward him. It was quite improper. She glanced over at Papa, but he wasn't looking back. She swallowed again. The Duke of St. Fell had very large hands. Huge hands, actually. With very long fingers. If he put his hand on top of her hand, his would completely cover hers. Just as his taller and broader body would—

"You know," he said, "you have the most expressive face of anyone I have ever seen. It reveals your every thought."

Hell.

He smiled. "So you may as well tell me what you are thinking. It is only a matter of time before I figure it out."

Hell. He couldn't really, could he? She goggled at him, trying desperately to think of a lie that was original and clever and meaningful, yet lighthearted and witty.

"I think you are cursing," he said.

Oh, for heaven's sake. She sagged back against the sofa cushions in relief. He was just going on about hell. Not that any power on earth would get her to tell him. She might not be a gentlewoman of the *ton*, but she wasn't completely backward. She had attended Miss Edgar's Academy for the Refinement of Young Ladies for two years, after Papa bought it. Young ladies most certainly did not say *hell*. If the Duke of St. Fell thought she was going to admit it, he could just go to hell himself.

"Is it thunderation?" he asked.

Thunderation? Her heart sank. He thought she was a dried-up old spinster!

"My apologies." He looked deep into her eyes and smiled. "Of course it is not thunderation. It is obvious you are not the thunderation type."

His words mollified her. Or perhaps the rasping tone with which he breathed his words mollified her. Either way, she was mollified. Or possibly liquefied. At least he had moved his hand from the back of the sofa. He had brought it back to his knee. She tried not to look at it.

"Is it dashed?" he asked.

"Lord Belcraven says dashed," she said.

He grinned. "Therefore it cannot possibly be dashed. You may as well tell me. I shall only imagine it is worse than it is."

Really? She didn't know any worse words than *hell*. Perhaps if she continued to say nothing, he would tell her.

He looked at her sideways. "You are deluded if you think I am going to start reeling off curses so you may improve your vocabulary. Just tell me. I am quite mature enough to handle your secret shame."

"For heaven's sake," she said, "I am not going to tell you."

"It is hell!" he declared.

Hell.

He pointed his finger at her. "There! You just said it again!" He leaned back against the cushions, a self-satisfied smile on his face. He looked like a five-year-old who had dropped a snake down his governess's dress. "Miss Arabella Swann says hell!"

"Keep your voice down!" she hissed. Honestly. Why did he have to act as if discovering that she had rude unladylike thoughts was delightful? "In any event, I most certainly do not say it."

"You think it," he crowed in that same smug singsong tone.

"What I think is my own business," she said primly.

"Ah, but it will be my business once we are married," he said, mimicking her sanctimonious tone of voice.

She had actually managed to forget for a minute that he was Papa's pet fortune hunter. Hell.

He slapped his hand over his heart. "You are saying hell again! You do not wish to marry me?"

"Of course I want to marry you," she snapped. "It is merely that I am being measured for my new pelisse this afternoon. I am wondering when I can fit the wedding in. Papa informs me you are going from town the day after tomorrow."

He burst into laughter outright now. "Miss Arabella Swann is naughty."

"You are being ridiculous," Arabella said, anxiously glancing over at the far wall, but everyone was still inching their way across the Belcraven family portraits.

The duke sighed. "Furthermore, your endearments leave much to be desired. I shall have to instruct you in the language of love."

"Completely ridiculous," she said.

"You are beginning to make me feel unwanted."

"Is that possible?"

He gave her a knowing look and a slow smile. "Probably not."

He should not be allowed to smile at women that way. She took a deep, steadying breath.

"I do not see how you could possibly feel unwanted after Papa's display," she said.

He nodded smugly. "Your family seems a touch eager for our union."

"They have done everything but offer to wrap me in brown paper and stuff me in the boot of your carriage!"

He shrugged. "The afternoon is still young."

She ended up snorting when she tried to smother her laughter, and Papa and Aunt Ophelia must have heard, because they looked over. Papa nodded curtly, while Aunt Ophelia waved and smiled, but then they both returned their attention to Lord Belcraven.

"See? Your aunt likes me," the Duke of St. Fell said.

"She likes everyone," Arabella replied in a dampening tone.

"And do you like everyone, Miss Arabella Swann?"

She shrugged. "Some people like themselves so well, they do not need anyone else to like them."

"You did not answer my question." He leaned forward and Arabella felt herself pinned beneath his gaze. "Shall I answer it for you? You like me very well. Since the first moment you set eyes on me, just before we were introduced when you looked me over—"

"That was your fault!" she said. He had ogled first! And he was a cad for mentioning it.

"I certainly hope it is my fault. You were looking at me."

"And I have never done anything like that in my life!" she added.

"You have never met me before." He leaned back again, the smirk in full bloom on his face.

She stared at him, dumbfounded. The man was not only a cad, he was completely in love with himself.

He shook his head sadly. "If you are going to insult me, I think you should say it aloud. It hardly seems fair to make me supply my own adjectives."

"If my face is so expressive," she said, "then you don't need me to say aloud how you must be the most conceited man in all of England."

He heaved a melodramatic sigh. "I do not know why you are so cruel to me. I want to marry you, your father wants us to marry—"

"I am not going to marry you just because that is what you and Papa want!"

"Then marry me because that is what you want," he said.

"I do not want to marry you!" Arabella said. "I barely know you!"

"You know everything of importance. I am a duke. You are a rich heiress. We are a perfect match."

She folded her arms across her chest. "To think that in all the years I dreamed of coming to London, I never dared hope I would receive so romantic a proposal."

"I thought you said you didn't read Minerva Press romances?" He had the nerve to sound injured.

"That does not mean I want to be married for my fortune!"

"But you have such a fine fortune!" he said. "Why not use it to acquire the best husband you can."

"Which would be a duke, I suppose," she said dryly.

"It is hard to do better than a duke. We are as scarce as hen's teeth, you know."

"So I have heard."

"And I have been told I am tolerably handsome and reasonably charming."

"Don't forget modest," she said.

"You see how you truly understand the depths of my soul?" He grinned. "You must marry me."

"Let us say we will marry," she said. "Do you know what people will say?"

"What should we give the couple who has everything?"

She shot him a withering look. "No, they will think I am too stupid to notice that I am being married for my money. That I came to London to find myself a husband and I was so pathetic that the best I could do was a fortune hunter."

"But I would know I was being married for my title." He held out his excellent hands, palms up, and gave her a choirboy smile. "Surely that would make me just as big a fool as you?"

"How do two fools make a better marriage?" she demanded crossly.

"They would keep each other amused," he said.

She looked down at her hands on her lap. Why did he have to be a fortune hunter? And weren't fortune hunters supposed to be less obvious? And why didn't he stop waving his hands at her? This whole conversation was happening too quickly. She barely had time to think of her answer before he had already said something else, and everything they said seemed very important, even though it was obvious he took nothing seriously.

She took a deep breath and looked back into his face. "I do not know what my father has told you, but I am going to choose my own husband."

The duke shrugged. "Choose me."

"I want to marry for love!"

"Love me."

He was impossible! "I want my husband to love me!"

"I love you."

Hell! Heat flooded her face. His lips were still curled in the smirk and his eyes were dancing with laughter. Not that she expected to see any expression of sincerity—it would have been worse if he had the nerve to look sincere.

"I wonder how many other women have heard you say that," she said, proud of herself for not squeaking.

"Excellent!" He grinned, looking as pleased as if he had said it himself. "Not cruel, but showing that you know enough not to get fooled by the wicked fortune-hunting rake." He took a deep breath. "Very well, you require something original. How about, 'I love you, Arabella.'" He paused again and looked up in thought. "'I love you, Arabella Swann.' There, I am quite positive I have never said that before."

She threw up her hands in resignation. "You would say anything to get me to marry you!"

He laughed. "Of course I would. I don't see why you have to make it sound so shameful. I would be flattered if you would say anything to get me to marry you."

Her fingers itched with the urge to slap the smirk off his lips. There could not be anyone in London more smug! In England! The man was the duke of smug.

"In any event," he continued, still merrily smirking, "it doesn't matter if I love you. You don't marry someone because they love you. What matters is whether or not you love me."

Of all the cheek! Arabella leaped to her feet.

"Arabella!" Aunt Ophelia shouted. She and Papa trotted back across the room, followed by Diana and Lord Belcraven. "Your papa has the most wonderful notion!"

Arabella lunged at her aunt in relief. Conversation with the Duke of St. Fell was like grabbing a maypole ribbon and spinning, after drinking two glasses of punch.

Aunt Ophelia smiled past Arabella's shoulder at the duke. "Your papa is wondering if you would like to sing for us, dearest."

"'Greensleeves,'" Papa said.

Arabella goggled at them. She had won a hundred pounds from Papa at Christmas when she was ten, one pound for each verse she managed to memorize. Otherwise she had the voice of a frog. A frog! Papa and Aunt Ophelia were the only two people on earth who did not think so.

"Certainly not, Papa." She gave him a fierce look.

The Duke of St. Fell snickered. She refused to look at him. It must be very amusing being a desirable duke that a merchant desperately wanted to marry his daughter.

As if she hadn't spoken, Papa beamed at the duke. "She knows one hundred of the verses." Honestly, Papa couldn't possibly make her look like a bigger antidote if he tried. She wondered if it would be noticeable if she reached over and pinched him.

"A very desirable talent," the duke drawled.

Papa nodded proudly. "And she wrote a poem when she was in school that was published in the *Ladies' Monthly Museum*."

For heaven's sake. It was the last straw of mortification. Also, it had been in the *Ladies' Almanac*. She looked around for Diana, but she and Lord Belcraven had stopped to stare at each other twenty feet away. Arabella squared her shoulders. She had to take action. "I must leave now," she said, keeping her eyes fixed on the mantel so she would not be tempted to look at the Duke of St. Fell's inevitable smirk and risk collapsing in a fit of giggles like a twelve-year-old girl while he, of course, would manage to keep a straight face.

"There is no reason to run away, dearest," Aunt Ophelia said soothingly as she resumed her seat. "We are going to have coffee and biscuits and then go for a lovely walk, remember?"

"And if you stay, you could sing," Papa said.

"A lot," the duke said.

"Diana!" Arabella shouted. "Papa wants me to sing!"

Diana finally looked over and her eyes widened in understanding. "Oh, no, Papa! Arabella cannot sing. She—she has a very putrid throat."

"Nonsense!" Papa declared. "Never sick a day in their lives, either one of them. Healthy as horses. It is merely nerves."

"Miss Diana looks as healthy as a horse!" Lord Belcraven cried.

The Duke of St. Fell's coughing barely covered his whoop of laughter.

"Perhaps we should go for our walk right away." Aunt Ophelia waved away Deakin and his coffeepot and rose to her feet. "It is a beautiful day for a walk." She walked toward Arabella, with the same coaxing look in her eye that Arabella's riding master had whenever a horse escaped from the paddock.

Arabella edged her way past the sofa, keeping her eyes averted from the duke. She made sure she didn't go near the hassock. The last thing she needed to do was to trip over it and fall into his strong arms like some henwit in a Minerva Press romance.

Aunt Ophelia took another step toward her. "A wonderful walk with the duke. The wonderful duke."

Arabella backed away slowly.

And fell over the hassock like an ungainly idiot. But thankfully Deakin caught her before she landed on her behind on the carpet in front of the Duke of St. Fell. She kept her eyes closed so she wouldn't have to see the duke completely collapse into gales of laughter. She would just pretend she had swooned.

"Arabella, dearest," Aunt Ophelia said, "I understand how much you want to continue your visit with the duke, but it is really not necessary to go to such lengths."

"I don't think much of this!" Papa bellowed.

"Ignore them," Arabella whispered without moving her lips. "Just take me to my bedchamber as soon as possible."

"It would be my deepest pleasure," a deep voice murmured in her ear. "But I think your family expects me to offer for you first."

Arabella's eyes flew open. She found herself staring into the laughing gray eyes of the Duke of St. Fell.

Hell.

"Oh come now," he said, his mouth so close to her face she could feel the puff of air from his lips on her cheek. "You are not going to tell me you weren't looking forward to this just as much as I was?"

"Certainly not," she croaked.

He shook his head. "What a bouncer. Next you will tell me that I shouldn't have moved that hassock."

"You tripped me?" Hell! He had made her squeak.

"I am a rake, you know," he said.

"I had no idea that was how rakes made women fall at their feet!"

He grinned. "God, but you're perfect."

"Set my daughter down immediately, St. Fell." Papa's voice sounded in the distance.

"Yes, a walk would be perfect right now," Aunt Ophelia said. "A nice bracing walk. With chaperones."

Arabella stared into the duke's eyes, unable to move. She was quite certain she was having a heart seizure. Her heart was pounding so loudly she was sure he could hear it. And she was panting in a most undignified way.

The duke kept his arms wrapped around her, one curved under her back, the other curled around her legs, pressing her body against his hard chest as casually and as confidently as if he carried women around every day, which, being a rake, he might very well do.

She swallowed. She was being carried by a man. By a duke. By a handsome duke. A handsome duke who was a rake and a fortune hunter, and completely smug and conceited, but still. It was her first carrying by a man. She shivered in pleasure. Her first carrying by a man was by a handsome duke.

Diana hadn't been carried by Lord Belcraven.

"This is exactly why a nice walk would be perfect," Aunt Ophelia said. "Just the thing to work off excess spirits."

"Put the girl down, son," Papa snarled.

The duke shifted her in his arms as lightly as if she weighed no more than a feather, and suddenly their faces seemed even closer. She watched the smirk fade from his lips. His breathing seemed to slow down. His lips parted.

"Damnation!" Papa's red face loomed at the duke's shoulder. "Drop her!" he shouted. "Now!"

The Duke of St. Fell looked up at Papa and blinked, a blank look in his eyes for an instant, as if he didn't understand what he'd been told. Then he nodded and slid her down the length of his body to her feet.

"A nice, long, vigorous walk." Aunt Ophelia caught her and hooked her arm through hers and dragged her to the door. "In broad daylight. In plain view."

"Damned right in plain view," Papa muttered.

Chapter 3

"Not so fast," Joseph Swann said grimly when St. Fell moved to follow Arabella through the door.

Arabella looked back over her shoulder and frowned. "Papa! You are not—" She paused, and her cheeks turned pink. "You are not!"

"Certainly not, my dear, certainly not." Swann laughed heartily. "The duke and I have a matter of business to discuss. Nothing to do with you, nothing at all."

"Truly?" She gave her father a piercing look. St. Fell stepped back into the room out of her sight. She had an excellent piercing look.

"Absolutely, my dear," Swann said soothingly. He lowered his voice. "We are just having a small drink of brandy, that is all."

"Then I think I shall join you." Belcraven stepped back into the room, completely oblivious to Swann's warning look.

It must have satisfied Arabella, however, because Swann nodded and smiled and closed the door on the women. He walked back to the fireplace and turned on St. Fell with a glare. "Well?" he demanded.

"I'll take her," St. Fell said.

Swann nodded. "Done." He pulled out his handkerchief. "Do you want to tell her, or should I?"

The coward. "You know perfectly well we cannot tell her," St. Fell said. "She wants to pick her own husband."

Swann's face turned red. "But she isn't going to do better than you!"

"She is going to pick me!" St. Fell said. "She just needs some time to realize it. We are going on a walk, aren't we?"

"I could just tell her she has to marry you to get her money." Swann dabbed at his forehead. "I know her. She'll complain for a few days—weeks possibly, but in her heart she'll be happy." He turned even redder. "She likes you," he muttered. "I knew she would."

"Yes, she likes me." St. Fell smiled. She had a particular fondness for his hands, even though she had no idea what he wanted to do with them the minute he got her alone—

"Damnation! Get that look off your face!" Swann shouted.

"I say, what about the brandy?" Belcraven said quickly.

"Forget the damned brandy," St. Fell said. Arabella Swann was too quick-witted for brandy.

Belcraven smiled. "Just like you forgot to find out what her marriage portion was before agreeing to marry her?"

Damn.

Swann burst into laughter and patted the idiot on the back.

"I suppose you're both entitled to know what their dowries are now." He tucked his thumbs into his waistcoat and swiveled his gaze between them. "Each girl gets fifty thousand."

St. Fell nodded. Exactly what he had expected.

Swann's smile turned into a smirk. "And a wedding gift outright of one hundred thousand."

Belcraven squeaked and fell into an armchair.

Swann preened even more. "Oh, and did I mention they each get a ten-percent share in the business?"

Belcraven moaned.

Swann gave St. Fell an evil smile. "Are you still certain that you want to leave it entirely up to Arabella?"

St. Fell looked down his nose at him. "Of course." She belonged to him.

Swann folded his arms across his chest. "You know she wants to marry for love?"

"I know." It wasn't a problem. St. Fell smiled. Miss Arabella Swann was head over heels in love with him.

"I am completely infatuated with him, of course." Arabella tugged the bottom of her spencer to fit more snugly over her bosom. The crimson silk would look very well in contrast to the Duke of St. Fell's navy blue superfine jacket. "He is outrageously charming and handsome and a rake. Any girl who spent five minutes in his company would feel exactly the same way."

"I am not infatuated with him." Diana stepped in front of the looking glass and scowled at her reflection.

"That is because you are infatuated with Lord Belcraven," Arabella said. "One cannot be infatuated with two men at once—it is forward."

"I am not infatuated with Lord Belcraven!" Diana said. "I am in love with Lord Belcraven!"

Arabella snorted. "You are no more in love with the Earl of Belcraven than I am in love with the Duke of St. Fell!"

Diana rearranged the folds of her pelisse. "Perhaps we are both in love."

How ludicrous. Arabella plucked her bonnet off the end of her bed, where Marie had placed it. "It is infatuation, quite obviously," she said. "It is hardly a mystery why. We have never been to London before. He is the first powerful man that we have met and he is a high-ranking peer. He is handsome and clever and witty and he does this little hitch with his shoulders that is really quite fascinating." She flushed at the memory.

Diana's face creased in puzzlement. "I do not recall Lord Belcraven having a hitch."

"Belcraven?" Honestly, her sister's infatuation was turning her into a henwit. "No one cares about Belcraven, Diana! I am talking about the Duke of St. Fell."

"I care about Lord Belcraven! Lord Belcraven is amiable and kind and handsome. Whereas the duke smirks and speaks too quickly."

"Will you stop saying 'Lord Belcraven' over and over again? I know perfectly well which moonstruck dolt you are gabbling about!" Arabella tried to tie the white silk ribbons of her bonnet into the rose at the left side of her chin as Marie had shown her, but the slippery silk was a lot harder to control than it looked when the maid had done it.

Diana reached over and took the ribbons from Arabella's fingers and started to tie the bow for her. "Lord Belcraven may be moonstruck, but he isn't a dolt. He is merely shy. And I like saying his name. Lord Belcraven. Lord Belcraven and the Countess of Belcraven."

Arabella lifted her chin so that her sister could see better. As if anyone would want to say Belcraven when they could say the Duke of St. Fell. His Grace, the Duke of St. Fell. And Her Grace, the Duchess of St. Fell, who would be the wife of the Duke of St. Fell. St. Fell.

Hell. She was beginning to sound as witless as her sister. "How do you know you love Lord Belcraven?" she asked. Even though the question was completely ridiculous.

Diana's face lit up. It was obviously something she

had thought about. "Whenever I am with him, I am happy and I feel as though everything in my life is right and the way it should be. And I want him to be happy as well."

Which, Arabella could say with the utmost confidence, was not how she felt about St. Fell. She felt unsettled in his presence. Nor did she want the best for him. She wanted him to want the best for her. To think she was wonderful. Which was not the same thing at all. Obviously, she was infatuated.

"Do you think that Lord Belcraven loves you?" She felt compelled to ask her sister in the interest of being thorough. "Has he said so?"

Diana's cheeks turned pink, but she didn't look up from the ribbon. "Oh, Lord Belcraven is too shy to declare himself on such short acquaintance. I think he does, but it is not as if one can ever know for certain, of course." She smiled at Arabella. "I suppose one just has to have faith."

Faith. As opposed to incontrovertible evidence that the person wanted one for one's fortune. Evidence such as wanting to marry her before he had even met her. Arabella stifled a sigh. She was certain the Duke of St. Fell had fallen in love at first sight. With her fortune. Not that she could blame him. Hell, she would love to have her fortune. But she wanted to marry for love. And just because she came with a fortune didn't mean that she wasn't entitled to be loved for herself.

Diana spun her around so that she could see the ribbon in the looking glass. It was a perfect rose. Arabella thanked her.

"I still say you are in love with your duke," Diana said. "Although I do not see why. He tripped you!"

"He is a rake, you know." Arabella tilted her bonnet to the left side at a slight angle.

"Lord Belcraven would never trip me."

Poor Diana. Lord Belcraven would likely trip over the hassock himself and dash out his own brains. Arabella put her arm around her sister's shoulders. "Lord Belcraven is very nice, in his own way, I am sure, but the Duke of St. Fell does this most astonishing movement with his shoulders that frankly I do not think gentlemen ought to do in the presence of chaperones." She closed her eyes and pictured the way that St. Fell had hitched his shoulders, which had made her knees go quite weak.

She threw back her shoulders and pushed forward her chest and tipped her head back and slightly to the side. She glanced in the looking glass. It wasn't quite the same. She tilted her hips slightly forward. There.

"You look like a pelican," Diana said.

"Diana, you must not tease Arabella." Aunt Ophelia walked into the bedchamber, tugging on her gloves. "She most certainly does not look like a pelican. You are both very pretty. Well?" She looked at them both and smiled. "Are you ready? You are both going out for your first walk on the arm of a suitor! It is so exciting!"

"I do not know why we cannot just walk in the back garden," Diana said. "It is so much cozier for having a conversation than Soho Square."

Aunt Ophelia sighed. "I am afraid your father has concerns about the Duke of St. Fell and shrubbery." She looked over at Arabella and beamed. "He truly is a rake, isn't he!"

Arabella nodded modestly.

Aunt Ophelia put her arm around her and pulled her close. "I am so happy for you, dearest! To find such a fine man who is so obviously perfect for you and for you both to fall head over heels in love—"

"We are not in love!" Honestly. Why did everyone

insist on trying to turn the matter into a Minerva Press romance?

"But—but the way you spoke to each other," Aunt Ophelia sputtered. "The way you looked at him, Arabella! My stars! The way he looked at you!"

Arabella shook her head. "It is infatuation. An attraction based only on the most superficial of characteristics. His appearance. His status. The fact that he is a rake practiced in making women fall at his feet." And he was insufferably smug about it.

Aunt Ophelia's brow furrowed. "But he seemed so sincere in his appreciation of you."

"And I am certain his appreciation had nothing to do with the size of my fortune." Arabella pulled on her kid gloves. "Because there would be nothing more natural than for a handsome rake of a duke to fall head over heels in love at first sight with a completely green girl from a merchant family."

Aunt Ophelia's shoulders sagged and she sank down on the chaise longue at the bottom of Arabella's bed. "I suppose you are right. It is much too early. I am on Chapter Ten of *Love's Heartsick Longing* and Raphael still has not suffered enough to realize that he loves sweet Lady Delfinia."

Arabella snorted. "The cabbagehead does not realize it until—"

"Do not tell me!" Aunt Ophelia cried.

Arabella shared an exasperated glance with her sister. It was hardly a secret. Everyone knew how it was going to come out at the end.

"In any event," Aunt Ophelia said, "we are speaking of our duke. And I must say, Arabella, I think you are perfectly suited."

"Well, he is charming and clever," Arabella conceded,

"but he is also conceited and sarcastic and thinks he knows everything."

Diana snickered. "That is what Aunt Ophelia is saying. You are perfectly suited."

Arabella stuck out her tongue at her.

Diana blew her a kiss back, then put her hands on her hips and took one last frown at her appearance in the looking glass. "I cannot believe I let you talk me into a pelisse the color of a dead stoat."

"Stoat becomes you," Arabella said.

"Well, it will not do! Lord Belcraven's coat is puce. We shall clash horribly!"

As if it mattered. The man was only going to notice her shoes. "You look fine," Arabella said.

"But I am going to be out in public on the arm of an earl!" Diana wailed.

"We cannot ring for a maid and wait for an hour while you change, Diana," Aunt Ophelia said. "The men are drinking brandy."

"Oh, I do not like any of my clothes anyway." Diana sighed. "Unless Arabella would let me wear something of hers?" She went over to Arabella's wardrobe and opened the door and stared inside.

Arabella put her hands on her hips. "We do not have time."

"What about this one?" Diana pulled out the new blue jaconet muslin with the bows on the shoulders.

"I have not even worn it yet!"

Diana brought it to the looking glass and held it against herself. "But the color looks so well on me! And you want me to hurry. It will take forever if I have to go back to my room and try to decide which of my boring and completely inadequate dresses I want to wear."

"Absolutely not," Arabella said.

Thirty minutes later, they descended the staircase,

Aunt Ophelia in front, Arabella beside her, and Diana trailing behind, wearing Arabella's new blue jaconet muslin with the bows on the shoulders.

Amazingly, the men were standing in the foyer, waiting for them, their beaver hats already on. The Duke of St. Fell wore his tilted at an angle. Rakish of course. As soon as Arabella reached the landing on the stairs above him, he looked over his shoulder right into her eyes and smiled. As if he knew she was watching him and waiting for him to notice her. And then he pivoted to face her, and his shoulders did that particular hitch, and his body seemed to angle toward her and he got a silky look in his eyes, and suddenly Arabella found herself clinging to the bannister, no longer certain that her knees would hold her all the way down the rest of the stairs.

"My stars, Arabella," Aunt Ophelia breathed in her ear.

Arabella nodded, unable to speak. He was a rake. He was a fortune hunter. He was smug. But still. Hell.

St. Fell's smirk deepened, and his eyebrow quirked as if he knew perfectly well she was cursing.

"You know, Arabella," Aunt Ophelia whispered, "from this particular angle he does not appear to be hunting your fortune."

"Where is Lord Belcraven?" Diana asked.

Arabella gritted her teeth. What was the point of coming to London and meeting gentlemen if Diana was going miss something as exciting as this? A duke. Being a rake. It was better than any play they had seen in the theater.

Lord Belcraven appeared from behind the Grecian urn, and Arabella heard Diana catch her breath. Obviously her sister had missed St. Fell completely, her view blinded yet again by that lump of a Belcraven, whose face flared red like a sunset the instant he caught sight of Diana. Or rather, Diana's shoes, judging from where his gaze seemed to be fixed.

Arabella looked back at St. Fell, who immediately ran his eyes down the length of her body until he reached the toes of her half-walking boots, and he smiled and nodded as if he also found them admirable. Ridiculous man. She looked away and tried to breathe evenly. It was very warm in the Belcraven House foyer.

Diana gave her arm to Belcraven, who blushed so deeply as he took it he was now beet red from hat to cravat. The man couldn't look more self-conscious and awkward if he had tried. It was obvious he had never courted a woman before. It was probably the first time he had walked out in public with one on his arm. He was completely pathetic. Heaven only knew what Diana saw in him.

But her sister smiled up into his eyes as though he were the most thrilling man in London, and they went out the front door and down the front steps.

St. Fell held his arm out, and Arabella slipped hers through it, and the slide of her spencer's silk sleeve against the rougher wool of his coat made her catch her breath. She could feel the hardness of the muscles of his arm under hers as they stepped down the stairs and they followed Diana and Belcraven through the wrought-iron gate onto Dean Street.

Arabella's heart pounded, and her breathing became ragged. Who would have thought that linking one's arm with a man would be so exciting? Infatuation was really quite delicious. If this was what Diana was feeling, perhaps she ought not to have teased her so. And the best thing of all was that if this was infatuation, then when she fell in love, it would be perfect, because hopefully being in love was exactly like being infatuated, but without the nerve-wracking anxiety.

Such as the nerve-wracking anxiety with which she suddenly found herself gripped by over the right amount of pressure to apply with her arm. She needed to find the balance between holding her arm firmly enough to show she had a mind of her own, yet being yielding enough to show she was willing to walk with him. If the circumstances were right. If he went where she wanted to go. Perhaps! Hell. She stared at the red silk of her sleeve against the navy blue of his arm and willed herself not to think about it.

And to make matters worse, St. Fell was a foot taller than she, which meant that she couldn't see his face from underneath the brim of her bonnet without tilting her head all the way back, which would, of course, look completely affected. Not to mention as if she were begging for his attention, as opposed to merely strolling down Dean Street in an ordinary fashion, enjoying the sights of absolutely nothing because she was too busy trying not to think overmuch about the feel of her arm in his, as if she were a great green idiot of a Minerva Press moron who was struck completely brainless by being on the arm of a handsome duke!

His free hand reached over and he tilted up her bonnet with his finger.

"What the devil is going on down there?" he asked. "You're twitching like a landed trout."

How romantic. Arabella looked into his eyes, trying to remember to keep walking, and not to bite her lip. She was not going to tell him the truth, of course. In the first place, even though he was her first gentleman, she knew perfectly well young ladies did not blurt out their feelings of infatuation. Especially when the subject of the infatuation was a fortune-hunting rake. In the second place, he would gloat. Even though a part of her suspected he knew perfectly well she was infatuated with him and he was already gloating.

"It is a lovely day for a walk," she said, bracing herself for his smirk. It was better to have him deride the banality of her topic than to have him gloat.

"The weather?" He shook his head, deriding her, just as she had predicted. "Even Belcraven and your sister have managed to stumble their way past the weather."

Arabella followed his gaze. She hadn't realized that Diana and Belcraven were standing at the corner right in front of them, waiting for a donkey cart to go through the intersection at Carlisle Street. Not that Diana and Lord Belcraven noticed anyone else except themselves. They didn't even glance back at her and St. Fell.

"The blue of the trim brings out the sparkle in your eyes," Lord Belcraven said.

Diana, heaven help her, giggled.

"Sickening, isn't it?" St. Fell murmured. He held Arabella back so that Diana and Lord Belcraven walked ten paces ahead of them. "That is the sixth time he has complimented her on the color of her cloak. Once more, and I'd say he wants to wear it himself."

"He is completely ridiculous," Arabella said, feeling the muscles in St. Fell's arm as they stepped off the curb and into the street. His body felt as lean and as firm as it had when he had carried her. She tried not to think about it. Overmuch.

"Yet your sister seems amused by him," he said.

"It is mystifying. He is an idiot." Another pull of his arm as they stepped up onto the opposite curb.

"True. But he is a war hero idiot. He was wounded at Vittoria. And he is the most amiable dolt in creation and he and your sister are obviously head over heels in love."

"My sister deserves better than some idiot earl of a fortune hunter!"

"What does it matter if he's a fortune hunter if she loves him?" St. Fell's eyes glinted with laughter.

Arabella forced herself to stop gawking up at him like a complete goosecap and turn her head forward. She would keep walking just as he was, if it killed her. And she would breathe evenly. He was a rake, trying to manipulate her. Only a great idiot of a girl would allow herself to pant because of it.

"She cannot possibly love him," she said as soon as she was certain her voice would sound steady. "She is infatuated."

He laughed. "Of course, you are the great expert on the subject, having just arrived from Little Nowhere."

She opened her mouth to protest just as they were suddenly forced to swerve two steps to the left as an old man in a greatcoat pushed past them and their evasive maneuver allowed the skirt of her dress to brush up between St. Fell's legs. Possibly. She swallowed.

St. Fell halted in the middle of the sidewalk. Arabella looked up to find his eyes locked on hers. "Perhaps she is in love with him but too inexperienced to realize it," he rasped.

"She barely knows him," she whispered.

He slid his hands along her arms to her shoulders and Arabella swore she could feel the heat of his touch all the way through her pelisse. Then he jerked and let go of her. And cursed under his breath as he shot a scowl over his shoulder and rubbed the small of his back.

Arabella leaned to the side so she could see past him. She had forgotten all about Aunt Ophelia and Papa. Sure enough, they were standing directly behind St. Fell. Aunt Ophelia beamed and waved. Papa scowled and waved a walking stick. Which Arabella had never seen before. Sometimes she hated her father.

Honestly, Papa," she said. "We are in the middle of

Soho Square in broad daylight. I have no idea what trouble you think the duke and I could get into."

"That's the trouble, Arabella." Papa glared at the duke. "You have no idea."

St. Fell folded his arms across his chest. "Since I am trying to give her an idea, I do not see what the trouble is."

"Oh look!" Aunt Ophelia cried. "A confectioner is moving into Soho Square!" She grabbed Arabella by the arm and dragged her over to the shop front on the corner. Arabella looked over her shoulder. St. Fell stood at the curb with his arms crossed, his firm jaw clenched as he listened to Papa, who was talking without stopping, punctuated with repeated stick waving. Lord Belcraven and Diana retraced their steps as well, and Lord Belcraven joined the gentlemen.

"What is the problem?" Diana asked as she came to the confectioner's window.

"The duke was trying to kiss Arabella in the middle of Soho Square!" Aunt Ophelia squealed.

"No!" Diana's jaw dropped in an expression of horror.

"He is a rake!" Arabella said defensively.

"Lord Belcraven would never try to kiss me in the middle of Soho Square," Diana said.

Arabella and her aunt patted her sister's shoulder consolingly.

Papa and Aunt Ophelia decided that Lord Belcraven and Diana would be allowed to cross to the green and walk in a circle around the statue of King Charles in the company of the footman who had followed them from Belcraven House, both Papa and Aunt Ophelia being of the opinion that they did not truly need a chaperone except for form's sake.

Poor Diana actually tried to look pleased by this.

After much negotiation between Papa and St. Fell, they agreed that Arabella and St. Fell were to stand in the window outside the confectioner's, and Papa could watch them from the inside as Aunt Ophelia ordered confections, it being agreed that this would allow them to have a private conversation whilst still under the careful scrutiny of Papa and his stick. This compromise was arrived at as the duke did not feel that Papa could be trusted to allow them a private conversation without using the stick, and Papa did not think that the duke could be trusted out of stick's range. They were to have thirty minutes, and Papa and Aunt Ophelia were to eat an ice inside the confectioner's if necessary, to allow the full duration of time.

Papa gave St. Fell a lingering look over his shoulder as he followed Aunt Ophelia through the shop door.

"Yes, yes, I know," St. Fell muttered. "Facing forward with my hands to myself."

Arabella peered through the window. A little man with an enormous mustache nodded enthusiastically while Aunt Ophelia pointed at the bonbons heaped in silver trays on the mahogany counter. Papa stood in the middle of the shop, looking out the window at her and the duke. He had his stick in one hand and his pocket watch in the other.

Arabella sighed. "I hope she thinks to buy nougat. Apricot, preferably." She was going to require nougat this evening, she could just feel it.

"Yes, those were my thoughts exactly," St. Fell said.

"I have a fondness for apricot nougat," she said.

"I am just trying to show you that that is not the only thing for which you have a fondness," he said.

"Oh no!" She blinked up at him, while keeping her head forward. "I also adore cherry nougats. And I am passionately in love with peppermint drops, of course."

"You know, this whole business is going to take a lot longer if you are going to keep pretending you do not want me as much as I want you."

"I am not pretending anything," she said. "I do not want to marry a fortune-hunting rake, thank you for asking. Repeatedly."

St. Fell rubbed the back of his neck with his hand. "Fine, deny it all you want. But I know you want me."

"Be still my heart! The duke is being romantic again!"

"Pardon me? I am standing like a great idiot in the middle of Soho Square, staring at a shop window after getting jabbed in the back by an annoyed papa with a walking stick I am quite convinced he does not need for walking and you are complaining about romance."

"It is not my fault Papa jabbed you with the stick. You were the one being ridiculous." If she tilted her head back, she could see their reflection in the glass, instead of Papa. The duke looked taller and straighter in the glass than she had noticed before—for a minute. Then his shoulders adjusted themselves in the familiar hitch and he looked like he always did. Her stomach fluttered.

"Ridiculous?" he said. "Is that what you call my clever plan of seduction? I am beginning to feel my skills are wasted on you. If you move your head to the right a bit, then you will see us, not your father."

"I know." She nodded, watching her hat bob in the reflection. Her head was just at the top of his shoulder, even with the bonnet. He was easily six feet tall. Even with the hitch.

"That is another reason why we are perfectly suited—neither one of us is the slightest bit romantic," he said.

"I am very romantic," she said automatically. He snorted predictably. The quality of the reflection was good enough that she could see them both smile. He was smirking, of course.

"God, you're short, aren't you?" he said after a minute.

"If that is your idea of small talk with a woman," she said, "I am beginning to understand why you require a hassock."

He shrugged. "No woman with any sense is going to believe a man who starts spouting ridiculous compliments after only a brief acquaintance."

"You told me that you loved me after half an hour's acquaintance!"

"And you did not believe me."

"Well, honestly! It was most unconvincing. I expected better from a rake." She sniffed at him. "Perhaps you are merely a rogue."

"A rogue? Certainly not. A man may as well be a rascal as be a rogue."

"Or a roué."

"A roué!" He looked down his nose at her in the glass.

She burst into laughter. "You look just like a duke!"

"I am a duke, madam. But I will never be a roué."

"Oh dear. I have ruffled your feelings. Now I shall never get a decent declaration of love out of you." She was flirting with a gentleman!

"I do not think there is a thing in the world I could say to convince you."

"Oh, I don't know," she said. "I am completely green. I would likely believe any flummery you could come up with."

"Ah, you say that, Miss Arabella Swann. But I think you are trying to trick me. You are being naughty again. You want me to tell you that I love you, and then you will sneer and say it isn't true and feel very superior to the wicked London rake."

"I have just arrived in town, Your Grace, and you are so sophisticated. I am sure you will come up with something that will take me in completely."

"Well, I suppose, since I am trying to marry you, I could declare my affections again."

"Thank you."

"I think it would be more effective if it included a compliment, don't you?"

She nodded. She had always known it would be wonderful to be flirting with a gentleman, but she had never dreamed she would feel this happy.

"Let's see." He clasped his hands behind his back and rocked back on his heels, and Arabella could see him look up in the reflection in the window. "She is petite, has a superior figure, slender ankles—"

"How would you know about my ankles?" she demanded.

"I looked while I was carrying you, of course," he said. "Her face is very pretty, her hair just begs for my fingers to run through it, her eyes are warm and intelligent, she blushes only infrequently and most attractively when she does, she has superior sense of style in her clothes—oh and don't forget fascinating shoes . . ." he tailed off. "Difficult. So many good features, a man doesn't know where to start."

Arabella's stomach quivered in anticipation even though she knew they were just playing.

"Are you ready?" he asked after a moment.

She nodded, grateful that they were both facing the window and that he wasn't going to try to look in her eyes.

He cleared his throat. "I love you, Miss Swann. I have loved you from the very first instant I saw you, and I will love you until I take my dying breath. I do not love you for your money. I love you for yourself. For your wonderful sparkling personality, for your sharp sarcastic tongue, for your fine sense of the ridiculous."

Good heavens! Arabella reached out to the glass to

support herself. Hell! She snatched her hand back. Papa was scowling. She smiled weakly at him.

"That was very good," she said.

St. Fell bowed his head. "Thank you."

A minute passed while she tried to stop panting without putting her hand on her bosom and worrying Papa. St. Fell smirked the entire time.

"Well?" he asked. "I cannot endure the suspense a second longer. Did it do the trick? Will you marry me?"

"Certainly not!"

"Whyever not? It was excellent! For God's sake, this is taking forever!"

"Forever! I have barely known you three hours! You expect me to give less consideration to choosing a husband than I would to buying a hat!"

"Good lord, it doesn't take you three hours to buy a hat, does it? Because I am not going to be one of those husbands who sits in the milliner's—"

"That is not what I mean!" She flushed. "I mean, you are my first suitor—"

"No! Truly?"

"Yes! You have seen my father!" She shifted her head slightly to catch Papa scowling at them, then quickly moved her head back so she could see St. Fell again. "He has not encouraged suitors and Little Darking is very small and mostly consists of Swanns. You are the first suitor he has allowed—" She stopped abruptly, her heart sinking. "You and he did not agree I would marry you, after we left you in the north reception room, did you?"

"Certainly not!" St. Fell looked offended.

"I am terribly sorry!" She had forgotten he was a duke! One did not accuse dukes of sneaking. "It is just that my father is determined for me to settle the matter with you, even though he promised I could come to London and meet eligible gentlemen and decide for myself. So far, you are the only eligible gentleman to whom I have been introduced."

It was impossible to see the expression in St. Fell's eyes, since he was facing forward as Papa had instructed. But he didn't answer immediately, which was unusual. He probably thought she was too forward in her desire to make the acquaintance of other gentlemen.

She sighed. "I do not expect you to understand."

"Actually, I was thinking that your position is not completely unreasonable." He shrugged. "After all, I have had my fair share of hats."

"Yes, of course." He was a rake. She wondered how many women that meant. How many women he had told that he loved them. She sighed again. Of course, there was no point asking him. He would say anything.

"Ah," he said in a meaningful tone. He looked down at her, and his smirk evaporated, and the expression in his eyes turned urgent and honest. "I know what you are worried about, Arabella. You need not be. I promise I will be faithful."

Good heavens! She wanted to look away and say something sarcastic. She wanted to tell him she wasn't going to marry him. She probably wasn't going to marry him. There was a chance she wouldn't marry him. But all she was able to do was burn in the heat of his eyes, and the way he called her by her first name, and remember how Aunt Ophelia had said reformed rakes made the best husbands, and try to forget that he was a fortune-hunting rake whom she had only known a few hours, and if she showed the slightest interest in him Papa would make sure her whole trip to London was as boring as her life had been up until she had first set eyes on the duke.

Hell.

"You can say it aloud if you like," he whispered.

Hell. Surely her face wasn't that expressive? She didn't even know what the hell she was thinking.

"I beg your pardon?" she said. Hell. He had made her squeak again!

"You could say 'hell.'" He swallowed. "Aloud." His whisper was so low it was almost a moan.

There was a loud sound of a man clearing his throat.

Good heavens! Papa! Arabella looked over in alarm. But it was a captain in the guards, standing in front of them with his hands on his hips. She took a breath she didn't even realize she was holding. Of course, she ought to have known it wasn't Papa. Papa had the stick.

"I say, St. Fell, how amazing to find you here, in the middle of Soho Square, roaming unfettered with an innocent girl in your clutches," the captain said.

St. Fell cursed under his breath. "What an astonishing coincidence this is not," he said, and introduced Arabella to his brother, Captain Tobias Warburton, Lord Toby. She ought to have realized it immediately. He looked very similar to St. Fell, tall, lean, golden, with a smirk, except he was younger and softer and not in the least the Duke of St. Fell. Nor did he have the slightest hitch.

The captain shrugged. "I suppose if the Swanns' butler had not been so kind as to tell me where to look, I never would have happened to run into you." He bowed over her hand. "Is he annoying you overmuch, Miss Swann? He comes with a leash, you know."

"He needs a leash," Papa muttered, coming out of the confectioner's with Aunt Ophelia. They were each carrying two boxes of bonbons, thank heavens.

Chapter 4

"The slink?" St. Fell pinched the bridge of his nose to keep from strangling his mother. "What the devil is the slink?"

"The St. Fell slink." His mother settled herself against the squabs of the carriage so she could look down her nose at him with her usual irritatingly smug expression. "Toby told me that you were slinking around that rich potter's daughter in Soho Square yesterday."

"You bastard." St. Fell glared across at his brother.

"I don't know how many times I have asked you not to call your brother a bastard," his mother said. "After all, it is actually an insult to me."

"Yes, St. Fell," Toby said. "Don't be such a bastard."

"Shut up, Toby," his mother said. "In any event, the slink is a particular twist of the shoulders that a St. Fell does when he has fallen in love."

St. Fell closed his eyes. He was going to have to start keeping a bottle of whiskey in the carriage.

"You remember, St. Fell," Toby said. "Father used to do it all the time whenever Mother came in the room."

Two bottles.

"Belcravens don't slink," that idiot Belcraven said.

Two bottles and a gun.

"Oh, you can stop being all silent and brooding, St.

Fell," his mother snapped. "You are acting like a Minerva Press hero—a bad Minerva Press hero, at that."

"It is just like a Minerva Press romance!" Toby crowed. "The sweet innocent virgin, the wicked rake trying to get into her—"

"Shut up, Toby!" St. Fell and his mother shouted at the same time.

"—good graces," Toby concluded, his smirk even more moronic than usual.

"As for you"—Mother raised a jeweled lorgnette to her eyes and fixed her beady stare on St. Fell—"why don't you just offer for the girl if you are in love? You are a duke. Even if the girl was too green to want you, her papa would march her down the aisle so fast you would be married before the ink was dry on the bank draft for her marriage portion."

Belcraven sat up and opened his mouth, but Toby, who was sitting directly across from him, kicked him before St. Fell could and Belcraven sank back on his seat next to Mother. Not before her lorgnette had swiveled in the idiot's direction, though. Damn.

She aimed her lorgnette back at St. Fell. "Have you offered for the girl then?" she asked slowly.

"No, of course he did not!" Belcraven said proudly. "Miss Swann wants to pick her own husband and her father promised her she could and St. Fell and Joseph Swann did not make any agreement behind her back."

Then he and Toby glanced at each other and collapsed into gales of laughter. One week in his house and the idiot thought he was one of his brothers. St. Fell tried not to give either one of them the satisfaction of seething openly.

"You made a deal with the father behind the girl's back?" Mother threw herself back against her seat. "I would not blame her if she married someone else to spite you. A woman likes to believe she has a choice. Even where she has none."

St. Fell folded his arms across his chest. "Thank you for your interest, Mother. Now stay the hell out of it." Everything was perfectly fine. Arabella would be his by this evening.

"Well? You still have not answered." Her lorgnette magnified her eyes into bloodshot robin's eggs. "Are you in love with the girl or not?"

"What the devil is that?" He jerked his chin at the lorgnette.

"It is a lorgnette," she said impatiently. "I shouldn't have thought love would make you stupid, but you are a man, so I suppose it is inevitable. I certainly hope it is not one of those dreary situations where you are afraid of saying you love her because it is an unmanly thing to admit?"

"I mean, why have you sprouted a lorgnette?" he said.

"For goodness' sake, St. Fell!" She reached across the carriage and smacked his knuckles with the lorgnette. "I am a duchess and these people are from the merchant class. They are expecting a heartwarming scene where the dowager Duchess of St. Fell inspects their daughter and decides to accept her regardless of her humble, yet fabulously wealthy origins. I am going to peer at her through my lorgnette. I cannot believe you require me to explain it."

God. He clenched his teeth and tried not to moan. He had everything arranged perfectly. His courtship of Arabella had already been cocked up by her father. They didn't need any more help from his mother. And if his mother got the notion to help him today, she would defeat the whole purpose of Arabella going to the Carr party.

"Of course, I am assuming she has all the qualifications to become a duchess," his mother continued, still refusing to spontaneously combust. "Intelligence, determination, firm opinions, and a monkey."

"Miss Swann is clever, determined and has as many opinions as St. Fell," Toby said.

"No monkey, though," Belcraven said.

"Well, it doesn't have to be a monkey," Mother said. "I had a python when I met the duke. Any unusual pet will do. Either that or she curses."

"Dash it, I don't think she curses," Belcraven said.

"Oh, I don't know," Toby said. "Look at St. Fell's face. He's as red as your hair. I'm willing to bet money she curses."

St. Fell willed himself not to blush as he shot Toby his most threatening glare. Toby laughed, damn him.

"How much?" Belcraven said.

Toby shrugged. "Probably every time she speaks to St. Fell, poor girl."

"No, how much do you want to wager she curses?" Belcraven said.

"There will be no wagering on the girl your brother is going to marry!" Mother barked. "That is exactly the kind of thing which leads to misunderstandings that prolong a romance even longer. In any event, we are still discussing Miss Swann."

"We are not discussing Miss Swann," St. Fell said.

"Yes, I can see that," his mother said in a knowing tone. She turned to nod at Belcraven and Toby. "You are absolutely right. She is all he can not talk about."

"It's quite sweet, really," Toby said.

"Dashed aggravating if you ask me," Belcraven complained. "He's never going to get Arabella Swann out of the way of Diana's happiness if he won't even discuss the girl."

"I think I can manage my private life without the help of the three blind mice," St. Fell said.

"Your private life affects us!" Mother snapped. "Especially if she is wealthy. I only pray she redecorates the drawing room first. I am heartily sick of that Egyptian papyrus wallpaper."

St. Fell glanced at Toby, and they both refrained from mentioning how they and Father and every one of their brothers were all heartily sick of it the day before it went up, at her insistence, twelve years ago.

"Listen"—he leaned forward and used his best firm, yet casual tone—"this is one of those matters that will proceed much more smoothly without any more meddling from interfering relatives."

"Aha!" She flicked the damned lorgnette under his nose. "You nearly admitted you were in love with her!"

St. Fell leaned back with a shrug. "I nearly kill Belcraven every morning, doesn't mean I do."

"Look at that, Belcraven," Toby said. "St. Fell is beginning to like you. He didn't say 'that idiot Belcraven.'"

"I'd like him too, if he could persuade Arabella Swann to marry him," Belcraven said.

Mother's lorgnette quivered. "Does the girl not return his affection?"

Toby smirked. "Oh, Miss Swann returns it all most obviously."

"She does not realize it," Belcraven said. "Her sister Diana says Arabella thinks she is merely infatuated—"

"Merely infatuated while a St. Fell is slinking?" Mother bristled. "Who does she think she is? It is an insult to our family!"

"Just stay out of it." Please. God. St. Fell took off his hat and rubbed his temples.

His mother sniffed indignantly. "I am not going to interfere! You are a grown man. A duke and a rake. I should think you could manage to get yourself married without requiring your mother to pin a note to your jacket. Even if the girl is an obvious henwit."

Two bottles of whiskey, a gun, and a muzzle.

"In any event, you never answered the question. Do you love the girl or not?"

"Why, Mother," he said, "you will have to sneak into my bedchamber while I am out and peek at my secret diary where I write down all my deepest thoughts and feelings." He leaned back against the squabs and closed his eyes again.

"Seven sons," she moaned. "It is beyond all reason. Why couldn't I have had one daughter? One other person of sensitivity."

St. Fell tried not to smile. His mother would figure it out the minute she saw Arabella. It was obvious in her every move, from the way her eyes never left him to the way she tried to pretend she wasn't breathless when they spoke. Arabella Swann was head over heels in love with him. St. Fell shifted himself more comfortably in the corner of the carriage.

"Is that the slink?" that idiot Belcraven asked.

Toby brayed.

"Our first London party! Isn't it exciting!" Aunt Ophelia quivered on the edge of her seat as their carriage pulled up in front of the Carrs' elegant Mayfair town house. "I am so glad your father agreed you could both attend."

Arabella looked out the window. There were three carriages ahead of them waiting in line to disgorge their passengers. "You know perfectly well why Papa decided to let us come," she said. "He felt guilty because he went behind my back yesterday and agreed with the duke that he could marry me." Again.

"Now, Arabella, we do not know that for certain that is what transpired," Aunt Ophelia said. "Deakin merely said that the gentlemen were discussing the subject of dowries when he brought them the brandy."

Arabella rolled her eyes. What else could it be? It had taken six pineapple nougats to get Deakin to admit that much. He refused to tell any more on the grounds of masculine solidarity. Next time she would use strawberry ice. Of course she should have known that St. Fell and Papa would stick together. And that St. Fell would lie about it. He had told her he would say anything to get her to marry him. She just hoped he would not make a big fuss today at the party when she was meeting all the other wonderful, eligible gentlemen. She knew he was going to be here. His brother said St. Fell and Gabriel Carr were best friends. That was how Papa had come to meet St. Fell yesterday when he had called on Mr. Carr.

"In any event," Aunt Ophelia said. "The wonderful thing is that your papa has allowed you to go to Mrs. Carr's party. It was very wise of you not to make a fuss about it."

Arabella folded her arms across her chest. She wasn't stupid. Arguing with Papa would just give him a reason not to let her come to the Carrs' party. And she certainly wanted to attend the Carrs' party. It promised to be very amusing. Everyone knew that Mr. Gabriel Carr was head over heels with Lord Belcraven's sister, Lady Nola. Everyone, except Mr. Carr, who apparently did not want to marry a woman from the *ton*. Not that Lady Nola was the slightest bit *tonnish*. They had met her and Mrs. Carr last week when Lady Nola was canvassing support for war widows. Lady Nola was quite drab and just as amiable as Lord Belcraven. Mr. Carr's mother proposed to prove to her son that he preferred Lady Nola by throwing a party and inviting marriageable girls from merchant families who met his criteria. But best of all, Mrs. Carr had invited a choice selection of London's most eligible bachelors to pretend to pay court to Lady Nola in order to make Mr. Carr jealous.

Thirteen of London's most eligible gentlemen. And the lying, smug Duke of St. Fell.

He had better not interfere with her meeting gentlemen. Papa was already going to be trouble enough. He had spent the morning grumbling and puffing and waving his stupid stick. He was coming to the party from Swann's Fine China Emporium. Hopefully he would not insist she spend the entire afternoon with St. Fell.

"Well, I am glad that Lord Belcraven and Papa have agreed we will be married," Diana said as they descended the carriage. "I am looking forward to meeting his aunts."

Aunt Ophelia nodded. "I am sure the Countesses of Belcraven are just as amiable as Lord Belcraven and Lady Nola."

"I am so pleased you could come after all!" Mrs. Carr trotted across the foyer to greet them as soon as the Carrs' ancient butler had taken their cloaks. "Mr. Swann is already here, but he is in the study waiting for Gabriel. Everyone else is in the drawing room."

As if to directly contradict her, there was a loud thumping above them on the staircase. They all looked up. Mrs. Carr sighed. Two elderly women were descending the stairs at the same time, each one clinging to opposite sides of the bannisters. The thumping sound was caused by each one striking her walking stick on each step. One was tall and wore a powdered wig and a patch on her wrinkled cheek and a laced-up stomacher, and either her dress had hoops or she was hiding a smuggler. She looked as though she had stepped out of a painting from fifty years ago. A very ugly painting. The second old woman was tiny and wore a filmy white muslin gown that Arabella would have found too young for herself when she was sixteen.

They landed in the foyer, and Mrs. Carr performed the introductions. The tall bewigged one was Lady Hortensia. The tiny one was her sister-in-law, Lady Caroline.

The Countesses of Belcraven. Lord Belcraven's aunts. Arabella and Diana curtsied.

"Which one of you thinks she is good enough to marry an Earl of Belcraven?" Lady Hortensia demanded.

Diana thrust out her chin. "I am."

Lady Hortensia sniffed. "In my day, wealthy merchant heiresses did not fling themselves at eligible earls."

"Why, you nasty old cow!" Diana exclaimed.

"Diana!" Aunt Ophelia squealed.

Arabella choked on her laughter.

Lady Caroline struck Lady Hortensia smartly in the ankles with her stick. "Yes, do not be such a fusby-faced old muttonhead, Hortensia," she cackled. "This one looks like a prime goer. Lord only knows what she sees in that slowtop."

"My stars!" Aunt Ophelia clutched her heart.

"How dare you!" Diana's hands clutched spasmodically as if she were wishing for her own walking stick.

"We shall see what she sees in him!" Lady Hortensia hooked her arm through one of Diana's, and Lady Caroline took the other, and they started dragging Diana up the stairs at a very quick clip for old ladies who were using walking sticks. Arabella and Aunt Ophelia charged after them.

But Mrs. Carr grabbed their arms to hold them back. "There is no point," she said. "Sooner or later she is going to have to deal with them. In any event, she looks like she can look after herself."

"But they are horrid!" Aunt Ophelia said.

Arabella shuddered. Exceedingly horrid.

"They certainly are," Mrs. Carr agreed. "But they will not actually eat her." Her smile took on a fixed edge. "I do not think."

Before they could protest any further, the butler opened the front door, and Lord Belcraven and Lord Toby walked into the foyer.

"Speaking of horrid, here is the Duchess of St. Fell," Mrs. Carr said brightly. She leaned close to Arabella. "She is yours, is she not?"

"Certainly not!" Arabella said, and narrowed her eyes at the knowing look the woman exchanged with Aunt Ophelia.

"A chaperone can tell a lot about a man from the way he treats his mother," Aunt Ophelia whispered.

"Good Lord! I certainly hope not," Mrs. Carr said.

"Damn you, Mother, keep that blasted thing away from me!" St. Fell's voice rang out. He stepped into the foyer, took one look at Arabella, and hitched. Despite herself, her stupid stomach fluttered and her pulse started racing. Honestly, she was completely bubble-brained. Then he smirked at her as if he knew exactly what she was thinking.

"Shut up, St. Fell." A tall, boxy, middle-aged woman elbowed her way past him.

The dowager Duchess of St. Fell. St. Fell's mother. The woman Arabella would want to impress if she was going to marry St. Fell.

"Eleanor"—the duchess inclined her head in an imperious gesture to Mrs. Carr—"I see your son is still hopelessly in need of your assistance in the simple matter of courting."

"Piffle!" Mrs. Carr waved her hand airily. "You know Gabriel. It is the least I could do for him since he is so busy making a success at business and not gaming or drinking to excess. And how is your son's courtship progressing? I hear the Guards had to be called out to Soho Square yesterday."

St. Fell winked at her.

"He is a rake, you know," the duchess said.

He certainly was! He was flirting with his best friend's mother! Mrs. Carr's cheeks had turned pink, and her hands fluttered to her bosom.

"Where is Miss Diana?" Belcraven asked.

"She is making the acquaintance of your aunts," Aunt Ophelia said accusingly.

The earl paled, and then dashed up the stairs. Lord Toby galloped after him. "They're old, but they're wiry," he cried over his shoulder. Mrs. Carr followed on the grounds that the drawing room had breakables. Leaving Arabella with St. Fell. And his mother and Aunt Ophelia, of course.

"So this is Miss Arabella Swann," the duchess intoned in an ominous voice when it was Arabella's turn to be introduced. She raised an emerald-studded lorgnette to her watery blue eyes and made a great show of inspecting her through it.

St. Fell stood behind his mother's shoulder and rolled his eyes.

Arabella bit her lip to keep from laughing as she offered her moderate curtsy. The duchess must have been reading Minerva Press novels.

"Opinionated," the duchess said.

Hell. Arabella flushed. It was her wretched expressive face.

"And she curses," the duchess continued.

"She most certainly does not," St. Fell said. "I know. I have tried to make her."

"Your Grace being the great expert in eliciting curses from women," Arabella snapped. Why in heaven's name did he have to act like such a donkey when she was meeting his horrible mother?

He shrugged. "Curses, wails, moans—"

"St. Fell!" The duchess jabbed him in the ribs with her lorgnette. "You are being a complete jackass."

"She started it." He pointed at Arabella, and perhaps it was her imagination, but his finger seemed very close to her bosom. And it lingered. She flushed and looked away from his hand. He was completely impossible.

The duchess raised her lorgnette once again and peered through it at St. Fell, who smirked and shrugged his shoulders with a patently false innocent expression. Then the lorgnette swung back at Arabella. Then back at her son again for a very long moment. She opened her fingers and let her lorgnette dangle impotently on the long ribbon round her neck.

"I know." Aunt Ophelia sighed. "If I read it myself in a Minerva Press novel, I would throw it against the wall."

"Why don't you two run along to the drawing room," St. Fell said to Aunt Ophelia and his mother. "Miss Swann and I will be along shortly."

"Certainly not, Your Grace," Aunt Ophelia said. "I am afraid that you require the utmost in chaperoning."

St. Fell pointed at the Carrs' butler, who was standing at the door doing a very poor job of pretending not to listen. "Bartlett will supervise us."

The butler collapsed in wheezing laughter. St. Fell shot him a glare. The old man winked, then shuffled out of the foyer.

"I think I will chaperone you as well," the duchess said.

"God no!" St. Fell blenched.

"Oh, do not fuss! I am not Eleanor Carr. I have no intention of interfering." The duchess waved the lorgnette at him. "Carry on with your courting."

Aunt Ophelia gave him an encouraging smile. "I will not interfere either."

St. Fell folded his arms across his chest and looked down his nose at them both. "Your mere presence interferes."

"Yes, that is the point of chaperones," the duchess said. "Go ahead, tell the girl something romantic."

St. Fell pinched the bridge of his nose, and Arabella had to pinch herself to keep from dissolving in giggles.

The duchess smirked at him. "Well, if you are not going to be able to help yourself, why do you not slink off somewhere so that Miss Swann and I can get acquainted."

"No, I think I will stay here," he said. "I have a feeling if I leave, I will be the topic of conversation."

The duchess shrugged. "You have a great deal of faith in the persistence of your appeal."

"I have a great deal of faith in the persistence of you, Mother."

Arabella looked at Aunt Ophelia. If you could tell a lot about a man from the way he treated his mother, the Duke of St. Fell considered women equal combatants in a war.

"St. Fell!" Mrs. Carr called down from the landing. "Why don't you come join Mr. Swann in Gabriel's study? You know she is going to corner your Swann sometime. You may as well let her do it now while her aunt is present."

St. Fell looked at Arabella. She nodded. Mrs. Carr was right. And if Diana could face two Countesses of Belcraven, she could handle one duchess.

He leaned over her. "You can take her," he whispered, then ducked the lorgnette and went up the stairs.

The duchess shook her head. "Eleanor Carr has a passion to interfere," she said. She looked at Arabella. "Now, Miss Swann, what is the delay?"

Arabella goggled at her. Honestly! "What is the hurry?" she asked.

"You ask me that when you require a chaperone in a foyer?" the duchess said. "In any event, it is Michaelmas. Tomorrow St. Fell must go to Fairfield for the Harvest Festival and he will be gone a week. Surely that is reason to hurry."

Arabella wasn't the slightest bit surprised at the pang of disappointment that struck her at the thought that she would go a week without seeing him. She was completely infatuated. But she met the duchess's eyes. "I am not convinced your son wants me for myself, and not for my fortune."

The duchess's jaw dropped. "How green are you? Can you not see him? He is slinking!"

Arabella flushed. "I can see him." Hitch. "But that does not mean that he loves me."

"It means that a duke is wandering around like a complete beefwit."

Arabella shrugged. "Perhaps the thought of all of my money has made him dizzy."

"You are very cynical for a girl who has done nothing!"

Said by a woman who knew everything.

"Has he not told you that he loves you?" the duchess demanded.

"Yes. But—"

"Arabella!" Aunt Ophelia clapped her hands together. "That is wonderful! He told you he loves you!" She nodded sagely. "That is the hardest thing for a man to admit."

The duchess looked at her as if she were feebleminded.

Aunt Ophelia's face fell. "But it is always the last thing a Minerva Press hero says. Why, I am on Chapter Ten of *Love's Heartsick Longing* and Raphael still—"

"That Raphael is a complete idiot!" the duchess barked. "He should have told that insipid Delfinia he loved her the minute he set eyes on her. She is the only

woman on earth who would not have the good sense to
bash in his skull with a poker while he slept. Anyway, he
is nothing like an actual man. I should know. I was married to a rake and I have seven sons. All of whom are
rakes!" She lifted her lorgnette and looked through it
with authority. "The hardest thing for a man to say is
'You are right, dear, I have no idea where we are and I
shall ask that nice coachman to direct us.' As for 'I love
you'? Why the little bas—beasts say it at the drop of a
woman's—" She shook herself and took a deep breath,
then looked at Arabella. "Are you saying he has said that
he loves you and you do not believe it?"

"He lies," Arabella said.

"Of course he lies!" The duchess snorted dismissively.
"All men lie! Men are like wild beasts, except that you
cannot keep them in cages when they are young. The
neighbors complain that you are insensitive."

"Are men all like wild beasts because they are full of
lustful animal passions?" Aunt Ophelia asked hopefully.

The duchess shot her a worried look. "No, they are like
wild beasts because they do not want to be domesticated.
They want to live their lives according to their own pleasure and when they face an obstacle, they take the way that
will cause them the least effort. And frequently, that is
lying." She turned the lorgnette on Arabella. "In any
event, whether or not he loves you is completely irrele-
vant." She poked the lorgnette in Arabella's face. "Because
you are obviously head over heels in love with him."

"That is ridiculous," Arabella said. She turned on her
heel and marched up the stairs to the drawing room
before she could see if Aunt Ophelia was nodding
in mindless agreement. She was here to meet eligible
gentlemen. The Duchess of St. Fell could go to hell. The
old bat.

"Just because men are idiots," the duchess called up at

her from the foot of the stairs, "it does not mean that a woman cannot be a fool."

Yes. Arabella gripped the bannister more tightly. She must remember to embroider that on a pillow. And use it to smother the Duchess of St. Fell.

Five minutes. That's how long it would take Arabella to shed his mother and make her way to the drawing room. She was hell-bent on meeting those suitors. St. Fell smiled to himself as he opened the door to Gabriel's study. It was a shame there wasn't enough time for a wager on it.

Swann was sitting in one of the chairs opposite the monstrous mahogany desk, already drinking brandy.

Excellent.

Swann's scowl deepened when he saw who it was. "I don't know why you are making me do this!"

St. Fell fetched a glass from the cabinet. "Oh, stop grumbling. It will all be over in a few hours." He sat down in the chair next to Swann's.

"She is in the drawing room with every fortune hunter in London!"

"Exactly." St. Fell poured himself some brandy. "I told you, it's the only way. She will spend one afternoon in the company of London's most eligible bachelors and she'll be ready to marry me by dinner tonight."

"I still don't like it!" Swann drained his glass.

St. Fell refilled his glass for him. "Well, it is all entirely your fault."

"My fault?" Swann's entire head turned red and he struggled to push himself upright in his chair. "I'm not the one who can't convince one green girl about the merits of marriage. You had three hours!"

"That is because no one left us alone. I keep telling

you, five minutes in a nice dark corner and I could have persuaded her—Ow!" Damn. St. Fell rubbed his left ankle. He hadn't realized that Swann had brought his walking stick. He must have leaned it against the desk in front of his chair.

"Keep your hands off my daughter!" Swann rested his stick on his lap and took a sip of his brandy.

"We would have been married by special license today if you had let me put my—Stop that!" St. Fell put his glass down and wrested the damned walking stick out of the idiot's hand.

"You're talking about my daughter!" Swann shouted.

"No, we are speaking of my wife." Arabella belonged to him. St. Fell stowed the stick on his side of the desk, out of Swann's reach.

Swann drained his glass. "Which is why I don't understand why you would want her to hang about a house full of eligible men!" Swann pulled out his handkerchief and mopped his head. "You are courting trouble!"

"It is exactly what you should have done from the beginning, instead of trumpeting me in her face as Papa's great choice."

"It worked well enough with Belcraven!"

St. Fell shrugged. "Your other daughter is obviously more amenable than Arabella."

"Actually, Diana's the stubborn one. That's why Belcraven's perfect for her."

"Well Arabella is the one you promised could pick her own husband," St. Fell said. "And you were supposed to introduce her to eligible men." If Arabella had met him in a roomful of suitors, they would be deciding whether to marry by banns or by license right now.

"I brought you home, didn't I?" Swann said resentfully. The door slammed open. Belcraven wordlessly marched to the cabinet, took out a glass, marched over to the desk, poured himself a full glass of brandy, drained it, poured himself a second full glass, marched to the window seat, and flung himself down without spilling a drop of brandy.

"Aunts?" St. Fell asked.

Belcraven nodded.

St. Fell shrugged. "Arabella's talking to my mother."

"My sympathies, but dash it, there's only one of your mother." Belcraven took a long draw of brandy. "Although Diana is holding her own."

"My daughters can manage anyone!" Swann said. "They are diamonds."

The three of them raised their glasses in a toast.

"I could just have a talk with Arabella," Swann offered, reaching for the bottle again.

"Oh, yes," St. Fell said. "That will help tremendously."

"You don't have to be sarcastic! I can just explain that I was only introducing you as a possibility for her to consider. I misspoke."

St. Fell propped his boots up on the desk and tilted his chair back. "I've known her for one day and I know she will never believe that." In any event, Arabella likely knew he and Swann had agreed she would marry him.

"I still say my idea was better," Belcraven said. "You pretend to be Compton just back from the Continent, and you court her and she realizes she loves you and then you tell her it was actually you all along!"

"I thought I told you to stop reading those Minerva Press romances." St. Fell drained his glass.

"But it's dashed clever! Works all the time. You see, Roderick in *Passion's Sweet Promise*—"

"That was a good one." Swann grunted. "Plenty of carriage accidents."

"Arabella isn't some Minerva Press mousewit," St. Fell said. For God's sake. She'd not only never be fooled, she'd brain him. "She just wants to meet other men before she decides."

"But she isn't going to do better than you!" Swann said for the hundredth time.

St. Fell sighed. "I know that, and you know that, but she doesn't. Anyway we wasted the afternoon yesterday talking and eating our tasty bonbons. I still don't see why we didn't just go for a walk in your back garden." Where there was undoubtedly excellent shrubbery.

"Because you are a damned rake!" Swann slammed the brandy bottle down on the desktop.

St. Fell shrugged. It took one to know one. In any event, Arabella liked that he was a rake. Just thinking about it made her pant. And then she'd realize she was panting and put her little hand on her excellent chest to stop herself from panting and that, of course, only made her pant more—

"Get that look off your face!" Swann snatched up the bottle again and filled his glass to the brim. "All I know is that this stupid notion of yours had better work."

"Of course it will work." St. Fell pushed his chair back further on its back legs. "Trust me, one lovely afternoon in the company of London's most eligible bachelors and she will be completely ready to admit she is in love with me."

Belcraven sighed. "I hope so. Diana and I are waiting on you. Your trouble courting is holding us up."

"I still don't like this!" Swann said.

St. Fell shrugged. "It's either that or the dark corner—"

"Damnation! Don't even think of it!"

St. Fell rocked back in his chair. How could he possibly not think about it?

Chapter 5

It ought to have been a perfect afternoon. Arabella looked out from where she stood in the corner next to the aspidistra. There were easily forty people crowded into the Carr drawing room. Fifteen marriageable daughters of merchants and their mammas or aunties and thirteen eligible men and no sign of Papa's stick. She looked over at Papa. He was still slumped in an armchair in the far corner of the room. His face was red, and his strand of hair drooped down over his nose.

He was foxed, of course. It was probably the only way he could cope while she and Diana were meeting eligible gentlemen.

Not that Diana had met many eligible gentlemen. The Countesses of Belcraven still had her trapped in the corner. Arabella and Aunt Ophelia had tried to rescue her several times, but the countesses had walking sticks and, like Papa, weren't afraid to use them.

Arabella sighed. On the other hand, if Diana insisted on marrying that idiot Belcraven, she would have to learn to cope with his aunts. And frankly, a few times one of the countesses had tried to walk away, and Diana had stepped in front of her.

Of course, Arabella herself had benefitted by the unceasing presence of the Duchess of St. Fell hanging over her shoulder like a funeral fog. Except when she marched off to snipe at Mrs. Carr, which, thankfully, the old bat felt compelled to do frequently. But most of the time she followed Arabella around, pronouncing on the advantages of being a duchess. Chief among them, as far as Arabella could tell, was that no one was allowed to tell them to shut up.

"What about Mr. Downley?" Aunt Ophelia asked around a mouthful of seedcake. "He seemed very nice."

Arabella lifted her glance from where St. Fell sat on the sofa talking to Lady Nola and looked around the Carr drawing room to refresh her memory. Mr. Downley was either the pale earnest man who had the youngest Miss Coulter cornered between the pianoforte and the wall in order to demonstrate his bird calls, or he was the bluff man with the big forehead on the blue sofa in the far corner who possessed London's largest collection of snuffboxes. Either way, Arabella didn't like him.

She shook her head. St. Fell must have followed the direction of her glances because the smirk he shot her over Lady Nola's head increased in intensity. Arabella schooled her face into a mild expression. The last thing St. Fell needed was to know what she thought of the afternoon's selection of eligible gentlemen. His head would puff up so large it would explode.

"Do you think Mr. Carr is jealous enough to propose yet?" she asked. St. Fell had been leaning over Lady Nola on the sofa for fifteen minutes while Mr. Carr glowered at him from his armchair in front of the fireplace.

The Duchess of St. Fell paused on her way to hector Mrs. Carr to swivel her lorgnette over to Mr. Carr. "The dolt is never going to declare himself in a room full of people." She marched on to the refreshment table in the corner.

Arabella sighed. She hated to admit it, but the old bat was right. It was perfectly obvious the dolt was head over heels in love with Lady Nola. He couldn't take his eyes off her for more than a few seconds. Arabella watched St. Fell once again nod his head as if in agreement with something Lady Nola was saying. Mr. Carr literally twitched with jealousy. But it was all his fault. If he would get his silly declaration of love over with, then the entire company would be able to stop being obliged to pretend to be interested in Lady Nola.

St. Fell looked over at Arabella and tilted his head in the direction of Mr. Carr and gave an exaggerated sigh. Arabella rolled her eyes. Lady Nola, of course, didn't notice anything, because she was too busy looking at Mr. Carr, poor woman. It was obvious that she completely adored him. Just as he could not see anyone else in the room. It was a shame no one would just knock some sense into his stunningly handsome, yet incredibly thick, head. St. Fell could do it, but he was too busy laughing at him.

Aunt Ophelia took a sip of her orgeat punch. "What about Mr. Durwood, Arabella?"

Arabella shuddered. "Mr. Durwood was moist."

"Lord Alward?"

"Lord Alward looks like a pug dog." Also, all he could talk about was what a great friend he was of the Duke of St. Fell and how much he owed him. There were thirteen eligible gentlemen in the room. They were supposed to take turns making Mr. Carr jealous. Surely it was someone else's turn by now? St. Fell obviously enjoyed being the center of attention. And pretending affection.

Not that St. Fell's pretended interest in Lady Nola extended to shifting his shoulders in the hitch. He only hitched at Arabella. She had noticed it when Mrs. Carr had dragged him around the room, introducing him to the other marriageable heiresses. He greeted them each with a half smile of a smirk, bowed over their hands and made what seemed to be charming conversation from their simpering demeanors. But he only hitched his shoulders when he was looking at her.

Not that it mattered in the least if he hitched. She was merely infatuated with him, no matter what anyone thought. He could hitch at other women if he liked. She was not agreeing to marry him. Even though he and Papa had already decided.

"Well, what about Lord Kennally?" Aunt Ophelia asked. "He wasn't moist and he didn't collect anything."

Arabella tried to think. "Was he the one who liked my dress because it reminded him of his mother?"

"No, dear, that was Lord Simpson. Don't you remember? He had a locket with her picture. And her latest letter from Shropshire. I must say, I would have liked him better had she at least been dead. Lord Kennally was the one who liked your dress because it reminded him of the hills of Scotland." Aunt Ophelia frowned. "Although I did not know the hills of Scotland were Naccarat tangerine."

Arabella sighed. Compliments about her dress had been offered by most every gentlemen. It was obviously a conventional source that eligible gentlemen mined when paying compliments to young ladies. Which she would not know about, of course, previously only having been flattered by St. Fell who never said anything seriously.

The sound of Lady Nola's laughter chimed out across the drawing room in appreciation of something St. Fell had said. The idiot could be perfectly charming when he wanted to be.

"Why are you scowling?" Aunt Ophelia asked. "I thought you liked Lord Kennally."

"Lord Kennally is very nice," Arabella said. Or at least, he wasn't completely atrocious. He was tallish and fairish and mostly attractive. Arabella looked around the room until she spotted him. He stood next to the sofa table, where the cakes had been set out. He picked up a piece of seedcake between his fingers and sniffed it. Then he licked it. Then he put it back on the cake plate and picked up a slice of the spice cake and sniffed that.

"My stars!" Aunt Ophelia blenched. "I must go warn Diana!" She squared her shoulders and marched off.

Arabella clutched her plate to her stomach. Thank heavens she had already taken her cake. It was very delicious. She had one bite left and she was saving it. Mrs. Carr had said it was made by their chef, Mr. Karl, who was also the confectioner in Soho Square. Where Arabella and St. Fell had stood in front of the window yesterday. Arabella's knees weakened at the memory. Even though he had lied.

St. Fell smiled up at Arabella and look his leave of Lady Nola, but he had barely walked five paces toward her when he was intercepted by Mrs. Coulter and her two eldest daughters, Vivian and Elvira. Mr. Coulter owned the largest bank in the City and he was nearly as rich as Papa. Nearly, but not quite. Still, the Misses Coulter had very nice dowries, and Miss Elvira had not been the slightest bit embarrassed to tell Arabella that there was nothing she and her sisters would like better than to marry a title, and they didn't much care much for the condition of the holder. A young and handsome duke like St. Fell would be a windfall of unimaginable order. And the Misses Coulter were not precisely homely. In fact, they were tall and shapely, and most gentlemen might actually think they were stunningly beautiful.

Arabella waited, and predictably, like a complete feather-headed henwit, she was gripped by a fierce urge to go over and make faces at St. Fell behind the backs of the Misses Coulter. She glared down at her plate, exasperated with herself. As if she should care if a fortune hunter was hunting another woman's fortune. Infatuation made one stupid.

She looked over. St. Fell bowed over the eldest Miss Coulter's hand, and his hair fell forward over his forehead, and his hand completely engulfed Vivian's while she tittered at him. He looked up past her and winked at Arabella as if he knew exactly what she was thinking. She glared back down at her plate. It was a Swann, the Imperial series. One of Swann's Fine China best, gold-rimmed and delicate and very interesting. Much more interesting than watching St. Fell watch her watch him with another woman.

"I see my mother has been haunting you." St. Fell's hand reached around from behind her and picked the seedcake off her plate.

Arabella spun around. He was eating it, of course, the selfish beast.

"I was saving that!" she said.

"Yes, thank you." He shot her the grin that made her feel that they were the only two people in the room. She caught her breath. He really could be quite wonderful.

"So?" he asked. "Are you not going to marry me because of my mother?"

"You know perfectly well I have other reasons to not marry you." She clutched the empty plate to her chest like a shield. "However, your mother hates me."

"She hates everyone." He pried the plate out of her fingers and dropped it in the aspidistra behind her. He smiled. "Your dress looks expensive."

Well, she hadn't heard that dress compliment. Arabella willed herself not to start panting as usual like a great green ninny just because he had touched her and was looking into her eyes. "That is hardly fair," she said, "I have an aunt who likes everyone."

St. Fell winced. "Yes, but you forget your father. He is most definitely not living with us."

"Neither is your mother!" Hell! She sounded like she agreed they would marry.

St. Fell grinned, of course. Grinned and took a step closer. "Go on, say it," he whispered. "I dare you."

Arabella swallowed. He was so close that she had to tip her head all the way back to look into his face. He tilted his head to the side as if he were taking a better look at her, and his eyes darkened.

"What on earth are you doing!" The duchess inserted her lorgnette between them.

Aunt Ophelia bustled to their other side. "I was only gone for a few moments!" she exclaimed, her tone of voice more awed than admonishing.

"This is a drawing room!" the duchess said. "You cannot stand six inches away from the girl in a drawing room! Whatever is the matter with you?"

"It really is not proper, dearest." Aunt Ophelia patted Arabella's arm. "I am afraid it might give the other eligible gentlemen ideas."

St. Fell sighed and took a step back.

"Very well, Miss Swann and I will endeavor to be perfectly innocuous." He inclined his head toward Arabella. "I trust you found the selection of hats to your satisfaction, Miss Swann?"

For an instant, Arabella looked at him blankly. Then she saw the glint in his eyes and she felt a thrill of excitement. They were going to talk about gentlemen in front of her aunt and his mother!

She smiled primly. "Yes, Your Grace, I have never seen so many hats."

"And were any to your liking?" he asked.

"Hats?" The duchess's eyebrows met in a scowl over the top of her lorgnette. "What the devil are you talking about, St. Fell? Stop wasting everyone's time and court the damned chit! Hats! No wonder this is dragging on forever!"

Arabella shot her a glare. "Forever? You know perfectly well we only met yesterday!" Honestly, the Duchess of St. Fell was as big a know-everything as her son.

"Perhaps hats is a metaphor," Aunt Ophelia said. The duchess rolled her eyes.

"Shouldn't at least one of you go chaperone Diana and Belcraven?" St. Fell said.

The duchess laughed derisively.

Aunt Ophelia's lip quivered. "But I have waited a very long time to actually chaperone something."

Arabella patted her aunt's shoulder.

St. Fell bent his head toward Aunt Ophelia. "And in your opinion as a chaperone, Miss Swann, do you think Arabella has met a better prospect for a husband than I?" He rocked back on his heels with his hands behind his back, his smirk in full bloom, and looked down at Arabella.

He knew he was the best prospect in the room, the conceited pest. Although one would have thought someone so conceited wouldn't need reassurance. "What about the ladies, Your Grace?" Arabella asked, matching his purring tone. "Mrs. Carr made a point of introducing you to every heiress in the room. Did you meet any other worthy women?" The twitch of his lips showed that he understood her use of the word *worthy*.

He shrugged. "None that I would care to hassock."

"Now, that is most definitely a metaphor," Aunt Ophelia whispered to the duchess.

The duchess snorted. "Probably for damned hats."

"You are not helping," St. Fell said to his mother.

She scowled at him. "We are not here to help, St. Fell. We are chaperones, not nursemaids."

"We have already told you we would not interfere," Aunt Ophelia said. "Although it is natural to keep being tempted to point out the obvious."

"I have pointed," St. Fell said. "Obviously."

"Well, how green can the girl possibly be?" the duchess said. "Makes me glad I had sons. And I have never said that before."

"Will you stop talking about me as if I were not here!" Arabella said. "I know perfectly well everyone wants me to think we are in love. But I am not. Nor is he. If he were, he would leave me alone and let me make my own choice." She jutted out her chin. "And not make arrangements with my father behind my back."

His eyes didn't show the slightest surprise at her declaration, nor did his smirk falter. She gritted her teeth. The man obviously thought he knew everything. He probably smirked in his sleep.

"No one can force you to marry me." He shrugged his most annoying, most superior shrug. "You are over the age of majority. Your papa is not going to drag you down the altar, crying and kicking."

Arabella folded her arms. "No, but he can sulk. And he could not like my husband for the rest of his life, which is not very pleasant . . ." she trailed off and looked down at the carpet.

"Is that the only reason?" St. Fell drawled.

She tilted her chin back up and spat out the words he was waiting for. "You know perfectly well he might not give me as lovely a dowry if I do not marry the man he has chosen! Not that that it is any concern of yours, the Duke of Know-Everything!"

"Arabella!" Aunt Ophelia squealed.

Arabella glared back down at the carpet. St. Fell would be gloating that she had finally admitted that the money was important to her, of course. She didn't know why she felt obligated to look up at him since she knew perfectly well he was. But like a little puppet on a string, she did. And he was looking right at her, waiting for her. He smiled at her over her aunt's head and mouthed the word "hell."

Arabella snorted. "I am not saying *hell!*"

"Arabella!" Aunt Ophelia squealed again.

"I suppose we can forgive her, given the company." The duchess turned her lorgnette on her son. "I do not know why he does not just pull her braid or throw mud at her and run away and be done with it." She sighed. "I am beginning to understand her father's need for brandy."

"Oh look!" Aunt Ophelia pointed at the doorway, her voice sinking to a tone of hushed awe. "It's Lord Stonecroft! London's most eligible bachelor!"

St. Fell coughed.

"Apart from you, naturally, Your Grace," Aunt Ophelia said.

St. Fell nodded in satisfaction. The great baby.

Arabella turned to observe the latest arrival. A tall, dark-haired and square-shouldered gentleman stood in the doorway. He had a classically handsome face, like Apollo on the Swann Grecian urns, and one lock of dark brown hair tumbled down over his broad forehead. He looked around uncertainly, an expression that probably never once crossed St. Fell's smirking smug face. Every woman in the drawing room turned to look at him. Except Lady Nola, of course. She was looking at Mr. Carr. Arabella looked up at St. Fell. He looked at Lady Nola and Mr. Carr and winked at Arabella. She smiled. They really were completely ridiculous.

Mrs. Carr wove her way through the drawing room crowd and pounced on Lord Stonecroft. She dragged him off to Lady Nola's sofa.

Aunt Ophelia followed him with her eyes. "There was

an article in the *Times* about him—a series, actually." She turned to Arabella. "I didn't bother to point it out to you, dearest. I didn't want to get your hopes up, given your papa." She looked back at Lord Stonecroft and sighed. "He was one of Wellington's bravest dispatch officers. He was badly wounded at Waterloo."

The duchess bristled. "Compton was one of Wellington's bravest dispatch officers and he was so badly wounded at Waterloo that he nearly died! He has never mentioned any Stonecroft. I have never heard of him."

Compton. Lord Toby had told Arabella about him yesterday. He was St. Fell's next younger brother who was still convalescing on the Continent, under the tender care of the nuns that St. Fell had arranged to look after him.

"Major Masterson was just made Baron Stonecroft for his wartime service," Aunt Ophelia said.

"St. Fell got Compton made an earl for his wartime service," the duchess declared smugly. "Masterson. That is a very common name." She stressed the word common. "What is his given name?"

"Raphael," St. Fell said. The idiot.

"It is Blade," Aunt Ophelia said.

St. Fell rolled his eyes. "You're not serious."

"I believe the *Times* mentioned that his mother is one of the Cheshire Blades," Aunt Ophelia said defensively.

"What is your first name, Your Grace?" Arabella asked sweetly. Typical of the smug idiot to mock the only other decent eligible gentleman in the room.

St. Fell shrugged. "No one has ever called me it."

"He was born the Marquis of Hanford," the duchess said in a condescending tone of voice, as if Arabella were too stupid to know he would have a lesser title.

"He still has to have a given name," Arabella said. It must be completely ridiculous if he and his mother were being so cagey about it.

"It's August," St. Fell said.

"August is an excellent name," Arabella said. "Very dignified and important." She waited until St. Fell's shoulders broadened the way they did when he preened. Which was just as often as his mother was superior. As in always. "It does not suit you at all," she said. He merely laughed and shook his head.

"Lord Stonecroft is a poet," Aunt Ophelia said.

St. Fell snorted. "Of course."

"A published poet," Aunt Ophelia continued. "He is reading a poem this Monday to celebrate the opening of Mr. Carr's new business on Pall Mall, Garrard House."

Arabella eyed Lord Stonecroft again. He was perched on the edge of the sofa, trying to make small talk with Lady Nola. A published poet who was a baron and a war hero. That was more like the kind of man she wanted to marry. The kind of man any woman would like to marry.

Except Lady Nola of course. She kept leaning past Lord Stonecroft's broad shoulders to look at Mr. Carr. Arabella looked up at St. Fell. He smiled and rolled his eyes.

"Lord Stonecroft boxes," Aunt Ophelia said.

"Poets?" St. Fell asked.

"All Warburtons box," the duchess said.

"And Lord Stonecroft is a rake," Aunt Ophelia continued.

The duchess gave a dismissive shrug. "Anyone can call themselves a rake nowadays," she said. "He's likely just a rogue."

Arabella smiled. "Or, heaven forbid, a roué."

"That's my girl!" St. Fell beamed and looked around proudly as if he wanted to make sure everyone heard that she had said something amusing. It was really quite endearing. In a completely manipulative way.

"And Lord Stonecroft is a fortune hunter," Aunt Ophelia said. "His eldest brother died in a carriage accident and he now he must support his five younger brothers and two sisters."

Before the duchess could proudly declare that St. Fell was also a fortune hunter, Mrs. Carr walked to the center of the room and clapped her hands until everyone stopped talking and looked at her. Then she motioned for Lord Stonecroft to step forward.

"I do hope he reads from his latest book of poems," Aunt Ophelia whispered. "They say he is the new Byron."

"Keats is the new Byron," the duchess declared.

"Really?" Aunt Ophelia frowned. "I thought Keats was the new Wordsworth?"

The duchess gave her a pitying look through her lorgnette. "Shelley is the new Wordsworth. Your Stonefield must be the new Blake."

"Stonecroft," Aunt Ophelia said. Arabella didn't bother to tell her that there was no point trying to make a St. Fell remember anything they didn't think was important.

"I don't know why there's a need for a new anything." St. Fell yawned. "Surely the old was boring enough."

Lord Stonecroft patted his broad chest under his tight-fitting tobacco brown superfine coat and pulled out a thick sheaf of papers from his jacket pocket. He shuffled the papers with a modest look on his face until everyone in the drawing room was silent and watching him. A sigh rippled through the assembled women. Arabella joined in. He was extremely fine-looking. And a poet—a published poet—and a war hero and a baron.

Lord Stonecroft cleared his throat and began to read.

> *"My ease of spirit wanes,*
> *For nothing good remains,*
> *To raise the lingering burden from my weary heart.*
> *I look to the east and pray for the strength to start."*

He had an excellent baritone voice that carried nicely across the room and a very engaging speaking manner, because at the end of each page he would look up and smile and scan the room as if seeking approval for his continued delivery. Arabella made sure she nodded and smiled whenever his eye caught hers. The poem itself was about a young man's journey of self-discovery whilst under the thrall of a wood nymph.

St. Fell took another step closer to her, and Arabella had to concentrate to make certain the sound of her breathing couldn't be heard. What was it about him that made her knees weak?

Lord Stonecroft was a highly desirable eligible gentleman. A war hero. A poet. But there was something about the Duke of St. Fell that was making her stupid. Because here she was, a rich, pretty heiress, finally in a Mayfair drawing room, listening to London's most eligible bachelor, and instead of concentrating on him, she was thinking about the unromantic, lying, fortune-hunting, conceited, know-everything rake of a St. Fell, who was standing next to her, far enough away to avoid being jabbed with the lorgnette, but just close enough so that she had to be careful where she swayed, in case she brushed up against him. Because touching him was all she could think about. It was ridiculous!

"God, this is a long poem," St. Fell whispered.

"I do not wish to hear your snide comments during Lord Stonecroft's poem," Arabella snapped, since it was all his fault she was not able concentrate on the poem.

"Quite true," he said. "You are perfectly capable of making your own snide comments." He dodged his mother's attempt to stab him with her lorgnette. One would think after enduring nine-and-twenty years of the man, the woman would think of carrying a fan. Fans were much longer and sturdier.

Arabella forced herself to pay attention to Lord Stonecroft.

"Though should I linger long,
The spell you cast so strong
That I may not hope to untangle myself from the threads."

It was a very enduring thrall. Arabella made sure she smiled encouragingly and nodded whenever Lord Stonecroft's glance fell upon her. There was no reason why she shouldn't find him attractive. She wasn't like Gabriel Carr, with a preconceived notion of the kind of person she wanted to marry. Lord Stonecroft was extremely handsome. His hair curled down around his ears, instead of being straight and heavy like St. Fell's. He was nearly the same height as St. Fell and more solidly built. Where St. Fell was golden and smirking, Lord Stonecroft was dark and brooding. Lord Stonecroft's legs were not as long as St. Fell's, but his thighs in his buckskin breeches looked thicker. They both wore polished Hessian boots.

"You aren't listening to the poem anyway," St. Fell said. "You are looking at his legs."

"I most certainly am not looking at his legs!" Any longer.

"Arabella!" Aunt Ophelia squealed at the same time the Duchess of St. Fell hissed her son's name.

Lord Stonecroft raised his eyes from his sheaf of papers and looked up at them.

Arabella blushed so hard she could feel the tips of her ears burn. Stupid St. Fell. He was determined to make them both look like idiots. She smiled and nodded at

Lord Stonecroft, and he cleared his throat and began reading again.

> *"Enchanted, I am taken,*
> *"Never wanting to awaken,"*

It was an apparently interminable thrall. Arabella kept her eyes on Lord Stonecroft's face, in case St. Fell was still looking. Which he was, she had no doubt, but for once she wasn't going to give him the satisfaction of looking back at him. She looked at Lord Stonecroft. He had a very handsome face, with a cleft chin, something the high-and-mighty Duke of St. Fell did not.

"You couldn't care less about the poem," St. Fell whispered, his lips so close to her she could swear they brushed her ear. "You are not fooling anyone. Your face is completely transparent."

"I love the poem," she said, trying to breathe through her nose to hide the fact she was panting. It was very exciting. Being in a London drawing room, listening to a dashing war hero read his published poem. With the Duke of St. Fell in a jealous snit about it. And trying to seduce her in front of everyone.

"Now you are thinking of me," St. Fell said, his voice still so low no one but she could hear it.

"You wish I were thinking of you," she said in a dampening tone, glad she couldn't see his face. He would probably quirk his eyebrow and smile in that knowing way.

"You are always thinking of me," he said. "You are head over heels in love with me."

Could he be more conceited? "I am not!"

The duchess had the nerve to hush her. Arabella shot St. Fell a glare, but he just smirked. She hid her clenched fists in the folds of her dress. "I am not in love with you!"

she hissed. "I am infatuated!" Why didn't he ever talk about how he was in love with her? Because he wasn't. He was just trying to make her believe it so she would marry him.

"You are in love with me, you are just too green to know it." His voice was so low, she could barely hear it. "Five minutes alone in a dark corner will persuade you."

Good heavens. She had to keep standing. If her knees buckled, everyone would look at her. And St. Fell would gloat.

"I do not want to go off to a dark corner with you," she whispered as soon as she was sure her voice would not squeak. Lord Stonecroft had achieved a climactic moment in the poem, thank heavens, and his eyes welled up with tears and his voice quavered. She glanced around the drawing room. Everyone seemed to be listening to the poem, except for the duchess, who appeared to have fallen asleep standing up.

"You know you do," St. Fell whispered. "It is writ as plain as day on your face."

"I most certainly do not," she whispered back. Hell. St. Fell was going to ruin a perfectly lovely social occasion. Lord Stonecroft pulled his handkerchief out of his pocket and dabbed at his eyes.

"Miss Arabella Swann is lying," St. Fell sang under his breath.

"Shut up!" Arabella swung around and stamped her foot down as hard as she could on the toe of his over-polished Hessians. "Lord Stonecroft is crying, you insensitive pig!"

She looked up in horror, the blood roaring in her ears. Lord Stonecroft was goggling at her. She looked around the room. Everyone was goggling at her. Even the two youngest Finnamore sisters who had spent the afternoon hiding behind the pianoforte were peeping over the top of it, goggling at her. The entire room was silent.

Except for the sound of St. Fell snorting in laughter beside her.

Then Lord Stonecroft smiled and began to walk toward them.

Chapter 6

"Now look what you have done," St. Fell said. "The great clod is lumbering our way."

Lord Stonecroft plowed his way through the daughters and mamas who surged in front of him and kept walking toward them, with his eyes fixed on her. Arabella smiled at back at him. To hell with St. Fell.

"Isn't this exciting!" Aunt Ophelia squealed. "Lord Stonecroft is coming to see Arabella!"

St. Fell shot her an evil look.

Aunt Ophelia shrugged defensively. "I like everyone."

Arabella felt a sudden surge of hatred for St. Fell. Because here was this perfectly wonderful man, Lord Stonecroft, London's most eligible bachelor, a war hero and a poet—a published poet! Who, by the way, was not in the least bit lumbering. He was walking toward her, and all she could think of was how ridiculous St. Fell was twitching beside her, and wondering what St. Fell was thinking. What St. Fell was thinking of her.

It was her first social gathering. Her first London party. She was surrounded by eligible men. She should be flirting. She should be making sparkling conversation with a crowd of admirers. She was pretty. She was clever. She was filthy, stinking rich. Instead, all she wanted to do was sneak off to some dark corner with stupid St. Fell, the fortune-hunting, conceited, smug, self-absorbed bas—

"Arabella!" Aunt Ophelia poked her in the ribs.

Arabella looked up. Hell. Lord Stonecroft had lumbered over when she wasn't paying attention.

He bowed over her hand. Not overlong. Not like St. Fell, who had already had her down to her shift before he knew her name.

She smiled at Lord Stonecroft. He had a very pleasant face, open and honest, not sneaky and smirking. He looked like the kind of man who would be sincere when he made a simple declaration of love.

"Arabella!" Aunt Ophelia poked her in the small of the back again. Hell. Lord Stonecroft had said something, and she had missed it. She smiled up at him with what she hoped was a neutral, yet encouraging expression.

"There is no use trying to talk to her." St. Fell looked directly at Lord Stonecroft. "She is completely insufferable."

Insufferable? Arabella snatched the lorgnette out of his mother's hand, but St. Fell wrested it from her fist without taking his eyes from Lord Stonecroft. "Insufferable," he continued, his voice completely unruffled, "in the sense of having opinions on matters about which she knows nothing."

She glared up at him. "You would know, Your Grace, being the world's foremost expert authority on nothing."

"You are too hard on yourself, Arabella," he said, his eyes still on Stonecroft. "You are not nothing, you are just green."

Lord Stonecroft thrust out his chest and straightened his shoulders ever so slightly. "I am sure Miss Swann could be everything," he murmured, "to the right man."

Good heavens! Arabella held her breath. How delicious! She was being fought over by two London rakes!

St. Fell tilted his head back and looked down his nose at Lord Stonecroft in his best ducal manner. "I am afraid Miss Swann is not a romantic," he said. "Don't waste your breath giving her compliments. She doesn't believe them. Or want them."

Lord Stonecroft turned to her. "What do you want, Miss Swann?" he asked. His lips quivered in a half smile.

Arabella swallowed. What she really wanted to do was squeal and call for Diana and then ask St. Fell and Lord Stonecroft to repeat their conversation. Preferably slowly enough so she could make notes.

Lord Stonecroft kept gazing into her face. He had very nice eyes, the same azure blue as the ribbons on her new jaconet muslin that Diana had now claimed as her own. Arabella had not gotten to wear it once, which was hardly surprising.

Lord Stonecroft kept staring at her. For heaven's sake. He didn't expect her to answer, did he?

St. Fell shifted beside her. She glanced up. Sure enough, he was watching her, his smirk back in place and his eyes dancing with laughter. He knew, damn him. He knew! The smug, conceited beast knew that she was enjoying being fought over by two fortune-hunting rakes. Immensely.

She glared back at him. He thought he knew her so well. It was smug and annoying. And presumptuous. And overwhelming. Which fairly described everything about him. For the hundredth time since she met him, she longed to do something to wipe the smug smirk off his face. To make him stagger and suffer and fall to his knees in a rush of remorse and say she was perfect and beautiful and brilliant and that he wanted her for herself, not for her fortune. And she would tell him to go to hell.

She wanted to hurt him. She wanted to make him cry.

Lord Stonecroft cleared his throat. Hell! She had forgotten to speak to him again. He inclined his head, and his lips curved into a sad smile. "Perhaps another day," he murmured, and he turned around and walked away.

A perfectly wonderful London gentleman whom she had missed out on because of her infatuation with St. Fell. She watched as Lord Stonecroft was engulfed by Mrs. Coulter and her daughters. They must have been hovering behind him the whole time.

"How sad," St. Fell drawled. "Lord Stonecase does not want to play with us."

"Stonecroft!" Arabella snapped. "And you know perfectly well what his name is!"

"Oh?" St. Fell raised his eyebrows. "Is he important?"

Arabella took a deep breath and turned on her heel and marched out the drawing room doors. She knew that people were watching her. What did it matter? She and St. Fell had been putting on a show for hours.

She didn't need to turn around to know that St. Fell had followed her into the hallway. She could hear the clatter of his overpolished Hessians on the hardwood floor. And behind him, the puffing of Aunt Ophelia and the duchess's muttering.

He sprinted past her just as she reached the staircase, and grabbed the bannister and swung around so he was facing her. And completely blocking her path down the stairs because he was so much taller and broader than she was. He wasn't even the slightest bit out of breath, while she was panting. Of course. Aunt Ophelia and the duchess stopped in the middle of the hallway.

St. Fell spread his arms, with the palms of his hands up, and offered her a sweet choirboy smile. "Come now," he said, in his silky purring voice. "Don't tell me you didn't find that diverting."

She glared at him. Diverting. Their whole courtship was a game to him. He stood on the edge of the landing, the back of the heels of his boots an inch from the edge of the step. One little push and he'd sail down the steps backward, the smirk of St. Fell forever erased from his face.

Arabella took two steps back. He followed, away from the staircase. She folded her arms across her chest. "Thanks to you, the most eligible man in London thinks I am an idiot."

His smile deepened. "I keep telling you, I just think you're green."

Which he thought he would remedy by taking her off to some dark corner, the arrogant rake. "You know I meant Lord Stonecroft," she said through clenched teeth.

"Oh, him." St. Fell shrugged. "He'll be back."

"Because of my great fortune?" she couldn't stop herself from saying.

"Not just your fortune," he said.

She threw her arms in the air. "More silver-tongued flattery from the great rake of St. Fell!"

St. Fell grinned. "You know damned well you are clever and pretty, Miss Arabella Swann, or you would not be so confident you could come up to London and snag yourself a fine husband even with your great fortune."

"You see?" Arabella spun around to appeal to her aunt and the duchess. "That is his idea of a compliment! The man doesn't have a single romantic bone in his body!"

He laughed. "I am afraid it is obvious to everyone that I do have a romantic bo—"

"St. Fell!" The duchess lunged at his ribs with her stupid lorgnette. Thank heavens he was far enough away from the stairs.

"You are only sorry you didn't get to say it first." He rubbed his side.

"That is beside the point," the duchess said.

"Yes, I keep getting the point," he said. "Which is why I wish you would give me that damned lorgnette."

"I have known him one day," Arabella continued, even though she knew perfectly well no one was listening. "He is my first suitor. Ever! If you can call him that, since he is all smug assumption and no courting. He is ridiculous!"

"I completely agree," St. Fell said. "That is why we are perfect for each other." He leaned his shoulder against the wall and folded his arms across his chest.

"I cannot believe this is happening." Arabella tried not to moan.

"Believe it." St. Fell smirked. "It is happening."

Arabella grabbed her aunt's arm. "It cannot be love," she said urgently. "It cannot be!"

"I would not know, dearest," Aunt Ophelia said. "I have never been in love."

"Of course it is love, you ninny!" the Duchess of St. Fell said. As if anyone had asked her!

"It is infatuation," Arabella said. The old bat was as big a know-everything as her son. No doubt there was a St. Fell dowager cottage. And possibly a separate town house in London.

"I have never been infatuated either," Aunt Ophelia said.

"You are both head over heels in love," the duchess declared. "I have been married. I should know."

"You just want me to marry him!" Arabella said.

"Everyone wants you to marry me," St. Fell said. "You want to marry me. If you weren't so green you would know."

"Greener than grass," the duchess muttered.

"I have to admit, dearest," Aunt Ophelia said, "you are making me feel wise about love. And I am fairly certain I know nothing about it."

"No, it is not possible!" Arabella shouted. "I have known him one day!" She held up her index finger and waved it under the duchess's arrogant nose. "One day! I have not gotten to do anything! No parties, no dancing, no first kiss under the moonlight!" She rounded on St. Fell. "It is all you! Just you! And I don't want you. You are smug and conceited. And you are a fortune hunter! You think you know everything about me when you do not! And you are very sarcastic!" She probably shouldn't have pointed out that last one.

"You forgot about gaming," he said, his voice as casual as if they were discussing the weather.

"You game?" She glared at him. Wonderful.

"Not excessively." He paused. "But constantly."

"Anything else?" she asked in a long-suffering tone.

"No, I think that describes being a duke and a rake. You could ask my mother, though, to see if I have omitted anything."

The duchess shook her head. "We will not interfere."

"But we are not leaving," Aunt Ophelia added breathlessly.

"Actually, I am leaving," the duchess said. "I need to go speak to Mrs. Carr."

"But you will miss it!" Aunt Ophelia cried.

The duchess rolled her eyes. "Believe me, this will not be resolved before I return." She marched back down the hall to the drawing room.

Arabella turned to St. Fell, who was still leaning against the wall, his arms crossed over his chest, the light in his gray eyes as mocking as always. She wanted to ask him if he truly did love her. Of course, he would say yes, and she wouldn't believe him. Or he would say no, and she might possibly cast up her accounts on the Carr's Mayfair town house hall floor.

Or perhaps he would say yes and she would believe him. He might take her hand and hold it in the heat of both of his and look deeply into her eyes and say he loved her truly and for herself and forever. Just as he had done yesterday in Soho Square.

Hell.

"You always curse at me," he said, with a shift of the muscles in his shoulders. "It is a good thing for you that I like it."

She flushed and looked down at the floor. He just had to look at her and her heart started pounding and her breathing became ragged. He wanted to sneak her off to some dark corner. Because he thought that once she went with him, she wouldn't have any choice but to marry him. Which was exactly why she wasn't going to go. No matter how much she wanted to, because this was marriage. Forever. And she wouldn't marry someone who wasn't as deeply affected by her as the way she was by him.

She took a deep breath to steady her voice. "I know perfectly well you went behind my back and made an agreement with my father after I told you I wanted to pick my own husband."

"I didn't make any agreement with your father!"

She shot him a glare. Did he think she was stupid? "You are lying."

He lifted his hand and opened his mouth as if to argue. But he didn't. He pressed his lips together and his chest heaved in a sigh and the laughter went out of his eyes.

He was silent. For the first time since she had met him, the Duke of St. Fell had nothing to say. The light in the hallway seemed dimmer.

He looked down and studied his boots for a minute, then he took a deep breath and squared his shoulders and raised his eyes and held her gaze straight on. For a few seconds. Then dropped his head down again as if he could not bear to face her.

"You're right," he rasped as though it pained him to force the words past his throat. "I have not told you the truth."

She nodded, unable to speak past the lump in her own throat. He had dealt with Papa behind her back. She took a deep breath. If she started to cry, she would kick him.

She knew it, of course. But Papa had promised on Mama's grave. How could he have? A part of her wanted to tell St. Fell to never mind, to not tell her. Another part of her wanted to gloat in triumph. She knew they had done it. They were pathetic to try to hide it from her.

St. Fell's head remained bent. "There is no agreement with your father," he whispered.

A flash of fury surged through her. She planted her hands on her hips. For heaven's sake! Was he going back to his ridiculous story?

He ran his hand through his hair and glanced up at her. "I just wanted you to think there was, so you would"— he trailed off, and bent his head back down so she couldn't see his expression. He took a shuddering breath—"so you would choose me."

Her heart was pounding so loudly she could barely speak. "So you did not offer for me?" Her voice came out in a croak. She was not disappointed. She was merely surprised.

His laugh was bitter. "I tried to offer for you. Several times. But your father refused. He kept saying he had promised you could choose your own husband." St. Fell shook his head as if he could not believe he was actually admitting it. "I pleaded. I begged him. But nothing would convince him to break his word to you."

Arabella released the breath she didn't realize she had been holding. Poor Papa. She had been quite curt to him this morning at breakfast, and he had not deserved it. She ought to have known he would not betray her just for the sake of getting a duke for a grandson. "I made him swear on Mama's grave," she said.

St. Fell pursed his lips and heaved a heavy sigh. "He mentioned that. Often."

She squared her shoulders, a glow of pleasure warming her heart. St. Fell wanted to offer for her. Of course, it was only because of her fortune—she shot him a sideways look—he smiled hesitantly, as if he were ashamed that he had been forced to confess that he had asked for the chance to marry her and had been refused. She supposed it must make him feel vulnerable. Which must be difficult for him because he didn't seem to be a man who was refused much. Ever.

"I suppose you think that was very wrong of me," he said, "to ask your father for you in marriage when you had already told me you wanted to decide for yourself." His gaze fell back to the toes of his Hessians. He was probably afraid she would say something sarcastic about his skills of persuasion.

Arabella sighed. When he stopped being smug, he really was completely endearing. She had a sudden urge to run her hand along the length of his arm to console him. She shot a look over her shoulder. Aunt Ophelia was watching from the center of the hallway, dabbing her streaming eyes with her wadded-up handkerchief. She motioned for Arabella to continue.

Arabella turned back to St. Fell. "You probably could not help yourself," she said.

He nodded, eyes still on his boots.

"What with the great temptation of my fortune," she added.

"Yes." He sighed again. "Your fortune," he said in a flat voice. "I was quite overcome by your fortune." He glanced up and gave her a trembling smile.

Good heavens. A wave of guilt washed over her. She never meant to make him cry.

"I have not said I would not marry you," she said. "I am just not ready to choose. It is very sudden."

"I know." He finally lifted his head and looked into her face. His gray eyes were clear and not the slightest bit mocking. And his sensitive lips actually did not have a smirk, just a hesitant smile.

"And I want to be married for love," she added, "not my fortune." She braced herself for his bark of laughter and sarcastic comment.

But he didn't laugh or make snide jokes. Instead he looked even deeper into her eyes. "Then marry for love, Miss Arabella Swann."

And before she could say anything, he spun on his heel and brushed past her and Aunt Ophelia and strode down the hall to the drawing room. His head was bent and his shoulders shook, almost—Arabella very nearly could not believe her eyes—almost as if he were trying to hold back his sobs. His mother emerged from the drawing room, and he shouldered past her without looking up. The duchess shook her head at him, then walked down the hall.

Good heavens. Arabella looked at her aunt in amazement. She had broken the Duke of St. Fell.

"You have missed the most romantic thing you could ever imagine!" Aunt Ophelia told the duchess. "He loves her!"

"I have been saying so all day," the duchess said impatiently. "Eleanor Carr is inviting a few guests to stay on for dinner. Your family and mine and a handful of others."

Arabella and Aunt Ophelia looked at her expectantly.

"You have a theater box, do you not?" the duchess continued. "I have mentioned it to Eleanor Carr. She will suggest it as an evening activity after dinner. If that is what Arabella wants."

"Why would Arabella want to go to Drury Lane?" Aunt Ophelia said. "She is not much for the theater."

"It is a dark corner, Aunt Ophelia," Arabella said, her knees already beginning to feel weak.

"And what does Eleanor Carr have to do with it?" Aunt Ophelia continued in the same bewildered tone. "Where will we be?"

"We are not staying for dinner!" the duchess snapped.

"But we must chaperone them, you see what they are like. Why anytime anyone leaves them alone they are panting," Aunt Ophelia said. "I fear Joseph is too foxed to be any use . . ." she trailed off at the duchess's know-everything expression. "Oh."

The duchess turned to Arabella. "Of course, only if you want to, my dear."

Arabella clutched her hands to her fluttering stomach. She wanted to go to a dark corner with St. Fell. She had wanted to since she had first set eyes on him. And now that she knew that he was in love with her, why shouldn't she go and see if he could show her that what she felt was more than infatuation? She nodded and tried not to grin. Overmuch.

"Excellent." The duchess patted her arm. "Now that the matter is arranged perfectly, I wanted to ask, just now, on his way back to the drawing room, what on earth was St. Fell laughing about?"

"You're not serious!" Swann gulped back his brandy and poured himself another. "I absolutely forbid it!"

"Lower your voice," St. Fell said. After an interminable dinner, throughout which Arabella had quivered, the women had finally left the men to their after dinner brandy and port. Swann, Gabriel Carr, Belcraven, Toby, and he were huddled at one end of the dining room table. The rest of the men were at the other end discussing politics. He damned well didn't need every idiot in London to know his plans for Arabella.

"Do you want to know what I think?" Gabriel Carr waved his glass and port slopped over the sides onto the dining room table.

"No," Swann said.

"Not again." Belcraven poured himself another brandy.

Toby just rolled his eyes and continued to shuffle the deck of cards he had taken from the dining room sideboard.

"Nobody wants to hear what you think, Gabriel," St. Fell said. "It is bad enough we are obliged to watch what you do." As if obliging everyone to participate in his mother's idiotic pantomime wasn't bad enough, the dolt had come up with the novel solution of coping with his unexpressed affection for Lady Nola by becoming back teeth awash in port. Next he would be staggering around the table, trying to make someone punch him.

"I think that marriage is a huge step," Gabriel said. "It cannot be decided in one day."

"For God's sake," St. Fell said. "You either know the woman is right or you don't. And if she's right, you do what you have to do to marry her. This is hardly your first crush. You know damned well what you're doing. Just get on with it, and leave the rest of us out of it." He had problems with his own courtship, never mind trying to make the idiot realize the obvious with poor Nola.

"Damnation!" Swann glared at him from across the table. "Carr may be a saphead, but he's better than you! What you're suggesting is completely insensitive. She is my daughter! I don't want to hear it!"

"It's the only way," St. Fell said, "and you know it. She

wants experience. She is not going to be happy until she has some." In fact, it was perfectly obvious that if the world allowed women to be rakes, Arabella would be one. However, that was not the kind of thing one pointed out to the girl's father.

Swann mopped his head with his dinner napkin. "It's immoral! It's bad enough that I've been forced to watch the way you look at her!"

"That is the same look he has on his face when he talks to my wife," Gabriel muttered.

"That's my sister!" Belcraven snarled at St. Fell.

St. Fell reached for the bottle. "I am only pretending about his wife—I mean your sister."

"You bastard!" Gabriel shouted.

Belcraven turned to Gabriel. "Dash it, she isn't your wife until I say so."

"You're completely insensitive!" Swann slammed his glass down on the table. "I can't believe you would ask me."

"I am not asking." St. Fell leaned back in his dining room chair and folded his arms across his chest. He wasn't asking. Arabella may be Swann's daughter, but she was going to be the Duchess of St. Fell.

Toby cut the cards. "A completely insensitive bastard, that's St. Fell."

Take a Trip Back to the
Romantic Regency Era
of the Early 1800's

4 FREE BOOKS ARE YOURS!

4 FREE
Zebra Regency Romances!
(A $19.96 VALUE!)

**Plus You'll Save Every Month With
Convenient Home Delivery!**

We'd Like to Invite You to Subscribe to Zebra's Regency Romance Book Club and Send You 4 Free Books as Your Introduction! (Worth $19.96!)

If you're a Regency lover, imagine the joy of getting 4 FREE Zebra Regency Romances and then the chance to have these lovely stories delivered to your home each month at the lowest price available! Well, that's our offer to you and here's how you benefit by becoming a Regency Romance subscriber:

- *4 FREE Introductory Regency Romances are delivered to your doorstep (you only pay for shipping & handling)*
- *4 BRAND NEW Regencies are then delivered each month (usually before they're available in bookstores)*
- *Subscribers save almost $4.00 off the cover price every month*
- *You also receive a FREE monthly newsletter, which features author profiles, discounts, subscriber benefits, book previews and more*
- *There's no risks or obligations…in other words, you can cancel whenever you wish with no questions asked*

Join the thousands of readers who enjoy the savings and convenience offered to Regency Romance subscribers. After your initial introductory shipment, you'll receive 4 brand-new Zebra Regency Romances each month to examine for 10 days. Then, if you decide to keep the books, you pay the preferred subscriber's price, plus shipping and handling.

It's a no-lose proposition, so return the FREE BOOK CERTIFICATE today!

to 4 Free Books!

Complete and return the order card to receive your FREE books, a $19.96 value!

If the certificate is missing below, write to:

Regency Romance
Book Club,

P.O. Box 5214,

Clifton, NJ 07015-5214

or call TOLL-FREE
1-800-770-1963

Visit our website at
www.kensingtonbooks.com

FREE BOOK CERTIFICATE

YES! Please rush me 4 FREE Zebra Regency Romances (I only pay $1.99 for shipping and handling).I understand that each month thereafter I will be able to preview 4 brand-new Regency Romances FREE for 10 days. Then, if I should decide to keep them, I will pay the money-saving preferred subscriber's price for all 4... (that's a savings of 20% off the retail price), plus shipping and handling. I may return any shipment within 10 days and owe nothing, and I may cancel this subscription at any time.

Name _____

Address _____ Apt. _____

City _____ State _____ Zip _____

Telephone (____) _____

Signature _____

(If under 18, parent or guardian must sign)

Offer limited to one per household and not to current subscribers. Terms, offer and prices subject to change. Orders subject to acceptance by Regency Romance Book Club. Offer Valid in the U.S. only.

RN054A

REGENCY ROMANCE BOOK CLUB
Zebra Home Subscription Service, Inc.
P.O. Box 5214
Clifton NJ 07015-5214

PLACE
STAMP
HERE

Chapter 7

"Impossible!" The Duchess of St. Fell swiveled her head and blinked at Arabella, Aunt Ophelia, and Diana, her blue eyes bulging without the aid of the lorgnette.

Arabella folded her arms across her chest and jutted out her chin. It was obviously the first time the old know-everything had ever not known everything.

"Are you saying Arabella is lying about what happened at the theater last night with your son?" Aunt Ophelia, God love her, bristled on the sofa beside Arabella.

The duchess scowled. "No, it is obvious she is telling the truth. Her face is completely transparent. It is merely that I never would have believed it of St. Fell." She sniffed. "Ever." She reached for the box of bonbons Aunt Ophelia had brought from Monsieur Karl's.

Even though the duchess had dismissed him as being inferior to Gunter's, when she had finished giving the Swann women a tour of the St. Fell Mayfair home and they had retired to the drawing room, the first thing the old bat had done was tear into the box and begin stuffing herself with apricot nougats. She had already gobbled down four before Arabella even started her third.

"He did not mention anything about last night before he left for Fairfield?" Arabella asked, not caring if the question made her look green. She was green, for heaven's sake! Completely green.

"It is hardly the kind of thing a man would discuss with his mother!" the duchess said. "Of course, he seemed very smug this morning." She popped a peppermint drop in her mouth. "But he is always smug."

She put the bonbon box on the chaise longue cushion next to her and awkwardly half rose to her feet to reach the sofa so she could pat Arabella's shoulder with her heavily beringed claw. Arabella ground her teeth. Of course the old bat felt guilty. It was all her fault for suggesting they go to the theater.

The duchess dropped back down on her chaise longue with a thump and a heavy sigh. "For goodness' sake, how foxed was your father?"

Diana leaned forward in her chair. "Papa was completely foxed when the gentlemen came out of the dining room after their cigars and brandy. He continued to drink all evening long. I think he even brought a bottle of brandy with him to the theater."

"Papa is still foxed now," Arabella said. She flushed. "Well, part of it is due to the celebration the gentlemen apparently had earlier today at White's, when Mr. Carr finally decided to propose to Lady Nola!" No reason to suggest to the duchess that Swanns were prone to excessive consumption of alcohol. Not that the Warburtons were in much of a position to cast stones.

"Oh, I know! Do not glower at me, Miss Arabella Swann!" the duchess snapped. "St. Fell was completely castaway when he left for Fairfield. It has nothing to do with it!"

Arabella leaned back against the sofa cushions and smiled.

"Henry was foxed last night as well," Diana said, just to say Belcraven's first name aloud for the ten thousandth time since last night, since surely she couldn't truly believe that the idiot's sobriety would ever make one bit of difference to his behavior. Belcraven had spent the whole evening staring at her shoes again. Poor Diana. She would probably never have children.

"Henry?" the duchess barked. "I called my husband St. Fell. Or the duke. Not by his first name." She snorted. "That idiot Belcraven has no idea how to go on."

For once the old bat was right. Arabella reached for the box of bonbons. As if she would ever call St. Fell anything but St. Fell. He was a duke, for heaven's sake. She would be a duchess, if she married him. Which after last night, she was no longer certain she wanted to do. The arrogant, conceited, smug bas—

"What about the ladies?" the duchess demanded. "Were they foxed?"

Aunt Ophelia's outrage was evident in the quaver of her voice. "Apparently not, yet they were completely oblivious the entire time! For hours!"

"I am not surprised that Eleanor Carr was useless," the duchess said. "Or those wretched Countesses of Belcraven—"

"Do not mention the Countesses of Belcraven!" Diana lunged for the bonbon box and scrabbled in it until she found a pineapple cream. "I do not see why Henry had to go to Fairfield and leave me alone with them!"

Aunt Ophelia smiled up at her. "But, dearest, if you and Lord Belcraven marry, he will take back his leased properties. And he has to learn something of estate management. I think it was very kind of the Duke of St. Fell to agree to instruct him."

"Since he obviously knows nothing," Arabella said.

The duchess snorted. "It is about time someone taught that idiot Belcraven his responsibilities as an earl!"

"In any event, the countesses have gone to Kent with Lady Nola, dearest," Aunt Ophelia pointed out.

"Kent is not far enough!" Diana wailed, and her chin angled upward. "Henry is going to have to do something about them, or I am not certain I will marry him."

They allowed her a moment of silence as she applied herself to her bonbon. The Countesses of Belcraven made the Duchess of St. Fell seem pleasant. Almost.

"What about Lady Nola? What was she doing last night in the theater?" the duchess asked. "I would have thought she would have had some sympathy for the situation."

Diana snorted. "Lady Nola is so deeply in love she would not have noticed if the theater had caught fire." She shot the duchess an evil smirk. "Ask Arabella what the play was last night."

Arabella flushed. "I know perfectly well it was *Richard III*."

"She had to ask this morning," Diana crowed.

Arabella glared at her. She hadn't asked, so much as requested a point of clarification. She knew it had been something by Mr. Shakespeare. One of the dramatic ones. With a horse, possibly.

"In any event, the women were all sitting in the front row," Diana said. "They could not have seen anything."

Aunt Ophelia nodded. "So Arabella and the duke were alone in a dark corner whilst Joseph was completely foxed and oblivious. A very dark corner, I might add, since that is our special box and I have been myself to the theater several times and often imagined—"

"Aunt Ophelia!" Arabella said, before Diana interrupted yet again to explain that she and Belcraven were also there, doing nothing. "The point is to tell the duchess what happened last night!"

"You have told me what happened!" the duchess bellowed. "Absolutely nothing!"

"Yes! Nothing! For two hours!" Aunt Ophelia cried.

Arabella clenched her teeth at the memory for the countless time since last night. Alone for two hours with the rake of St. Fell, and he had not once tried to kiss her. She had sat there next to him in the dark theater, inches away from him, her skin tingling, catching her breath every time he moved, and he had not touched her.

A few times she thought he was going to put his hand on hers because he had reached out toward her. But at the very last instant he had run his hand through his hair. Or rubbed the back of his neck. Several times he pinched the bridge of his nose. And cursed. Not always under his breath.

And yet, when they had walked out of the theater—or staggered out, in Papa's case—even though they had spent the evening merely talking, St. Fell's hitch was still there. If anything, more pronounced.

It was ridiculous. Her entire love life was ridiculous! She had waited all night for a rake to make advances so she could leap to her feet in the Drury Lane Theater box and spurn him. And he had spent the entire evening talking to her.

She glared at the Egyptian-style papyrus wallpaper trailing up the side of the wall. Hideous. This room would be the first to be redecorated. If she married St. Fell.

"Perhaps St. Fell was excessively foxed," the duchess said. "On occasion, a man can be too foxed to—"

"Your Grace!" Aunt Ophelia squeaked. She turned bright red. "I thought we were speaking of a few stolen kisses. Perhaps a hand on her knee. Surely the duke would not think of actually—"

"Of course he would not think of it!" the duchess said

indignantly. "Well, he might think of it," she added after a moment, "especially if he were foxed. But he certainly would never do it! I know my son."

"But St. Fell was no longer foxed by the time we reached the theater," Arabella said, not certain if this made matters better or worse. "All the other gentlemen kept drinking, but he did not." She slumped back against the sofa cushions.

"That is true!" Diana said. "He made the Carrs' butler bring him coffee and made us late. Henry was most vexed with him for it. He kept shouting about how the duke was holding everyone up."

The duchess wolfed down another caramel praline. Her third. "So St. Fell was cold sober, and you and he sat in a darkened theater box, side by side, together for hours, with nobody watching you and absolutely nothing happened." She sounded like she were reeling off a list of symptoms of a fatal disease. She shook her head mournfully. "It is a blot on the St. Fell family honor."

"Well, now I feel worse!" Arabella snatched up the box of bonbons. Caramel pralines were her fourth favorite kind of sweet. She would have to get the duchess her own supply so she would not unbalance the box. If she married St. Fell. "In any event, we didn't do nothing," she said defensively. "We talked." She took the last caramel praline from the box. If the duchess cared so much for them, she could just fetch her own from Gunter's.

Actually, the talking had been quite nice. Wonderful, really, when she stopped worrying about him making advances so she could spurn him. St. Fell was just as quick-spoken when he was describing his childhood being groomed for the dukedom as the eldest son of an eldest son. And his affection and sense of responsibility for his brothers was as clear as his cursing them. He obviously adored Compton, although Arabella hoped he wasn't in any great rush to return from the Continent. He sounded expensive.

She leaned back against the sofa cushions and tried to make the caramel traces on her tongue last as long as possible. They had not only discussed St. Fell's life, although his was considerably more exciting. It was more exciting being a poor duke in London than a rich heiress in Little Darking. Of course, St. Fell would argue that neither one was as nearly as thrilling as being a rich duke and duchess in London. But last night, St. Fell had encouraged her to talk about herself, and she had told him all about their lives in Little Darking. Also she had been able to explain the whole matter of knowing one hundred of the verses of "Greensleeves" so he did not think she was a complete antidote. St. Fell had been impressed that she had earned so much money on a wager at such a young age.

And like every minute she spent in his company, the time had flown by. The whole evening was over before she even realized that nothing had happened. Nothing! She was supposed to wait until he made his advances, then roar to her feet and announce she knew he had been lying about his arrangement with Papa. But nothing had happened, and nothing had happened so quickly, she didn't even know it until she was home in her nightgown, alone in the dark of her bedchamber, still aching for him.

And now he was gone to Fairfield for five days. She hated the Duke of St. Fell.

The duchess sat back with a smirk. "You know what he is doing, of course?"

"Of course I know!" Arabella leaped to her feet and stormed to the fireplace. "He wants me to chase him!" She was Arabella Swann, of Swann's Fine China. One of the richest heiresses in England. If he thought she was going to chase after him, when he was already the most conceited man in England, he was going to have to think again.

"Yes, and I do not care if it happens all the time in the Minerva Press romances," Aunt Ophelia said. "I do not think it is quite fair to expect a young woman with no experience to seduce a rake."

The duchess scowled. "I agree. I had hoped St. Fell would display a little more originality. But I am beginning to think he is hopeless at courting."

"Exactly," Arabella said. "And because of his incompetence, I am going to be five-and-twenty next week and I have never been kissed."

Aunt Ophelia extracted a candied violet from the bonbon box. "Not all girls have to be kissed before they are married, you know. I have never been kissed."

The duchess shrugged. "There is nothing wrong with saving your first kiss until you are married. It is just boring."

Diana sniffed. "I do not think being kissed is the most important thing in a courtship. Some gentlemen are not so forward."

Aunt Ophelia passed her the box of bonbons.

"But I am a wealthy heiress!" Arabella said. "An extremely wealthy heiress! Being courted by a rake. And last time I looked, I was reasonably attractive. One would think I would have a good chance of being kissed."

Diana rooted through the box. "Perhaps the duke is no longer a rake. It is possible that being around Henry has had a positive influence on him." She sighed at a sugared almond. "It is possible."

Honestly. Arabella shot her a glare. As if making everyone else miserable was going to solve the problem of Belcraven.

"Why would St. Fell reform before she realizes that she

loves him?" The duchess smirked. "The fact he is a rake is one of the things she loves best about him!"

Arabella flushed. "It is not!" She did not find that aspect of his character appealing. Very much.

The duchess snorted and Diana snickered and Aunt Ophelia diplomatically looked down at her hands on her lap. Arabella gritted her teeth. Obviously smugness was catching. "In any event I do not love him!" Why should she love him when he didn't love her?

"How can you be so certain?" Aunt Ophelia asked.

Arabella planted her hands on her hips. "Diana, why do you think you love Belcraven?"

Diana beamed. "Because whenever I am with him I feel as though everything in the world is right. I am happy when I am with him and I want him to be happy as well."

Exactly. The same answer she had given every time Arabella asked her.

The duchess nodded. "That is true. When you love someone, you want the best thing for them."

Arabella didn't need to say it aloud to be told that taking Papa's walking stick and beating the smirk off St. Fell's face probably wasn't the best thing for him. "I am infatuated," she said.

The duchess rolled her eyes. "I am ringing for brandy," she said. "In the meantime, there is nothing to do but wait until St. Fell returns."

"No." Arabella walked over to the box of bonbons and picked out the last peppermint drop. "In the meantime, I am going to go shopping."

Garrard House in Pall Mall was a wonderful innovation because five separate stores were all contained in the same elegant building. Which explained why the opening ceremonies were so ardently attended by the ladies and gentlemen of London that it was difficult to press through the crowd to walk from the front door to the wide central staircase.

"I am telling you, dearest, I do not think this is a very wise idea." Aunt Ophelia managed to stay right at her shoulder as Arabella darted between an elderly couple who were dawdling between the haberdashery and the perfumery.

Arabella put her head down and kept walking. Her aunt knew perfectly well it was the only way she had of meeting Lord Stonecroft again. It was not as if the poor man would ever come to call at Belcraven House. Not after she had ignored him in the Carrs' drawing room while St. Fell had puffed up his chest and scratched the ground like a great big ridiculous rooster. Nor could she possibly ask someone for Lord Stonecroft's direction, never mind actually write him. He was a bachelor and she was an unmarried woman. It was not done. Even by Arabella Swann of Swann's Fine China. Never mind Papa.

Although in the two days since St. Fell had left London Papa had managed to spend all day at Swann's Fine China Emporium, and all night in the Belcraven House study with a bottle of brandy. Obviously, he was disheartened by the thought of losing a duke for a grandson. And too foxed to object to Arabella's suggestion that they have a small party Friday night to celebrate her birthday. Of course, she and Diana and Aunt Ophelia told Papa it was a small party. Otherwise he might possibly think it was a ball, given that they had hired an orchestra to play in the Belcraven House ballroom. Not that he would be so overset if he sobered up. St. Fell was returning to town Friday morning. She would be dancing with him on Friday night. Which was why she needed to meet Lord Stonecroft now, on Monday. It would give her four days with a gentleman other than St. Fell. Assuming Lord Stonecroft was interested. He had certainly looked interested in the Carrs' drawing room. Four days of a gentleman who wasn't St. Fell. Two days more than she had actually spent with St. Fell. She could feel twice as strongly about Lord Stonecroft.

"I do not know why we are rushing," Diana said. "I am certain Lord Stonecroft's poem today is as lengthy as the one he read at the Carrs'." She tugged on Arabella's arm and pointed at the display of fox tippets spread out on the furrier's counter on the other side of the hall. "Why can't we actually do some shopping?"

"Because the only shopping she wants to do is for that Stonefort!"

Arabella whirled around. The Duchess of St. Fell was glowering at her through her lorgnette. Hell.

"Do not curse at me, Miss Arabella Swann! You are not a duchess yet!"

Arabella shot a glare at her aunt and her sister. Why in heaven's name did they have to tell the old bat?

The duchess snorted. "No one had to tell me! You are completely transparent."

Aunt Ophelia wrung her hands together. "It is not that I do not like Lord Stonecroft, dear. Naturally, I do. It is just that I like the Duke of St. Fell better."

"Everyone likes St. Fell better," the duchess said. "Including you, you big ninny."

"I am sure that he loves you, Arabella," Diana said. "You just need to have a little faith."

Arabella turned on her heel and continued her march to the staircase. It was easy to have faith when your suitor was as pathetic as Belcraven. She reached the foot of the staircase just in time to be bowled back by the rush of ladies and gentlemen who streamed down the stairs. The opening ceremonies must have just ended. She kept her hand on the carved marble bannister and ducked to the side to avoid being trampled.

"I do not think Lady Delfinia would chase after a man just to make Raphael jealous, dearest." Aunt Ophelia's voice sounded in her ear. "I am sure she would stay at home and wait faithfully until Raphael had suffered enough to realize he loves her."

"Actually, she goes out to look for little Ruby and falls down a well," Diana said.

"Do not tell me!" Aunt Ophelia clapped her hands over her ears for an instant, then lowered them and peered at Diana anxiously. "Does she die?"

"Of course she does not die!" the duchess barked. "It is a Minerva Press romance!"

"How long is it taking you to read it?" Arabella could not stop herself from asking. "Last week you were on the chapter where Raphael has amnesia—"

"In the inn?" the duchess asked gruffly. "In the candle-light?"

Aunt Ophelia flushed. "I am still at that part."

"Well, Lady Delfinia falls down the well in the next chapter," Diana said.

Arabella rolled her eyes. As if anyone would have a carriage accident one minute and then fall down a well the next. Stupid Raphael and dim-witted Lady Delfinia would have had much less trouble if they had just stayed at home in their library with a good book. Not theirs.

She glanced up at the staircase and straightened her back. The amount of people descending had thinned enough for her not to be bowled over and she marched up the stairs to the top landing. She caught her breath when she walked into the first room on the third floor. It was magnificent—all bright windows and elegant columns stretching up to the high ceiling and around each column were rods from which hung a riot of colorful fine furnishing fabrics. While in the middle area there were tables where customers could drink tea and wine and eat sweetmeats.

Lord Stonecroft stood silhouetted against one of the central windows, a dozen women clustered in front of him. Arabella stopped twenty feet away. She couldn't very well loom up at him, but if he happened to notice she was there, that would be perfectly proper. The sunlight from the window made his dark brown hair appear lighter. Almost as golden brown as St. Fell's. Arabella recognized the Coulter women amongst the crowd. Lord Stonecroft obviously had many female admirers. Probably more admirers than St. Fell.

"You are bringing the name of St. Fell into disrepute!" the duchess hissed in her ear.

Arabella snorted. The hypocritical old bat had seven sons who were rakes. "I am not a member of your family," she whispered back fiercely and then turned around so she could chase her away with a glare. But her attention was caught by the bright swath of fabric hanging on the column just beyond the duchess's left shoulder. A luscious red chintz. Arabella took a step toward it. It would be perfect for the sofas in the St. Fell drawing room.

The duchess looked over her shoulder to follow the direction of Arabella's gaze. "The drawing room sofas?" she asked.

Arabella nodded, then jerked herself back to the moment. Honestly, the duchess was as bad as St. Fell at distracting her. "Go away!" She made a shooing motion with her hands and turned back toward Lord Stonecroft. He was still talking to his adoring crowd. Arabella looked behind her. Aunt Ophelia and Diana were admiring the fabric on the fourth column down. She didn't blame

142 *Nonnie St. George*

them. Silks in deep jewel tones. They would be perfect for ball gowns.

"I most certainly will not go away!" The duchess stepped in front of Arabella. "You cannot fling yourself at the man. It is not done!"

"Come along, Mother, there is a nice piece of raw meat in the corner." A tall, slender, golden-brown-haired man reached from behind the duchess to hook his arm through hers, and for an instant Arabella's heart stopped because she thought it was St. Fell.

But it wasn't. It was his brother, Lord Toby. Arabella swallowed nervously. She wondered if he was going to make a scene on behalf of St. Fell about her renewing her acquaintance with Lord Stonecroft. But Lord Toby merely smiled down at her with a perfectly pleasant expression.

"Don't mind my mother," he said. "Her love for St. Fell makes her overprotective. I'll look after her for you." And as Arabella watched open-mouthed, he dragged his sputtering mother off toward the front of the room where Gabriel Carr and Lady Nola stood receiving well-wishers.

Good heavens! How convenient of Lord Toby to remove his mother. It was obviously a good omen. Arabella shook herself and looked back at Lord Stonecroft. His admiring crowd had thinned down to the Coulters. Mrs. Coulter was talking whilst Elvira and Vivian were gazing. Lord Stonecroft looked over Mrs. Coutler's head and saw Arabella. He smiled. A pleasant smile. Not a knowing smirk like the one St. Fell always gave her.

Arabella felt a rush of satisfaction. Lord Stonecroft remembered her. She smiled back, and one minute later Lord Stonecroft walked to where she stood.

"A pleasure to see you, Miss Swann," he said, bowing low over her hand. His voice was very deep and smooth.

Much deeper than St. Fell's. Not that St. Fell's voice wasn't deep. Of course it was. But he spoke much more quickly than Lord Stonecroft.

"I am surprised," Lord Stonecroft continued. "I did not think I would ever see you again."

"Yes, my father is very overprotective." But still foxed. She smiled at the thought.

"I meant that when we met in the Carrs' drawing room, I received the impression that the Duke of St. Fell thought you belonged to him."

She refused to enjoy the shiver that ran down her spine at his words. She did not belong to St. Fell, the manipulative rake. Lying his head off. Pretending to cry. And then expecting her to feel sorry for him and chase him around some dark theater box, as if she were so desperate for his hands on her body she would resort—

"Do you belong to the Duke of St. Fell?" Lord Stonecroft asked.

She shivered again. "I most certainly do not, my lord."

He smiled. "I thought not."

"Really?" she blurted out, hoping her voice was not as shrill as it sounded to own her ears. Because everyone thought she and St. Fell belonged together. Not that she minded the fact that Lord Stonecroft was immune to the assumption. But still. It was peculiar.

"Yes, I could tell from your face that you did not belong with a man as insensitive as the duke." Lord Stonecroft shrugged apologetically. "I know his brother, Frederick."

"The Earl of Compton?" she said. After all, he was the Earl of Compton now. There was no reason not to call him that. She wouldn't call Stonecroft Blake Masterful or whatever his name was before he was made a baron. She looked past Lord Stonecroft's head out the window. There was a magnificent view all the way down to St.

James's Park and Westminster. And in the distance, she could swear those were the Surrey hills. Where St. Fell was right now.

"The Duke of St. Fell is not known as a romantic," Lord Stonecroft said. "You need romance in your life, Miss Swann. It is obvious you appreciate the finer things that the world has to offer."

Yes, it was obvious. To everyone but that know-everything St. Fell. This was a much better caliber of compliment than St. Fell ever gave her. It made a woman feel tender and gentle to be called romantic. "I do have an appreciation for the finer things in life," she said. Like shopping. She wondered how much the silk cost that Aunt Ophelia and Diana were still fingering. She smiled at Lord Stonecroft. She wasn't forgetting to answer him this time. Not when she wasn't being distracted by St. Fell.

"Yes," Stonecroft said, "you appreciate the finer things like poetry."

Which was a perfectly legitimate thing for him to say. He was a poet, after all. Of course, St. Fell would insist the man was completely self-absorbed if he truly thought she liked poetry. But St. Fell wasn't here. He was lounging in Fairfield. Probably laughing at her.

"I love poetry," she said, not needing to brace herself for a bark of derisive laughter. Talking to Lord Stonecroft was very relaxing. Lord Stonecroft did not argue with her. He believed everything she said, no matter how ludicrous.

"I know you love poetry," Lord Stonecroft said. "While I was reading my poem in the Carr drawing room, I was completely transfixed by your face. Your eyes shone as brightly as if you had swallowed the stars. Your expression was the definition of bliss, Miss Swann." He leaned in closer. "You looked like you had caught your first glimpse of paradise."

"I did?" Good heavens! What an excellent compliment! She'd like to see St. Fell come up with anything half as good. He couldn't, she'd wager. Well, he wouldn't, that was for certain. She struggled to remember a detail of Stonecroft's poem. She would look very clever if she could casually quote a line from one of the verses right now. There had been something about enchantment, she remembered that. And elves. Or nymphs. Or both. She would know for certain, had St. Fell not been nattering at her the whole time.

Stonecroft nodded. "That was the reason I came over to speak to you in the Carr drawing room."

"I am very glad you did," she said. Otherwise, her entire store of compliments would have to be the backhanded and mocking ones given to her by St. Fell. And the ones about her dress from the boring eligible gentlemen in the Carr drawing room. Lord Stonecroft knew exactly what kind of compliments to give a girl.

"Did you like my poem today?" he asked. He held up a sheaf of papers which she hadn't noticed he was holding in his hands.

"I am afraid that I missed it." She looked over her shoulder and smiled Aunt Ophelia and Diana, and they came over, and just as her aunt had promised, she invited him to Arabella's ball. He accepted quickly. He was probably an excellent dancer. As Arabella listened to him declare how much he was looking forward to it, she had a sudden vision of herself at her ball, dancing with him. While St. Fell prowled at the edge of the dance floor, lashing his tail in fury.

Aunt Ophelia explained that they needed to pay their respects to the Carrs. Arabella was flattered when Lord Stonecroft offered to accompany them.

"Perhaps afterwards, we could take a table and I could read you my poem?" he said.

"Certainly." It would be soothing to listen to his poem. She could use the time to plan what was needed for her ball. Because it was a private ball, after all, and she could have any arrangement of dances she wanted. So if she wanted to start the ball with a waltz with Lord Stonecroft and then have a supper dance waltz with St. Fell, it was no one's business but her own.

He smiled and offered his arm. Arabella took it. She did not feel the same jolt of self-consciousness she had endured when she had taken St. Fell's arm for their walk to Soho Square. But then again, Lord Stonecroft was not the first eligible gentleman whose arm she had taken. She was not as green about touching a gentleman's arm. Therefore it was natural that she was less of a henwit and more aware of her surroundings and not brooding overmuch how the gentleman's arm felt or what he was thinking of her. Not that all the worry in the world about what St. Fell was thinking would help anyone fathom what was going on in his head.

Lord Stonecroft looked down at her, and Arabella gave him her sweetest smile. The one she had been practicing in the looking glass ever since she was sixteen.

It was very pleasant to be thinking of another gentleman besides the Duke of St. Fell.

Chapter 8

It was finally Friday. The day St. Fell was to return to London.

Arabella took three hours in the morning to decide what to wear to receive afternoon callers, mostly because Diana insisted on howling like a great bubblebrain about her own choice of dress, as if it mattered. It had taken all of Arabella's power of will to refrain from pointing out that Belcraven would likely only notice her sister's shoes. Although she may have mentioned it once, in the heat of the moment, whilst she and Diana were wrestling over a white satin fichu embroidered with daffodils, which anyone could tell would make Diana's complexion look sallow.

In any event, the dress Arabella finally selected did not need the silly fichu. It was a white muslin morning dress with long sleeves and small silver ribbon frogs that ran up the front of the bodice to a high lace collar. It was demure, and not the slightest bit forward. As if St. Fell returning to London was no special event requiring the display of her plumage.

Besides, it would be the perfect contrast to the extremely low-cut rich pink silk ball gown she would wear tonight. Arabella smiled to herself as she made her way to the east drawing room. This afternoon's call would be brief, as a matter of manners. But tonight she would spend the entire evening with St. Fell. And Lord Stonecroft, of course. Her birthday ball. When she would celebrate turning five-and-twenty. When she might very well decide to be kissed. Depending on how St. Fell behaved.

Aunt Ophelia and the duchess and sallow Diana in full fichu were already sitting in a line on the sofa when Arabella walked into the room.

"Isn't this exciting!" Aunt Ophelia beamed. She took a sip from her glass of something that was more the golden brown color of brandy than the paler ratafia.

"He is home." The duchess did not look up from polishing her lorgnette on the edge of her shawl. "He is telling me nothing. Except that he will be here and he still thinks he is marrying you."

Diana, of course, was nattering on about Belcraven and his aunts and their emigration, even though no one could possibly be listening. Ever since she had seen the Countesses of Belcraven at the Garrard House opening, she had decided that they would have to go to Canada or she would not marry Belcraven. Arabella hoped the earl had enough sense to stop at the docks on the way over and book their passage, because Diana had fixed her mind.

She waved to Papa, who was ensconced in his chair at the card table he had moved to the corner. He had stayed there all week during calls. He smiled hazily and lifted his glass in a toast. Arabella smiled back. He was still foxed. Everything was proceeding most excellently.

She decided to pace in front of the fireplace, where she could easily see the clock on the mantel. It was a quarter to three. Fifteen more minutes before the hour at which callers were welcome at Belcraven House, since they kept Little Darking hours. St. Fell wouldn't come early, of course. That would show weakness. Or perhaps he would come early to manipulate her into thinking he wanted her so desperately that he couldn't help but look like an eager love-sick moonling. So in actual fact it was meaningless if he came early. Similarly, if he came late, it would either be because he forgot or because he wanted her to think he forgot so that she would be so worried she would fall on him in gratitude and beg him to marry her.

Of course, she wouldn't put it past him to arrive exactly on time, merely because she wouldn't know what to make of it.

Hell. He was so annoying, so frustrating in every respect. No matter how many times she applied herself to the puzzle, she still had no idea if he had any true feeling for her or if he just wanted to get his hands on her fortune. Arabella sighed. The clock hands were moving as slowly as if they were dipped in treacle. Diana was still going on about Belcraven. Aunt Ophelia and the duchess were most definitely drinking brandy, because they rose to refill their glasses from Papa's decanter.

At one minute past three, Deakin announced Lord Stonecroft. Arabella looked up with a guilty start. She had forgotten he would be calling as well. As he had every day since Monday. He always called on her first, then went on to the Coulters'.

He acknowledged Papa and then offered his greetings to Aunt Ophelia, Diana, and the duchess, even though the old bat glowered right through him as if he didn't exist, as always, then he walked over to where Arabella stood in front of the fireplace. He was holding a box of bonbons.

He ran his eyes over her dress with an appreciative smile. "You look like a birthday present that is just waiting to be unwrapped," he said in his deep smooth voice.

Arabella thanked him. He always gave excellent compliments. She did feel like a birthday present. That might be unwrapped tonight, by St. Fell. Depending.

Lord Stonecroft thrust the box in her hands with a proud smile. "And here is another present waiting to be opened."

"How nice," she said. The bonbons were from Mr. Karl's confectionary. Lord Stonecroft had already brought her a box of bonbons on Tuesday. And roses on Wednesday and her favorite essence of lavender yesterday, because even Lord Stonecroft had noticed that Papa was completely foxed, otherwise he would have not have dared give her such a personal gift as perfume. She must find a way to casually mention the perfume to St. Fell.

"Open it," Lord Stonecroft repeated.

Arabella pulled at the red satin ribbon. You'd think if the man was so desperate for bonbons, he would have just snuck one in his carriage on the way over. She would never have noticed. St. Fell would have done so. St. Fell would have eaten the entire box and claimed it was his birthday. She hoped he would bring her something more original than bonbons. She knew perfectly well his mother had written to tell him about her birthday. And the ball. She smiled to herself. And Lord Stonecroft.

She lifted the bonbon box lid. There were twenty bonbons, each one resting on a folded slip of parchment paper. She glanced past Stonecroft's shoulder at the clock. A quarter past three. Obviously St. Fell had decided not to look like an eager moonling. Not that it would have made the slightest difference in what she thought of him anyway. She hoped he realized that and didn't bother to make a show of waiting until the very last moment to pay his call.

Lord Stonecroft pointed at the bonbons. "I have written a poem for you and placed each verse under a bonbon."

Arabella smiled and nodded pleasantly. Twenty verses. One of his shorter poems, thank heavens.

"You see," Lord Stonecroft continued smoothly, "when you eat your sweets from your most favorite to least, you will be able to read the poem in order." He looked deeply into her eyes. "I remember all of your bonbon preferences." He shrugged. "You have firm opinions." He shrugged again. "About everything."

Good heavens! Arabella looked down at the box in awe. That was the most romantic thing anyone could possibly imagine! The man had written her poetry and remembered her bonbon preferences. She thanked him warmly. St. Fell would go completely insane.

She looked in the box for the apricot nougat but before she found it, Deakin announced the arrival of the Duke of St. Fell. And the Earl of Belcraven, obviously, since Diana squealed and leaped to her feet like a great featherbrained henwit.

Arabella shoved the box of bonbons at Stonecroft and wiped her suddenly damp hands on the back of the skirt of her dress. Then she snatched the box back so she would have it on hand to show St. Fell.

St. Fell stopped dead in the doorway and quickly scanned the room until he saw her. Then he hitched his shoulders, smirked his half smile, and strode straight toward her.

He still hitched! A surge of pleasure warmed her all the way from her toes to the tips of her fingers. Not that he wasn't a manipulative, lying, fortune-hunting snake, of course. But still. He hitched.

He came to an abrupt stop in front of her, just as tall and lean and ridiculously handsome as she had remembered.

"Did you miss me, Miss Swann?" he purred, his gray eyes shining with laughter.

She tilted her head and gave a casual lift of her right shoulder. "Were you away, Your Grace?"

He grinned. "How long did it take you to think of that one?"

An hour after breakfast, with Diana instructing her on the tone of delivery. "Fifteen minutes," Arabella said.

"Liar." His grin didn't falter. "It took me an hour to come up with mine. I debated between 'Have you missed me, Miss Swann?' and 'So, have you finally come to your senses and decided to marry me?' but I decided the latter was too complicated for a green little girl from the provinces."

"That was very sensitive of you." She grinned back at him. He was such an idiot. And he still wanted to marry her. Of course, she hadn't doubted it for a moment. Not really. She still had her fortune.

"Everyone says I am very sensitive," he said.

"Ha!" It was the duchess. She and Aunt Ophelia were standing directly behind St. Fell, each one clutching her glass to her bosom.

St. Fell turned around and looked down his nose at them. "Do we really need chaperones?"

"We have been waiting a week!" Aunt Ophelia's bottom lip trembled.

"You are not seriously going to suggest we follow around Belcraven and Diana," his mother said.

"That would be completely unfair!" Aunt Ophelia wailed.

"Fine," St. Fell pinched the bridge of his nose as if willing himself to find patience. "But you have to be quiet."

Aunt Ophelia bobbed her head in enthusiastic agreement. The duchess took a noncommittal sip of her drink.

St. Fell turned back to Arabella. His eyes were the most intelligent shade of gray. "Have you been trying on hats in my absence?" he asked.

The duchess snorted. St. Fell shot her a warning

glance over his shoulder. His hair had grown just the tiniest bit while he was away. It came down to cover the top of his ears.

Arabella smiled. "I found a very fine hat for my consideration."

Aunt Ophelia peered around St. Fell's back. "You have not been shopping for hats, Arabella," she whispered loudly. "You have been too busy parading around town with Lord Stonecroft."

"A very fine hat?" St. Fell asked, biting his lip but barely hiding his laughter.

"An excellent hat," Arabella said. If he could keep a straight face, so could she. "Very flattering in every respect."

"I have had enough of hats!" The duchess shrugged off Aunt Ophelia's hand on her arm and pushed herself between Arabella and St. Fell. "I am actually beginning to feel some pity for the girl."

St. Fell clenched his jaw. "You are not helping," he said to his mother. "Again."

The duchess snorted. "We keep telling you we are not here to help!"

"Chaperones merely observe," Aunt Ophelia said.

"And comment," the duchess said.

"Only where necessary," Aunt Ophelia added primly.

"Which is constantly!" The duchess tossed back the rest of her drink. "I have never seen such pathetic courting."

St. Fell sighed. "Perhaps we might have a better conversation were we not accompanied by a constant chorus of comments."

The duchess snorted. "Do not blame us for your poor conversation! You are the one who insisted on talking about hats."

"If you go away," St. Fell said pleasantly, "I promise for

the five minutes we will be allowed to speak in peace that I will keep my hands to myself."

The duchess rolled her eyes at Aunt Ophelia. "Now he is blaming us for his complete lack of action."

St. Fell shrugged at Arabella. "I give up. You have a try."

"It is pointless," she said. "They are drinking."

"Hardly anything!" Aunt Ophelia protested.

"Not nearly enough!" bellowed the duchess.

"Not as much as Papa, of course," Arabella said.

"Not yet." St. Fell's smile deepened and he shot her a conspiratorial look that made her catch her breath. It was very pleasant having Papa foxed. It would be even more pleasant tonight if Aunt Ophelia and the duchess were as well.

"How is your sister, by the way?" St. Fell asked. "Is she always infatuated? Or does she finally admit that she is head over heels in love with that idiot Belcraven?"

Aunt Ophelia tugged on his jacket sleeve. "Actually, Your Grace, Diana has always admitted being in love—"

"She will always be infatuated," Arabella said loudly, drowning out her aunt's voice, "as long as she doesn't know if the idiot loves her for herself or her fortune."

St. Fell laughed. "I suppose she will decide tonight at the ball?"

The duchess slapped her glass down on the mantel and planted her hands on her hips. "Can you imagine? Now they will not stop talking about that idiot Belcraven!"

"No," Aunt Ophelia said in the hushed tones of a play-goer in a theater, "I think it is another metaphor."

"It is all a metaphor," the duchess snapped, "and my lorgnette stands for 'get on with it'!" She aimed the stupid thing at St. Fell's ribs, but he easily caught it and held it up over his head. The ribbon was still around the old bat's neck, but it was too long to actually strangle her.

"She is not dead," Arabella pointed out helpfully.

"What would you like us to discuss, Mother?" St. Fell asked.

"That great idiot Stonecroft, of course!" The duchess snatched her lorgnette back and smoothed her shawl around her shoulders. "Do you not notice him mooning at her while you chat about headgear?"

Hell! Lord Stonecroft! Arabella had forgotten the poor man was actually in the drawing room. She looked over. He was sitting on the armchair facing the sofa, watching her and St. Fell. He must have gone over there when St. Fell had appeared. She gave him a guilty smile and prayed he wouldn't come over. At least, not right away.

St. Fell stepped in front of her to block her view. "I know perfectly well old Stoneface is here," he said, his smooth tone of voice not disguising the steel underneath.

"Stonecroft," Arabella corrected, bending her head so St. Fell wouldn't see her grin. He was insanely jealous of Stonecroft, of course. So predictable. Jealousy was the only true show of emotion that wiped the smug smirk off his face. Tonight would be delicious.

When she had schooled her smile, Arabella looked up. "Lord Stonecroft is a very wonderful gentleman." She held out the bonbon box she had forgotten she was holding until she looked down. "Today for my birthday he has—"

"Oh, yes, it is your birthday." St. Fell winced. "I meant to get you a gift—"

"You did not bring me a gift?" she said. She had actually forgotten it was her birthday in the thrill of just seeing him. But still. She took a deep breath and forced herself to loosen her punishing grip on the bonbon box. The man was beyond unromantic.

"I wrote you about it repeatedly!" His mother jabbed the small of his back with her lorgnette.

St. Fell glared at her over his shoulder. "Are you even pretending to look through that damned thing?"

"Are you here to talk to me or to her?" she snarled back.

St. Fell crossed his arms and returned his attention to Arabella. "I suppose you are overset because I did not buy you a present?"

"No," Arabella said, "I was overset because you did not buy me a present. Now I am overset because you did not even remember it was my birthday."

St. Fell shrugged. "I suppose Stonehead fetched you a present?"

"Stonecroft," Arabella corrected him. She hoped he wouldn't go over and punch poor Stonecroft in the nose this afternoon. Or tonight, of course. Although there would be so many more witnesses to St. Fell becoming undone tonight. She held out the box of bonbons.

"You are excited because he gave you bonbons?" St. Fell drawled. "God, you are green."

"Oh, but these are not merely bonbons!" She made her voice bright and enthusiastic. "They are a poem! Lord Stonecroft wrote me poetry and remembers my preferences for bonbons. And flowers! And perfume! Lord Stonecroft is considerate and romantic!" Let St. Fell top that, the unromantic, self-absorbed fortune hunter.

"Lord Stonecroft is so very romantic." St. Fell sighed. "And yet here you are, panting at me."

"I am not panting, you conceited, smug bast—"

"Arabella!" Aunt Ophelia shrieked.

St. Fell smirked. "Yes, Miss Swann, how dare you insult my mother."

Arabella's foot twitched with the urge to kick him. "At least Lord Stonecroft does not lie his head off every time he speaks to me!"

"The girl is right, St. Fell," his mother said. "We all know perfectly well you are spinning a Banbury tale about the agreement you have made with Swann to marry her."

"Yes, Your Grace," Aunt Ophelia said, her tone meeker, yet no less insistent. "We are all very interested in why you lied, given that you did not subsequently"—she took a mincing sip of her brandy as if for courage—"take advantage of the dark corner."

Arabella held her breath as she waited for his answer.

St. Fell grinned down at the three of them. "Because sometimes winning at whist depends on your partner."

Arabella goggled at him. Conversation with him was impossible!

"Conversation with you is impossible!" the duchess shouted.

For heaven's sake! Arabella shot her a glare. Why didn't the old bat keep her nose out of their business?

The duchess glared back at her and then turned to St. Fell.

"Just tell the ninny you love her," she barked, "and try to look sincere about it!"

St. Fell laughed. "Miss Swann would not believe me," he said. "She knows perfectly well I would say anything to convince her to marry me."

He was right, of course. Which didn't mean she didn't like to hear it. But she would never believe him. And she wanted to know—no she needed to know that he felt the same way that she did about him. That he was moved by her. The way she was moved by him. Arabella stared down at the bonbon box blindly. Hell.

"Come on," he whispered. "Say it."

She lifted her chin at him in challenge, but he tilted his head and smiled, and his eyes darkened, and the rest of the room faded along with any thought she had of arguing.

"Say it," he repeated, the rasp in his voice sending an ache all the way through her. "You know that you want to." He stood before her, swaying, his arms hanging down at his sides, his hands clenching and unclenching as if he wanted to seize her.

"What does he want her to say?" Aunt Ophelia whispered.

"That she loves him, of course!" hissed the duchess.

St. Fell cursed and spun around. "Could you possibly be more annoying?" he shouted.

"Oh, yes!" Aunt Ophelia beamed at him. "I think we would be considerably more annoying if we actually interfered. We are merely chaperoning. As is our duty."

The muscles in St. Fell's shoulders twitched, but when he turned around to face Arabella again, his expression held its usual smirk. "I look forward to resolving the matter while we're dancing tonight, Miss Swann. Alone."

He bowed to her, but didn't straighten up immediately. Instead he reached into the box and plucked out the apricot nougat and popped it into his mouth, and without lowering his eyes from hers, he picked up the parchment paper underneath it and crumpled it in his fist and dropped it back in the box. "Let us see tonight how I will deal with your Lord Stonecrate."

He turned on his heel and stalked off to join Papa at the table in the corner.

Good heavens. Arabella let go of the breath she had been holding and smiled at her aunt and the duchess. Tonight's ball was going to be perfect.

St. Fell took another slow sip of his half glass of brandy. Courting Arabella required a clear head. It was a good thing the afternoon was already enjoyable without needing to muddied by brandy. Arabella and

Stonecroft sat on the sofa with their heads together while the clod droned his latest epic and Arabella wolfed bonbons as required and tried desperately not to look over her shoulder at St. Fell.

She looked over her shoulder at him. He winked. She snapped her head back at Stonecroft, but not before cursing. St. Fell shifted himself in his chair more comfortably. It drove her mad when he could watch her and she couldn't watch back.

"It's a father's worst nightmare," Swann muttered into his glass.

"She is just having a little fun," St. Fell said.

"Fun?" Swann took a great gulp of brandy. "Wait until you're the father of daughters! We'll see how much fun you'll think it is then!"

St. Fell shrugged. He and Arabella would have sons, of course. He took another small sip of brandy. Hopefully. All Warburtons had sons. God help him, they were having sons. He grabbed the decanter and poured himself another half glass of brandy.

Arabella looked over her shoulder at him. St. Fell raised his glass in a toast. She lowered her eyebrows in a scowl and pursed her lips in a little disapproving pucker, trying to pretend that she didn't really want to be back here, sitting on his lap, instead of trapped on the sofa with the great epic bore.

St. Fell raised the glass to his lips to hide his smile. She obviously had her heart set on some sort of show at her ball tonight. Perhaps he'd wait until she was waltzing with Stonecroft, then he'd scowl and storm at the edge of dance floor.

She would love that.

"He's a rake and a fortune hunter!" Swann tossed back the rest of his drink.

St. Fell shrugged again. Who wasn't? Or perhaps he

would cut in while she was waltzing with Stonecroft. The height of bad manners, but it would be forgiven since everyone knew they would soon be married. Maybe Monday morning by special license, if Arabella was sufficiently impressed by his fit of jealousy tonight.

Swann pulled out his handkerchief. "Sometimes I think that you have been on her side from the beginning." He dabbed the top of his head. "Because if you had any loyalty to your sex you would not make me do this."

"No one is making you do anything," St. Fell said. "You lost at whist."

"I'd have won if Gabriel Carr had not been foxed!"

St. Fell didn't bother arguing that he and Toby had been foxed too. Swann damned well knew it. He was just a poor sport.

Swann eyed Arabella nervously and lowered his voice to a whisper. "Anyway, if I had won, you would still have made me agree to let her chase after Stonecroft! You just would have blackmailed me with that ridiculous fairy tale you told her about me holding to the promise I made her."

St. Fell shrugged. He'd do whatever was required to have Arabella. But Swann must have been completely castaway all week if he hadn't noticed that Arabella already knew that the story was a bouncer.

Which was one of the many advantages of Swann staying foxed. St. Fell refilled the merchant's glass. "You were the one who promised her she could choose for herself," he said.

"It was a stupid promise!" Swann slammed his hand down on the table.

Arabella glanced over her shoulder in alarm. St. Fell gave her an innocent shrug and glanced meaningfully from the decanter to her father's crimson face. She sighed, but her lips curved in her usual smug smile before she looked back at Stonecroft.

She knew perfectly well the advantages of her father staying foxed.

"I should have just told her she had to marry you to get her full dowry." Swann glowered into his glass. "She'd have kicked up a fuss but by now she'd be perfectly happy."

"She is perfectly happy," St. Fell said.

Swann sighed mournfully. "I want my grandson to be a duke."

St. Fell took another sip of his brandy. So did he.

"What if he offers for her before she agrees to take you?" Swann demanded. "What am I supposed to do then?"

"She'll never let it go that far." St. Fell smiled and Arabella looked over, as if he had called her. God, but the clod's damn poem was taking forever. She was probably biting her tongue to keep from saying something sarcastic. "She's green, but she isn't the slightest bit stupid."

"I suppose you're right." Swann heaved a deep sigh. "She's a clever girl, my Arabella."

No. St. Fell smiled. She was his Arabella.

Swann shook his head. "I can't believe Belcraven hasn't blurted out anything. If Diana found out, she'd tell her sister for certain."

"Belcraven isn't that stupid," St. Fell said. Nor did the idiot want anyone to suggest to Diana that she stop wearing the black kid leather lace-up half boots she favored.

"Where is he anyway? Didn't he come in with you?" Swann peered around the room owlishly. His shoulders slumped when he couldn't spot the idiot, and he went back to staring sullenly at his glass. "Diana's probably taken him out to buy ship passage to the colonies for his aunts," he muttered.

Arabella glanced back. St. Fell looked at Stonecroft and rolled his eyes. She tilted her chin as if she didn't care about his opinion, but her eyes lingered on his before she turned back to Stonecroft.

Tonight. St. Fell shifted pleasantly in his chair. She would be ready to choose him tonight.

"At least she's wearing something modest today," Swann said. "You wouldn't believe what she wore when he took her driving through Hyde Park yesterday. She must have hoped you might come home a day early and hide in the bushes."

"Tenants' delegations went a day over schedule," St. Fell explained. Otherwise he'd have been home in time to hide in the bushes of Hyde Park and let her catch him spying on her and Stonecroft. Arabella's dress today had twenty catches up the front. He couldn't help but count them while they were talking. He smiled. A great deal of trouble to get off, but damned diverting while you're doing it. Stonecroft had probably given her the line about how she looked like a present waiting to be unwrapped.

The clod looked predictable.

Arabella looked over. St. Fell looked at the clock on the mantel, then back at Stonecroft, and closed his eyes and flopped his head down for a second as if he were falling unconscious. She snapped back to look at Stonecroft even more quickly than usual. St. Fell grinned. She must be afraid she was going to burst out laughing. The next time she looked over, he'd give her his best Minerva Press hero leer. That would tip her right over the edge.

"He gave Arabella her favorite perfume!" Swann poured himself another glassful from the decanter. "I had to get myself foxed at twelve noon not to face it."

Her favorite perfume? Stonecroft had been smelling Arabella? St. Fell slid his glass away from himself even though it still had brandy left in it. "You worry too much," he told Swann. "She knows what she's doing. And in any event, it's almost over."

"I hope so." Swann sounded doubtful. "Look at her face. That's the same look she gives you."

Arabella was shining up at Stonecroft as though her horse had just crossed the Epsom finish line first at a hundred to one.

"She is thinking of me," St. Fell said. She had been looking at him like that ever since he had sat down next to her on the Belcraven House north reception room sofa. Stonecroft didn't mean anything to her.

Stonecroft finally finished his poem. Arabella and her aunt applauded, and he took a bow. The noise made Mother sputter awake in the armchair and she shot Stonecroft her most baleful look. But the clod didn't notice because he was walking over to St. Fell and Swann's table.

St. Fell crossed his arms and leaned back in his chair. This had the potential to be highly amusing. He shot Arabella a warning glance to stay out of it. Not that she would for very long.

When Stonecroft reached the table Swann looked up, grunted once, and then lay his head down next to the brandy decanter and passed out.

Stonecroft stayed there, standing. "I wanted to mention that I fought alongside your brother Frederick," he said.

"Do you mean the Earl of Compton, er, Blade?" St. Fell smiled at him.

Stonecroft stared at him for a long minute. "Compton." He nodded. "And because of my respect for your brother, I thought you should know that no matter what happens, I always wished that my older brother looked after me in the way you take care of him."

St. Fell stood up. What in God's name did the clod imagine was going to happen?

* * *

Arabella sat on the sofa and pretended to listen as Aunt Ophelia and the duchess debated the merits of Lord Stonecroft's poem, even though the duchess had snored through it. In any event, it had just been another in the wood nymph thrall series. St. Fell was managing to look down his nose at Stonecroft even though he was seated and Stonecroft remained standing. She would have liked to have gone over, but St. Fell just shot her a warning glance to stay put. She would give them five minutes.

Diana came and sat down on sofa to Arabella's right. "Henry and I snuck down to the conservatory while no one was looking," she said in Arabella's ear.

Arabella bit her lip to keep from laughing. She had no idea why they bothered to sneak away to do nothing. Papa's head was slumped on the table. He had passed out again, poor dear. It was a shame it was so early. He would likely be awake again by the ball.

"I have decided marry Henry after all," Diana said.

Arabella nodded. No one ever had any chance against a determined Diana, never mind anyone as amiable as Belcraven. St. Fell stood up, his smug smirk never faltering for a second. "So do the aunts go to Canada before or after the wedding?" she asked Diana.

"Well, actually"—Diana lowered her voice to a whisper—"Henry has persuaded me that his aunts are really not that bad. They are just misunderstood."

"Really?" Arabella turned to stare at her sister. Belcraven's aunts were abominable and Belcraven's powers of speech were hardly impressive. "What in heaven's name could he have possibly said to persuade you of that?"

Two pink spots appeared high on Diana cheeks, and

she looked down at her hands. "It is not so much what he said . . ." she tailed off without meeting Arabella's eyes.

The blood drained from Arabella's face. She gripped her sister's arm. "Surely you did not—"

"Of course we did not!" Diana looked up, her eyes wide. "I never would, not before marriage! We have not even had the banns read!"

"You do not have to look so offended!" Arabella said, feeling guilty for thinking it. Obviously no good girl would think of it. She felt her own face flame the same color as Diana's.

Diana shrugged as if to say she had already forgiven her, and then looked up with a shy smile. "We did kiss."

Diana had kissed Belcraven? Diana was two-and-twenty and her suitor was Belcraven and she had kissed? Arabella clenched her fists and shot a glare over to the table in the corner.

But St. Fell was not there. She looked around the drawing room. St. Fell was gone. And so was Lord Stonecroft.

"They have left together!" The duchess loomed in front of her. "You know what that means, don't you?" Her ominous expression made Arabella's blood run cold.

"What?" Arabella croaked. She stood up even though her legs were unsteady.

The duchess's scowl deepened. "They have gone to duel over you, of course!"

Aunt Ophelia wrung her hands together. "Remember, Arabella? The duke said he would take care of Lord Stonecroft! That is manly code for dueling!"

"Don't worry," Diana said soothingly. "I will send Henry after them. He will find them and put a stop to it before anyone gets hurt."

The duchess's glare did not lift from Arabella's face for a second. "Look what you have done, you completely insensitive, smug, self-centered—"

"Your Grace!" Aunt Ophelia shouted.

"You have got my son killed!" The duchess threw her arms around Arabella's neck and burst into tears.

Arabella numbly patted the sobbing woman's back. Hell.

Chapter 9

St. Fell won the carriage contest handily, Stonecroft having come to Belcraven House in his grandmother's dogcart, claiming that one of his whiskey gig horses had just thrown a shoe. So St. Fell drove them to Mayfair at racing speeds in his high-flyer phaeton. Which was actually Toby's, but Stonecroft didn't need to know that.

As always, Ricardo cracked open the front door of the discreetly elegant St. James Street town house only a few inches until he knew the callers were welcome. "Your Grace!" He threw open the door and his weathered face broke into an enormous grin. "We haven't seen you in weeks!"

St. Fell patted the porter's stooped shoulder as he stepped into the foyer. Madame Martina's was highly exclusive. Not that he needed to impress Stonecroft.

Ricardo's smile didn't falter when he saw Stonecroft. "A pleasure as always, my lord!" he exclaimed. "Your usual table?"

St. Fell gritted his teeth as they followed the porter to the ground floor card room. Obviously in the past two weeks, Madame Martina's had gone sadly downhill.

Two hours and two bottles of Madeira later, they dispensed with the drinking match by mutual consent. Stonecroft had five brothers himself. There wasn't much of a gain in tolerance past the fourth brother.

And although they didn't speak of it, it was clear Stonecroft did not want to be three sheets to the wind at Arabella's ball any more than St. Fell did.

Similarly, the two hours of piquet they played while they drank gave neither one the clear advantage, Stonecroft having been taught to play by Compton.

Which meant that by seven o'clock in the evening there remained only one last field of competition for two London rakes.

St. Fell and Stonecroft climbed the stairs side by side to Madame Martina's first floor parlor. Where Madame Martina's finest women awaited.

"Dash it, of course they are not dueling!" Belcraven had suddenly taken on the demeanor of the captain in the Guards that he had been for all those years before he sold his commission. He stood at attention in the middle of the east drawing room, his voice confident and reassuring as he spoke to Arabella and Aunt Ophelia and Diana. And Papa, although Papa was still snoring softly at his table. "They're both the heads of their households. They have family and tenants dependent on them. They're not going to go do something as corkbrained as shoot each other over a woman they want to marry, especially since there's no guarantee that winning would mean you would marry either one of them, begging your pardon, Arabe—Miss Swann."

"Arabella is fine," Arabella said. He was going to be married to Diana, after all. And the idiot actually managed to sound convincing, as astonishing as that was. Besides, he had come up with the brilliant notion of having the duchess sent home right away so she could change into her evening clothes for the ball.

Lord Toby nodded. "My mother worries overmuch

about nothing where we are concerned. St. Fell and Stonecroft are rakes, not rakehells or hotheads."

Aunt Ophelia sighed. "It is a shame that gentlemen do not need chaperones. Their lives seem so interesting."

"That is because they do not have chaperones," Arabella pointed out.

Lord Toby shook his head. "I am sure St. Fell and Stonecroft aren't doing anything the slightest bit interesting. They are merely off drinking and gaming and—"

"Shut up, Toby," Belcraven said.

"—drinking," Lord Toby concluded smoothly.

Arabella smiled back and nodded, and suppressed the sigh that threatened to overtake her. She didn't want St. Fell and Lord Stonecroft to go to Rotten Row and fire pistols at each other, of course. But there was something about a contest of drinking and gaming—even if she was the object of the bet—that seemed to be so sadly lacking in passion . . . although surely rakes did not only drink and game?

"St. Fell!" Yvette ran toward him as soon as they walked into the parlor, an expression of delight on her face. The redhead was the most beautiful and exclusive lovely in Madame Martina's. "You have not been here in weeks!"

St. Fell looked over his shoulder at Stonecroft, but the clod had galloped over to the sofa and was too busy making ox faces at a blowsy blonde and a lumpish brunette to notice anyone else but himself.

St. Fell took Yvette's arm and steered her to the alcove at the far end of the room. It was an excellent dark corner. It had a perfect view of the sofa.

"Are we not going up to my room?" Yvette nestled close and trailed her scarf along the top of her low-cut—very low-cut—gown in a way that raised many happy memories.

St. Fell allowed himself a moment of reminiscence, then he shook his head. He was going to have Arabella. "I am afraid I am no longer interested," he told Yvette, his tone gentle.

He looked back at the sofa. Stonecroft had parked the blonde on one knee and the brunette on the other, and both girls were giggling.

"If it is a question of credit," Yvette leaned in close to whisper in his ear, "I could speak to Madame Martina."

"No, it has nothing to do with credit. I am just not interested." St. Fell moved his head out the range of her tongue. "And it has absolutely nothing to do with you, I swear. You are very lovely." Women never liked hearing about other women. He patted her shoulder in what he hoped was a brotherly way, never having tried it before. "I'm really only here because of the clod on the sofa."

Stonecroft hauled himself to his feet and draped one arm around the blonde. He pulled the brunette up as well and the three of them lurched out the door together. St. Fell rolled his eyes. The idiot obviously hadn't spent that much time with Compton if he thought St. Fell was going to be impressed by that.

As soon as he was sure Stonecroft was safely out of the room, St. Fell stepped out of the alcove. He'd give the clod ten minutes, then he'd send Ricardo up with a smoking rushlight to bang on the door and yell fire. Juvenile, but always amusing. Except when his damned brothers did it to him.

"St. Fell! You have not been here in weeks!" Marguerite, the second most beautiful and exclusive of Madame Martina's lovelies ran into the parlor and threw herself at him. "Ricardo told me you were here! You know I don't start work until nine."

St. Fell pried her arms off his neck and set her down

next to Yvette. "I am afraid, my dear, that I am no longer interested."

Marguerite laughed. "If it's a question of credit, I am sure I could speak to Ma—"

"It has nothing to do with credit," he said kindly but firmly. "I am simply no longer interested."

She curled herself around his left arm as if he hadn't spoken. "If you come to my room now," she murmured, "I won't begin charging you until nine o'clock."

"Thank you, but I am not intere—"

"Ha!" Yvette grabbed his right arm and leaned across his chest to glare at Marguerite. "If he comes up to my room, I won't charge him at all!"

Marguerite yanked his left arm. "If he comes up to my room, I will pay him!"

"You are both very kind." He wrested his arms free and dusted off his jacket. "But I am not interested in you—in any of the women here," he added quickly when their expressions turned stormy. He smiled gently but kept his tone firm. "I am only interested in Lord Stonecroft."

Yvette's jaw dropped. Marguerite burst into tears.

He pinched the bridge of his nose. "I did not mean it in that way."

Someone tapped his shoulder from behind. God help him, for the first time in his life he found himself praying it was not another beautiful and exclusive Madame Martina lovely. He turned around.

It was Stonecroft, fully dressed, his face ashen.

"I have to leave here immediately," he croaked. "I have just remembered a pressing appointment."

"I do not mind taking you," St. Fell said quickly. He shot Yvette and Marguerite a hurried smile over his shoulder and followed Stonecroft out the door. It was a good thing he was never returning.

But the two girls that Stonecroft had gone off with were waiting in the hallway outside the parlor door.

"Are you certain you don't wish to try again, my lord?" the blonde asked Stonecroft. She was wringing her hands, and her eyes were wide with concern. "Sometimes a few minutes of waiting can make all the difference." The brunette hovered at her elbow and nodded, a coaxing smile on her face.

Fifteen minutes later, Stonecroft was still grim-faced and silent as they sat at their table downstairs and waited for their beefsteaks and ale. As soon as the waiter brought dinner, St. Fell picked up his knife and his fork and began eating. He had every sympathy for the poor clod, but it was nearly eight o'clock. He still needed to go home and change for Arabella's ball.

Stonecroft took a small sip of ale. "This has never happened to me before," he said.

"It happens to the best of men," St. Fell said soothingly. Not to him, of course. That one time in Brighton didn't count. When they had gone back to her room and the girl had removed her bonnet, she had looked exactly like his mother. He shuddered.

"I have heard of it happening to other rakes, of course." Stonecroft stared at his plate as though it were empty. "But I always thought it was romantical Minerva Press rubbish that women told each other to make themselves feel superior."

St. Fell chewed his meat thoughtfully. He had never heard that explanation before.

Stonecroft looked up at him, his eyes sparking in fury. "I am a rake. A fortune hunter. A man of experience." He jabbed his steak with his knife at each point he made. "Do you know upstairs, just now, I actually felt guilty!"

"There is no need to feel guilty," St. Fell said. "After all, it's a commercial transaction."

"That is what I thought at the beginning! I told myself it was only about money." Stonecroft's voice grew wistful. "A great deal of money." He sighed. "But now it is obviously much more than just that."

Obviously. St. Fell nodded.

Stonecroft sighed again, more gustily. "I never expected this to happen."

"I don't think it is something that a man ever expects," St. Fell said.

"I suppose not." Stonecroft finally started eating. "Although as a poet, I suppose some small part of me must have known it was possible."

St. Fell concentrated on cutting his tasty steak into very small pieces. The poor clod was wounded. It was not the time for jests about the size of his part. "It is probably just a case of too much alcohol," he offered when he could speak without laughing.

Stonecroft shook his head. "I've hardly dared drink much of anything since Monday."

"Perhaps it's your war wound."

Stonecroft goggled at him as if he were demented. "What does my war wound have to do with the matter?" he demanded.

"How should I know?" St. Fell washed a mouthful of steak down with his ale. "I'm not a doctor." He had no idea where the clod had been wounded. It wasn't the kind of thing men talked about. "I'm sure the effect is just temporary," he said.

Stonecroft shook his head sadly. "I don't think so."

Good God. St. Fell looked at him with pity. No wonder the poor clod was taking it so hard. Or not, such as it were. St. Fell looked back down at his plate and willed himself to keep a straight face.

"Everyone knows you are completely insensitive," Stonecroft said sharply, "But I didn't expect you of all people to laugh, given that it is obvious that you are in exactly the same situation."

"I beg your pardon?" St. Fell sat up straight in his chair. He never should have told damned Compton about Brighton. "I have no idea what my brother has said but I was only sixteen at the time!"

"Sixteen!" Stonecroft gave a harsh bark of laughter. "I saw you upstairs, just now. You weren't taking anyone out of that parlor!"

St. Fell looked down his nose at him. "Unlike you, that had nothing to do with any failure on my part to rise to the occasion."

"Failure . . ." Stonecroft's brow sank even lower than usual while he considered St. Fell's words. "Failure?" His face turned crimson. "You think that upstairs, with those women, I was not able?" He leaned forward and planted his knife like a flag in his steak. "Damn you! I assure you I was perfectly able!" He maintained his glare across the table for a few seconds more, then his shoulders sagged and he buried his head in his hands. "I was able," he repeated, his voice sinking to a despairing whisper. "But for the first time in my life, I was not interested."

The Belcraven House ballroom glowed in the golden light from the hundreds of beeswax candles in the chandelier and the wall sconces and their reflections in the gilt-mirrored walls. The entire room was permeated with the scent of the twenty bouquets of white roses in the Swann Fine China vases that graced the shallow shelf tables lining the walls. The orchestra played softly in the background. A quarter of an hour before her ball was officially set to begin, the Belcraven House ballroom was a feast for the senses.

Of course, it didn't matter in the least. Arabella sank

down in one of the chairs against the wall next to Diana and watched the duchess and Aunt Ophelia pace the edge of the dance floor.

"I am sure the duke and Lord Stonecroft will be here any moment!" Aunt Ophelia's hopeful tone of voice was belied by the mournful list of the plum-colored plumes in her headdress. She and the duchess were already on their second glass of brandy.

"No one of any importance ever arrives on time," the duchess declared for the twentieth time. "St. Fell will likely not even show up until midnight." She pivoted on her heel so smartly that Aunt Ophelia had to duck to avoid being struck by the beaded fringe of her shawl.

Arabella's stomach knotted. The old bat was right, of course. The dancing was scheduled to begin at ten o'clock, and unless St. Fell and Stonecroft arrived early, Arabella would be obliged to promise the waltzes to the gentlemen that were present. Not that it was a very large ball, by *ton* standards. Barely sixty people, business acquaintances of Papa and the eligible gentlemen and marriageable young ladies they had met at the Carrs'. But still, it would be unspeakably rude of her to try to keep the waltzes free in the hopes that St. Fell and Lord Stonecroft would show up in time to claim them. Not to mention making her look completely pathetic, since no one had the least idea when they would return from whatever it was they were doing. Their drinking and gaming and drinking.

Their raking.

She folded her arms across her chest. St. Fell had been out all afternoon being a rake, and he would show up too late to make a fuss over her and Lord Stonecroft waltzing, and Papa was in the card room drinking coffee and sobering up. Her birthday ball had not even begun and it was a wretched disaster.

"Arabella! Your arms, dear," Aunt Ophelia called out. "Silk rumples."

Arabella unfolded her arms and smoothed the pink silk over her bosom. She would spend the evening wasting her lovely low-cut neckline on second-rate eligible bachelors.

Diana reached over and patted her knee. "Don't assume the worst, Arabella. Perhaps they are out dueling."

Wonderful. Arabella gritted her teeth. Now Diana was being sarcastic.

"Oh, come now!" Diana laughed. "I am just saying you should have a little faith in him."

Arabella sighed. "It is easy for you to have faith," she said. "You are being courted by someone insanely amiable."

Diana beamed. "You are beginning to like him. You did not think of him as that idiot Belcraven."

"At least you know he loves you," Arabella said, shooting the duchess a glare across the room, but the old bat merely shrugged and rolled her eyes.

"Henry loves everyone. Even his beastly aunts." Diana lowered her voice to a whisper. "He has just persuaded me that his aunts should stay with us when they come to London for the Season."

Arabella nodded bleakly. So far Belcraven had persuaded Diana that his horrid aunts should come to the wedding, that the horrid aunts should host the wedding breakfast and that he and Diana should travel to Kent to visit the horrid aunts for the duration of their honeymoon. Every time Arabella asked what it was that Belcraven did that was so convincing, her sister turned as red as her beau and giggled. Nor did anyone object whenever they snuck off together. The duchess and Aunt Ophelia had decided that Diana must be secretly teaching Belcraven how to dance. As for Papa, all of his cursing was confined to the subject of the Duke of St. Fell.

It completely unjust. Arabella swallowed her moan. She was the older sister. She was the one being courted by a rake—two rakes, counting Lord Stonecroft. She stared blindly at the inlaid patterns of rosewood that marked the edge of the dance floor. She was the one who was five-and-twenty and had never been kissed.

"So that is what you look like when I am not around."

Arabella looked up and her breath caught in her throat. It was St. Fell. He loped down the three steps into the ballroom and strolled toward her, his black silk evening clothes with snowy white linen making him look taller, even with the hitch. Her hitch.

"See?" Diana elbowed her. "I told you to have faith."

Arabella nodded. St. Fell was here. That didn't mean he was ready to show the slightest depth of devotion. Or that he hadn't spent the past five hours being incredibly vexing. But still. He was here. With his hair gleaming amber in the candlelight, strong clean-shaven jaw and gray eyes brimming with laughter. She swallowed and tried to steady her breathing.

He smiled. "No sarcastic comment, Arabella? Whatever is the matter with you?"

"There is no amusement in insulting you when you expect it," she said, pleased that her voice sounded casual. Good heavens, but he was handsome.

And a rake, she reminded herself sternly. A rake, who from his sleek demeanor, had obviously not spent the past five hours drinking.

"Better, but not up to your usual form. You seem distracted." He flexed his shoulders and rocked back on his heels. Arabella rolled her eyes. Honestly, the great showoff. He knew perfectly well he was gorgeous.

"Arabella has had a trying day, Your Grace," Aunt

Ophelia said. "First your mother convinced her you and Lord Stonecroft were dueling—"

"Dueling?" He snorted with laughter.

Arabella jutted out her chin. It was not so unreasonable as all that. At least dueling was more chivalrous than what he had probably been doing.

"It would be a stupid way of showing you love her," the duchess said.

St. Fell shrugged. "She would merely say I had got myself killed so I could get my hands on her fortune."

"Well, what have you been doing?" Arabella couldn't stop herself from asking over the shocked gasps from Aunt Ophelia and the duchess and Diana's snicker.

St. Fell slapped his hand over his heart. "Are you ready to marry me?"

"Certainly not!" Not until the smug little smirk was wiped off his face.

"Then I do not see how it is any of your business," he said primly. While smirking, of course.

Arabella made a show of shrugging with boredom. As if she would agree to marry him just to find out what he had been doing when he had gone off for five hours with his only rival and came back still looking as if the world belonged to him and whatever it was he and Stonecroft had been doing, it was obviously not drinking, and no wager could possibly require five hours! She narrowed her eyes and glared at him.

He merrily waggled his eyebrows and leered back at her like a penny melodrama lecher. The idiot obviously knew perfectly well what she was thinking and found it all very amusing.

"You do need a leash!" she snapped.

He mouthed the word "promise" and blew her a kiss at the same time that Aunt Ophelia squealed "Arabella" and the duchess lunged at him with her lorgnette and Diana giggled.

"Where is Lord Stonecroft, Your Grace?" Aunt Ophelia asked as soon as everyone had settled.

Arabella flushed. "Yes, where is Lord Stonecroft?" she echoed quickly, pretending she didn't notice St. Fell's knowing look or the duchess's snort of derision. She hadn't forgotten about poor Stonecroft. She was merely waiting for the right moment.

"Toby is fetching him. They'll be here shortly," St. Fell said. "Which reminds me, I am here early because I need to have a word alone with Arabella."

Arabella's pulse sped up. Ideally, she should not think of going off to a dark corner with St. Fell until he had shown some true feeling while she was dancing with Stonecroft, but one shouldn't be inflexible, after all.

"We all agree you need a word alone with her, St. Fell," the duchess said. "But now is hardly the time. She has to be present to greet her guests."

"But you said no one shows up on time," Diana said quickly, thank heavens, so Arabella did not have to look so forward.

"Yes, dearest, but Arabella's dress is silk," Aunt Ophelia explained as the duchess nodded authoritatively. "It rumples easily."

A delicious shiver went through Arabella at the word *rumple*.

The duchess gave Diana a knowing look. "Because it is a metaphor when he says he wants to have a word with your sister. Trust us, they will not be talking."

St. Fell rolled his eyes. "Actually, I did mean that I wanted to talk."

Aunt Ophelia's face fell. Arabella tried not to be disappointed. Overmuch.

The duchess shot him a glare through the lorgnette.

"If all you want to do is talk, then you can do it while you are dancing." She snorted. "Apparently, there will be two waltzes." Not that the number of waltzes were any of the old bat's business.

"I don't want to wait until the dancing." St. Fell turned to Arabella. "I need to speak to you now." He looked past her shoulder and cursed under his breath as footsteps sounded in the hallway.

"Are we too early?" Lord Toby called out as he and Lord Stonecroft walked into the ballroom. Arabella turned to greet them. They were also both very handsome in their evening clothes.

"Fine. Give me the first waltz," St. Fell said from behind her.

For heaven's sake! Arabella spun around to make a sarcastic comment about his romantic way of asking a woman to dance, but she saw his face and the words caught in her throat.

For the first time since she had laid eyes on him, St. Fell's expression was completely sincere. Not a trace of the smirk. He looked steadily into her eyes as if they were the only two people in the ballroom. The only two people in London. His smile was sweet and the light in his eyes told her they were in this together. That they were the only two people in the world who weren't utterly ridiculous.

Arabella's heart soared. This was the look she had always imagined. Not smug, not smirking, just the true light of passion. The look she had been dreaming of ever since she had first seen him.

The look of a man who was head over heels in love with her.

Chapter 10

It was finally time for the waltz. Her first dance with St. Fell, in the glittering ballroom of Belcraven House in London on her birthday. Arabella had to think about it now, because she knew the minute he touched her, everything else would fade into nothing, the way it always did when she was around him.

St. Fell stood before her, his expression still all shining sincerity. Arabella took a deep breath and tried to steady herself. This time, when he said that he loved her, she was going to believe him. No matter how outrageously unromantic he was when he said it.

His gaze flickered downward as he held out his hand for hers. His eyes darkened to nearly black. Arabella looked down. Good heavens. Her right hand was splayed across the top of her bosom above her gown's low neckline. She must have been trying to stop herself from panting. She lifted her hand and placed it in his. He bent over it slowly, and his eyes smouldered even more. When his lips brushed the back of her knuckles, a flame shot all the way through her body. Her knees buckled.

"See?" The duchess's voice hissed from behind her like a bucket of cold water. "I told you he was a rake!"

"Oh, yes!" Aunt Ophelia gave an awed sigh. "That was excellent!"

The muscle in St. Fell's jaw twitched, but he merely

shot a narrow-eyed glare at them over Arabella's shoulder before turning and escorting her to the dance floor. Then, before Arabella had any more time to think about it, the orchestra started playing and he put his hand on the curve of her back and she put hers on his shoulder and they were waltzing.

At least, Arabella thought they were waltzing. They were moving, but she had absolutely no idea what her feet were doing. Nor did she care. She was touching St. Fell and moving to music. Although the blood was roaring so loudly in her ears she wasn't quite sure there was music. Out of the corner of her eye she could see the blur of the other couples dancing and beyond them the people standing at the edge of the dance floor watching. She stared at St. Fell's shirtfront and willed herself to be calm. All she had to do was follow where he led her and not think about how heavy and hot his hand was on the small of her back. Or how small her hand felt in his. Or let her hand twitch where it rested on his lean muscled shoulder. Thank heavens she wore gloves, otherwise her palm would leave a snail trail of dampness on his black evening jacket. Now she knew why women wore gloves to a ball.

She took another peek out of the corner of her eye. Everyone else seemed perfectly able to talk and dance. Vivian Coulter was already tittering at something Stonecroft was saying. Even Belcraven could do it, because he and Diana danced by, and her sister was nodding. Therefore it couldn't possibly be that difficult.

By their second circuit of the dance floor she felt confident enough to let her eyes slide upward past the column of St. Fell's throat to his face. He was looking down, waiting for her, as always, with the gleam in his eyes that made her feel as though they were sharing a secret.

"So?" He dipped his head even closer to hers. "Is your first London ball as fine as you imagined?"

She nodded, not yet trusting herself to speak. It was the most perfect moment of her life so far, and it was about to get better. He was going to say that he loved her, she knew it. This time she would believe it. She didn't need to wait until she danced with Lord Stonecroft and St. Fell made a fuss.

His smile deepened. "That is excellent, my love—"

He had called her his love!

"—because that great clod Stonecroft has gone and fallen in love with you."

"Stonecroft," she said automatically, not really understanding the meaning of his words except that they were not what she had expected to hear. And they were possibly annoying.

"I said Stonecroft!" St. Fell's tone of voice was aggrieved. "The whole mess is ridiculous enough without my having to call the poor clod names."

She stared up into his clear gray eyes. There were so many things about his last statement with which she could take issue. But mostly she wanted to stop waltzing and grab him by his strong arms to hold him still so she could kick him in the shins. She bit her lip and looked down. The skirt of her dress brushed against his legs as they moved. Apparently they were still dancing.

She forced herself to take a deep breath. Perhaps she had misunderstood him. After all, there was music and dancing and a confusion of people. It was hardly the right venue for a serious discussion. She brightened. Or perhaps he had meant it as a metaphor and he was actually talking about himself being in love with her! She chanced a look back up into his face.

He was waiting for her, of course. "Stonecroft?" His mouth twitched into the smirk. "Surely you remember him, Arabella? Tall, dark, and rhyming. The other rake and fortune hunter. The one you have been using to make me jealous."

"I hate you," she said, pleased at the casual tone of her voice. She did hate him. He was completely insensitive. He knew perfectly well she was thrilled to be with him. What did he do? Not tell her he loved her with the slightest trace of sincerity. Again. "I hate you."

"No you don't," he said, completely predictable.

If he dared say she loved him, she would kick him. She didn't care if it disrupted the entire dance and caused a great scandal. It was her birthday ball. She was perfectly justified. Everyone knew Stonecroft was paying court to two out of the three Coulter sisters and was dashing and smooth to every marriageable heiress in London. Arabella was to waltz the supper dance with him, but he could have asked anyone. In the hour before the dancing began he had been engulfed in his usual crowd of adoring females while St. Fell skulked in the card room with Papa.

The whole story about Stonecroft was probably all some Banbury tale St. Fell had invented to drive her to marry him. Or to just drive her mad.

St. Fell sighed. "I am not just making it up," he said. "Why the devil would I?"

How would she know? She never had any idea what was going on in his head. "Why should I believe you? Everything you do is a lie or manipulative."

"I see," he said. "So, do you want to marry me, Arabella?"

"Certainly not!" Not until he proved that he loved her.

He gave her a knowing look and pursed his lips in that smug way he did when he was laughing at her. Arabella narrowed her eyes. She was not lying!

"You know perfectly well I want to marry someone

who loves me for myself, not my fortune," she reminded him.

"Well, then let me be the first to offer my congratulations to you, the future Lady Stonecroft."

"Just for once," she snapped, "you could try saying that you want to marry me for myself, not my fortune! In a sincere tone of voice," she added, since apparently that was still not obvious.

St. Fell shrugged. "Why? You wouldn't believe me anyway. Besides, I told you. You should marry me because you love me."

Hell. She glared back down at his shirtfront. He was beyond impossible!

His hand on her waist tightened. "Now is not the time to be cursing, Arabella. We are in the middle of the dance floor and everyone is watching. In any event, stop trying to change the subject. We are talking about Stonecroft, not me."

"Why do you think Lord Stonecroft loves me?" she demanded. "Is it the bonbons? Because I can tell you, I think he had that poem already written before he met me. It could have applied to any number of women." She did not look anything like a lily. Or a filly.

"It's not the poem, Arabella. Trust me, he loves you."

"Did he say so?"

She felt his sigh under her hand on his shoulder and looked up to catch his crooked smile.

"He may have mentioned it a dozen or so times," he said. "In between sobs."

"He cries easily!" Arabella couldn't stop herself from blurting out, even though St. Fell's immediate snort of laughter indicated he took it as a sign she was slightly insensitive. But it was true. Stonecroft did cry easily.

"It wasn't just the weeping," St. Fell said when he had stopped laughing. "It was something he didn't do. And don't ask what it was, I have already said I cannot discuss it with you now. Your father has that damned stick propped up against his chair in the card room. Anyway, it doesn't matter. If you don't believe me, then use your own judgment. The poor clod is completely head over heels in love with you."

Of course, St. Fell had no trouble maintaining a sincere expression when he talked about Stonecroft. Arabella gnashed her teeth in frustration.

"It's perfectly understandable," St. Fell continued, still speaking in his casual tone as if they were discussing the weather. "You have been making doe eyes at him all week."

"I most certainly have not!" She wasn't even nice to poor Stonecroft. But perhaps the fact that St. Fell thought so did mean he was jealous. She lowered her head and studied the billow of her dress against his long legs to hide her expression, because no doubt her face would reveal how pleased she was at the thought.

St. Fell shrugged. "Of course, the poor idiot has no idea you are thinking of me when you are with him."

How ridiculous! "You are so conceited you probably think Lord Stonecroft thinks only of you!" she said.

"Oh, he does, believe me." He grinned. "I'm afraid that Lord Stonecroft thinks I presume."

He wasn't the only one. "Why do you not warn him off then, if you are so concerned?"

St. Fell shook his head. "You are the one who wants to make her own decisions. I am not going to do it for you."

She sighed and turned her head to the right. Diana and Belcraven were still twirling beside them, beaming at each other in an irritating and completely unfair manner.

"You have to look left," St. Fell whispered in her ear.

She turned her head without hardly basking at all in

the rush of pleasure she felt when his lips brushed her ear. Vivian Coulter and Lord Stonecroft were gazing into each other's eyes with apparent adoration, for heaven's sake. Furthermore, as she watched, Lord Stonecroft looked up and right through Arabella and St. Fell as though they didn't exist, and then he returned his gaze to Vivian with an even more ardent expression.

"You see?" Arabella looked up at St. Fell in triumph.

He smirked. "Naturally, it would never occur to you that he might be using Miss Counter to try to make you jealous."

"Coulter, not Counter!" Arabella bit her lip to keep from screaming. He knew perfectly well she wanted him to be jealous of Lord Stonecroft. And he wasn't, of course. Because that would be romantic. And how in heaven's name had she managed to let him trap her into arguing that Stonecroft wasn't in love with her? Which he most certainly was not! But if she wanted St. Fell to be jealous, then she should encourage him to believe that Stonecroft was in love with her.

"Oh come now, I do not have anything against your trying to make me jealous," St. Fell said. "Quite the contrary. I enjoy our diversions just as much as you do. It was all very amusing, until he fell in love with you." He lowered his voice, and his eyes became serious again. "He is a war hero, Arabella. His family sent him to die for our country. They are like children or puppies. You cannot abuse them."

"It is none of your concern!" Now he was making her feel guilty about a rake and a fortune hunter, and she hadn't even done anything! In any event, why would Stonecroft love her when she hadn't encouraged him, and St. Fell not love her when she had?

"You have to deal with him, Arabella." St. Fell's voice

was still urgent. "And not in the middle of the dance floor either."

She looked at Lord Stonecroft. Vivian Coulter was smiling up into his face as if she could not believe her luck in finding herself dancing with such a prize. Vivian Coulter was dancing with Lord Stonecroft and looking radiantly happy while Arabella was dancing with St. Fell, feeling miserable and frustrated.

The most ridiculous thing about it was that it would be pleasant to be loved by Lord Stonecroft. He was straightforward. He didn't confuse her or annoy her by failing to appreciate her. The Misses Coulter found him attractive—every heiress in London found him attractive. He was attractive. He was a war hero and a rake and a broad-shouldered, handsome, published poet. She looked over at him. Extremely broad-shouldered, and just as handsome as St. Fell, in a beefier way, which was not necessarily bad. Also, Lord Stonecroft had a very attractive cleft in his chin. Perhaps the only reason she didn't take him seriously as a suitor was because she had been thinking overmuch about St. Fell. Because if Lord Stonecroft loved a woman, he would show it in a sincere and romantic manner. He wouldn't smirk. He would never lie. He would be kind and thoughtful and he would do what she asked and be jealous of other men and not think it was all a great game, and for once in his life he would look like he was suffering the agony of wondering if she felt as strongly about him as he felt about her without her having to beg him to show it.

"You cannot be serious." St. Fell's voice in her ear made her start. Arabella looked up. St. Fell's gaze went from Lord Stonecroft back to her, and he gave her a long-suffering look. If they weren't dancing, he'd be pinching the bridge of his nose.

"I do not know what you mean," she said primly. Lord Stonecroft didn't pretend he could read her mind.

"You don't want him, Arabella. You want me."

What she wanted was to not spend the rest of her life being one of those pitiful people who obviously loved their spouse more than their arrogant, smug spouse loved them.

St. Fell stopped dancing and let go of her. Arabella looked around in confusion until she realized that everyone else had stopped dancing as well. The waltz was over; the orchestra had stopped playing. Her first waltz was over, and she had spent most of it arguing with St. Fell about another suitor, and not in a way that was the slightest bit pleasant.

She was forced to take a step back as Lord Stonecroft and Vivian strolled arm in arm between them, Vivian's lilting giggles ringing out in counterpoint to Lord Stonecroft's hearty baritone chuckles.

St. Fell rolled his eyes and offered his arm. Arabella took it. It would be the height of rudeness not to do so and he knew it. They had only taken a few steps when she felt a shove at the back of her shoulders. Diana and Belcraven elbowed their way past. They were making such moon eyes at each other they were completely oblivious to everyone else. They dodged their way through the guests and headed for the doorway, then they darted into the hallway and disappeared from view.

"Library?" St. Fell asked.

"Conservatory," Arabella answered resentfully.

"Then we shall continue our discussion in the library," he said.

Arabella snorted. She wasn't going to the library so St. Fell could continue to ring a peal over her about Stonecroft. It was her birthday ball. She was going to enjoy herself. Next was the country dance, and she and

Lord Toby were going to be the lead couple. The lines of ladies and gentlemen were beginning to form on the dance floor. Lord Stonecroft was already there, having exchanged Miss Coulters. His partner was now Elvira.

Arabella tried to slide her arm from the crook of St. Fell's and looked around for Lord Toby. "I am supposed to dance the next set with your brother."

St. Fell held her arm firm in his. "I am sure Toby will not mind." As if he had conjured him, his brother appeared at his elbow. "We are going to the library if anyone is looking for us," St. Fell said curtly, and he tightened his hold on Arabella's arm and started pulling her toward the doorway.

She looked over her shoulder. Lord Toby gave her a helpless shrug.

"What in heaven's name are you doing?" she hissed under her breath at St. Fell. The orderly way in which people stepped out of their path made it clear they were the center of attention. Gabriel Carr rolled his eyes as they passed him, and the Countesses of Belcraven thumped their sticks.

St. Fell didn't answer. He just continued to march across the ballroom, his eyes fixed on the doorway, his jaw set at a determined angle. Arabella tried dragging her feet, but he just slid her along the hardwood floor without showing the slightest effort.

Good heavens! He was making a scene in public. She could scarcely believe it. She was being dragged out of the ballroom at her own birthday ball by the Duke of St. Fell as if she were a naughty little girl in need of punishment! It was completely outrageous and wrong, and only a very bad person would find it exciting.

He skidded to a stop in the hallway. "Where the hell is the damned library?"

"First floor, east wing, double doors at the end," Arabella said breathlessly. She was a very bad person.

He looked down at her with a knowing grin. "I know, sweetheart, we are made for each other." The pad of his thumb stroked her arm in a way that made her tongue thick and her stomach hollow, but she barely had time to lean into it before he released her with a lingering touch of his fingers. "But we cannot play any games until you have sorted out the matter of Stonecroft."

Stonecroft! She rubbed her arm where he had touched her and tried not to tremble. He was thinking about Stonecroft?

"St. Fell! What on earth are you doing?" The duchess's voice rang out behind them. "You cannot haul the girl out of the ballroom in front of everyone without causing a great scandal!"

Arabella looked over her shoulder, and her heart sank even further. The duchess and Aunt Ophelia puffed into the hallway, leaning against each other for support. They must have run to catch them. From the refreshment room, judging from the hectic flush on their cheeks and the glassy cast of their eyes.

"Yes, Your Grace. You cannot go off without chaperones!" Aunt Ophelia let go of the duchess and staggered a few steps in a circle as she adjusted her plumes. "It is not proper. I can only imagine exactly what might happen."

Arabella didn't have the heart to tell her that St. Fell wanted to take her to a dark corner so he could lecture her about Stonecroft. And now she could go in the company of foxed chaperones. She sighed. Her love life was completely hopeless.

She looked beyond the duchess, back into the ballroom. The country dance had already begun, but most of the guests were looking at them in openmouthed wonder. She turned back toward the hallway and sighed even more deeply. She could hardly go back to the ball-room now without looking like a complete idiot. It was one kind of scandal to get dragged off by one's irate suitor. It was completely another to return alone after only a few moments.

Besides, St. Fell might talk about Stonecroft, but she had felt his shudder when he had run his fingers along the length of her bare arm. Perhaps her aunt and his mother would distract him from his lecture. And perhaps her aunt and his mother would leave them alone. Either way, in the library, her chances of getting kissed were better than staying in the ballroom watching other couples dance. She smoothed down the front of her dress. St. Fell's eyes darkened. Much better. Arabella threw back her shoulders, lifted the hem of her skirt with her fingers, and marched up the stairs. St. Fell, Aunt Ophelia, and the duchess followed.

"What on earth are you fighting about?" the duchess demanded. "You were not going on about hats again, were you?"

"Certainly not," St. Fell said.

"We were!" Arabella called over her shoulder. "Your son believes I am trying on too many hats!"

"That is completely ridiculous," St. Fell said, pulling even with her on the stairs. "I have every sympathy for your complete lack of experience."

She shot him a glare. Her complete lack of experience which was due to him. While he had spent the afternoon in a hattery. "How many hats have you tried on, Your Grace?" she asked sweetly.

"A gentleman never tries on hats and tells—Ow!" He jerked and reached for the small of his back. The duchess must have remembered her lorgnette.

"We know that is not true!" the duchess shouted. "All you can do is talk about hats."

Arabella turned down the east hall on the first floor. "Well? How many hats have you tried on?"

"I do not know what you are asking me to count." St. Fell loped easily beside her.

"What do you mean? A hat is a hat, isn't it?" The number was so great he probably couldn't count that high.

Aunt Ophelia trotted to catch up on Arabella's other side. "I think what His Grace means, dearest, is are you asking him how many women he has courted, or are you asking him how many women he has . . ." She tailed off and flushed.

The duchess snorted. "Or are you asking him how many women he has pulled down to the brim!"

St. Fell winced. "And they say I am insensitive. Stop fussing about this afternoon. You know perfectly well nothing happened. I do wish you would have a little faith." He flung open the library doors and went over to the fireplace.

Arabella threw herself down in the window seat in the corner. Everyone wanted her to have faith. It was completely patronizing.

"It is very cold in here." Aunt Ophelia fell into a chair at the circular library table in the middle of the room. "I think we should ring for the fire to be made."

"The temperature is perfect." St. Fell lit a spill with the tinderbox on the mantel and held the flame up to the wall sconces on either side of the fireplace.

The duchess's face brightened as she spotted a decanter and glasses on a tray on the writing desk in the corner, and despite Arabella's prayers, she managed to carry the tray to the library table without falling. She wedged herself in the chair next to Aunt Ophelia and pushed the tray between them.

"Storming off to some dark corner when you are both in a temper is not the solution," the old bat said as she poured two tumblers of brandy. "This is not some Minerva Press romance where you show a girl you love her by ripping her bodice"—she shot a scowl at Arabella—"not that her bodice would require much ripping."

Arabella ground her teeth. Her dress was the latest London fashion. Not that it was doing her much good. Yet.

Aunt Ophelia pounced on the brandy. "Actually, it is a misconception about the ripping of bodices," she said. "Nowadays Minerva Press romances rely on the hero getting in a lovely carriage accident." She eyed St. Fell over the rim of her glass. "Preferably with amnesia."

"I am not going to get myself in a carriage accident." St. Fell lit the candelabra on the writing desk in the far corner. "I like knowing who I am."

Liked? Arabella snorted. The man loved knowing who he was.

"Never mind the carriage accident." The duchess shook her head and then righted her turban. She swiveled around until she was blinking at St. Fell, even though he was too busy lighting the wall sconces between the bookcases to notice. "Miss Ophelia and I determined the perfect solution while you were dancing. Arabella is going to dance with Stonecroft and you will be jealous. After the dance, you will take her in your arms and declare that you love her in front of the assembly. Then we will look the other way while you both come up to the library. It is so obvious I would have thought that one of you would have figured it out, even though you are both very dense."

"I'm afraid there has been a slight change of plans," St. Fell said, and Arabella could see his smirk all the way across the room as he walked back to the table. He knew perfectly well that had been what she had wanted, the great know-everything, and he still had not done it.

"Are you certain?" Aunt Ophelia watched St. Fell wistfully as he leaned in front of her to light the candelabra in the center of the table. "Because we have discussed it at great length, and that seemed to be the most sensible way to convince Arabella of the depth of your feeling. Although Her Grace wants you to throw a punch at Lord Stonecroft as well."

"His poems are very long, St. Fell," the duchess said. "You have no idea because you do not listen."

St. Fell stood up and brushed off his hands. "Yes, well, Arabella won't be dancing with Stonecroft, I won't be making a big scene in the ballroom—"

"And you are both going to go away now, not later," Arabella said. Why in heaven's name were they still here?

Aunt Ophelia shook her head, her eyes fixed on St. Fell. "I do not think we should leave you alone with Arabella when you are both in a temper. You might spank her."

"He would not dare!" Arabella cried.

"Hush, Arabella!" Aunt Ophelia brought a finger to her lips carefully. "Let His Grace answer."

"I am sorry to disappoint you, but I will not be spanking her," St. Fell said in a prim voice. "We are not yet married." He shot Arabella a grin. "And even then, she'll have to ask nicely." Idiot.

The duchess tilted her chin at a belligerent angle. "Of course he will not spank her! He never wants to upset her delicate sensibilities."

St. Fell wagged his finger at Aunt Ophelia. "She won't be spanking me either, in case you were wondering."

Two spots of pink appeared on Aunt Ophelia's cheeks. "I would never imagine any such thing!" She looked up at him from under her lashes. "Until now."

The duchess slammed her glass on the library table so hard that brandy slopped over the edges. "That is disgusting! He is my son!"

Aunt Ophelia bristled. "I am not related to him!"

"She is your niece!"

"Oh, but I am not imagining her at all." Aunt Ophelia's face had a faraway expression.

Arabella leaped up. Her aunt wouldn't be living with them either. If she married St. Fell. "That is quite enough." She plucked their glasses off the table and dumped the contents into the aspidistra in the corner. She dropped them back on the tray. "You are both leaving now."

Neither woman budged. St. Fell snickered.

The duchess lifted her lorgnette and blinked. "It seems very bright in here."

Arabella looked around the library. The room was extremely bright. St. Fell had lit every lamp and wall sconce and all the candelabra. The library was as bright as the summer sun at high noon.

St. Fell sighed. "I suppose I am not that much of a saint after all."

Aunt Ophelia's plumes trembled. "You have not actually come to the library to read, have you?"

"Read?" the duchess barked. "With this much light they could repair watches!"

"Out!" Arabella shouted.

"I do not think he actually is a rake!" Aunt Ophelia fumbled in her sleeve for her handkerchief.

The duchess reached for her lorgnette. "Of course he is a rake! It is all her fault! She has completely unsettled him. He has not been right in the head since he laid eyes on her."

Arabella sagged against the table. They were never going to be left alone. She was never going to be kissed. She may as well go back to the ballroom. The Scottish reel would be starting soon and Lord Stonecroft was her partner.

St. Fell threw her a pitying glance, then strolled over to

the table. "You know," he said, in a casual voice, "I cannot help but wonder why Arabella and I must be chaperoned when Belcraven and Diana are free to wander off where ever they please?"

The duchess waved her lorgnette belligerently. "You know perfectly well Belcraven could not find his way around a woman with a map and a compass. I do not know why Swann is so keen on the match. I would not be surprised if they never have children."

Aunt Ophelia nodded in mournful agreement.

"I see." St. Fell said with his best choirboy expression. "Why do we not ask Arabella what she thinks?" He looked straight at her. "Arabella? What is your opinion of Belcraven and Diana scampering about without chaperones?"

"I do not have an opinion!" Arabella did her best to blink and school her face to look innocent, but she felt herself flush hotly all the way to her ears. Hell. Her stupid transparent face.

"My stars!" Aunt Ophelia gasped. She lurched to her feet.

"I will not believe it unless I see it!" The duchess shoved back her chair.

"That was not very nice!" Arabella rounded on St. Fell as Aunt Ophelia and the duchess staggered to the door.

"I don't know." He grabbed the decanter off the library table. "There's nothing like humiliation by chaperones to bring a couple together. Wait!" he called out and Aunt Ophelia and the duchess bobbed to an impatient stop in the doorway. He handed the decanter to Aunt Ophelia. "Take this. You might need it."

She glanced at Arabella. "Perhaps we should leave it for Arabella. I am finding that it makes the ridiculous more tolerable."

He shook his head. "Arabella doesn't need brandy. She has me. Oh, and one more thing!" He whisked the shawl from his mother's shoulders as she turned to follow Aunt Ophelia. "It is freezing in here."

The women thundered out the door and down the hall.

Arabella's heart hammered. She was alone in the library with St. Fell.

Chapter 11

Arabella's heart pounded so hard she felt dizzy and her breath started coming in gasps. St. Fell's eyes darkened and he took a step toward her. She tilted her head back, and her eyes fell shut, and a small moan escaped from the back of her throat.

She felt the soft stroke on the back of her shoulders first, then the front, and down the length of her back, and the top of her bosom and—

She opened her eyes and looked down.

He had wrapped his mother's shawl around her shoulders and was holding it folded across the front of her chest without touching her.

She blinked up at him blankly.

He let go of the shawl and took a step back. "We cannot kiss, Arabella. Not yet." His voice was ragged, and his eyes were still black, but his lips twisted into his smirk.

She kicked him. She was only wearing kid dancing slippers, but she must have hurt his shin nearly as much as she hurt her own toe because he limped to the library table.

He limped, but he was laughing.

She lunged to the closest bookcase and yanked out a book, nicely heavy and leather, so it wouldn't slip from her gloved fingers.

He raised his hands placatingly. "The kick is totally

fair, sweetheart. I am not complaining in the least." He edged his way backward, putting the library table between them, his eyes going from hers to the book. "And the worst of it is, that once we do kiss and you see how fine it is, you will be even angrier."

That was doubtful. "If we are going to kiss anyway," she asked pleasantly, as she hefted the book from her right hand to her left, "why would we not kiss now?"

He glanced at the clock as he took another step backward. "In the first place," he said, "Stonecroft will be here at any moment. It would kill the poor clod if he came upon us kissing."

Lord Stonecroft was meeting them in the library? Arabella goggled, the blood roaring in her ears. In the flash of an instant, she understood exactly what St. Fell had been up to. He had planned the whole thing all along—timed his mother and her aunt's departures so he wouldn't be alone too long in the library with her in case he was tempted to kiss her. Just as he had brightened the lights and covered her bosom, all part of his scheme to avoid kissing her. She narrowed her eyes and tried to think of something to say, something to wipe the superior smirk off his face. Something that would hurt him more than a book topside the head.

"You are the most annoying, conceited, arrogant, and insensitive man in all of London!" she shouted.

He nodded. "Well, yes, quite possibly. But in the second place—"

"Lord Stonecroft would never do anything so underhanded and manipulative!" she added triumphantly.

"That was the second place," St. Fell said, and Arabella's jaw dropped as his smirk—impossibly—deepened.

She threw the book at him.

He ducked it easily. "You are mine, Arabella. But if you are going to keep brooding about Stonecroft, then you are obviously not ready to decide, and until you are, I am not kissing you."

She snatched another book off the shelf and pitched it at his head as hard as she could.

He batted it away with his forearm. "Once we kiss we will have to be married and then, for the rest of your life, whenever you were annoyed with me"—he leaned to the right and the next book sailed past him—"which might well be often, you would always wonder if you could have done better."

"Anyone would be better than you!" She glared at him, her chest heaving with rage and the exertion of book flinging.

He pursed his lips to hold back his laughter and shook his head in mock sadness. He was actually becoming more smug with every minute she knew him. She threw another book at him, but it barely skittered across the table.

"I am sure in a few years, your aim will be much better," he said soothingly. "In the meantime, you have to deal with Stonecroft. Do what you have to to make up your mind and let him down gently. Lack of experience is not an excuse if you break his heart, Arabella. Trust me, you will only feel guilty later."

She reached for another book. If it was the last thing she did, she'd erase that patronizing, smug—

"Miss Swann?"

Hell! Lord Stonecroft loomed in the doorway, his uneasy frown ricocheting between her and St. Fell. "Do you require assistance?" He stepped into the room and settled his scowl on St. Fell.

St. Fell straightened his shoulders, but his smirk didn't falter. "Miss Swann is perfectly able to look after herself."

Lord Stonecroft turned back to her with a concerned expression. Arabella flushed. She wanted St. Fell dead, but she wanted to kill him herself. She shot St. Fell her most evil glare and then took a deep breath, unclenched her fingers, and dropped the book down on the library table. She pasted what she hoped was a pleasant smile on her face. "His Grace and I were having a discussion about literature." She glanced at the book. "Possibly more of a debate."

"She is a poor loser," St. Fell said.

Lord Stonecroft frowned at the books scattered all over the floor. "I do not think I should leave—"

"Oh, I am the one who is leaving," St. Fell said in a breezy tone. "I must go to the card room and see how Swann is faring."

He was leaving? Arabella stared dumbfounded as he walked past Lord Stonecroft and turned around to blow her a kiss behind the other man's back. She snatched up the book and lobbed it, but St. Fell didn't even flinch when it hit the doorframe an inch above his head. She dashed over to the door and clung to the doorframe as he strolled down the hallway to the staircase without a single backward glance, even though he knew perfectly well she was glaring at him.

Lord Stonecroft picked himself up off the floor, where he had thrown himself to avoid being brained by the book, and came to stand behind her. "I am terribly sorry, my dear. I know he is completely insensitive, but I had no idea he would actually do anything to offend you."

"He did nothing to offend me!" Absolutely nothing.

"Are you certain?" Lord Stonecroft's voice was gentle. "You seem quite overset."

She stormed back into the library and flung herself down on the window seat. She was overset! Alone in the library with St. Fell, and it was only so he could order her to get rid of his rival. It was beyond insulting. And as if telling her she had to get rid of Stonecroft wasn't enough, he had the nerve to deliver the man to her so she could get rid of him according to St. Fell's order, according to St. Fell's schedule.

Lord Stonecroft hovered in the doorway. "We should not be alone together. I will escort you back to the ballroom."

"No!" Arabella snapped. He jumped. Poor Lord Stonecroft was not St. Fell. She had to be more considerate of his sensibilities. She softened her tone of voice. "I mean, I am too overset to return to the ballroom right now. I need a few moments to compose myself." She wasn't going back down to the ballroom until she had thought of a way to make St. Fell sorry. To humble him, once and for all.

"Perhaps your chaperones will be back shortly?" he asked.

"I doubt it," she said. Her sister would never speak to her again, and it had not even got her kissed. Her self-pitying moan was interrupted by Lord Stonecroft asking if he would mind if he lowered some of the lights. She waved at him to go ahead. St. Fell had lit them all to create the least possible romantic atmosphere. So he would not be tempted to kiss her. So she would be five-and-twenty and have a birthday ball in London and not be kissed, and be pathetically green until she was ready to choose him, the patronizing, self-absorbed, selfish beast.

She watched Lord Stonecroft go around the room dousing the wall sconces. He was very tall and reached them easily, just as easily as St. Fell had. He was just as handsome and had lovely fine muscles visible under his evening jacket. He kept looking over at her with a concerned and caring expression. He didn't smirk, or sneer, or issue stupid orders as if he had any right to. Conversation with him was always completely straightforward and very pleasant. He thought she was wonderful. Why should she feel guilty if he was in love with her? Every heiress in London would be thrilled to be in her position.

Interfering St. Fell. It was completely unfair. And none of his business. It was his fault she was not satisfied with Lord Stonecroft. How could she be? Poor Stonecroft had to come after St. Fell had already clouded her head with thoughts of him. St. Fell didn't know what he was talking about when he insisted that she kept thinking about him when she was with Lord Stonecroft.

She shook herself. She was thinking of St. Fell right now, which was completely unfair to poor Lord Stonecroft. She wouldn't do it any longer. From now on, she would think only of Lord Stonecroft when she was with him. For all anyone knew, perhaps she would fall in love with him for real. Which would make certain knoweverything dukes very sorry.

Lord Stonecroft extinguished the last wall sconce. "That is better!" He dusted his hands with a satisfied look and returned to the window seat and sat down next to her. "I am surprised that the duke didn't think of it."

"The Duke of St. Fell is a cabbagehead."

Lord Stonecroft shook his head sadly. "I cannot believe he had you alone in a dark corner and did not kiss you."

She did have some pride after all. "A lady does not kiss a gentleman and tell." She pulled the shawl closer and tried to look mysterious.

"It is cold in here, is it not?" Lord Stonecroft quickly went to the door and closed it and sat back down. "It will be less drafty. Just in case you want to take off that blanket. One cannot see your fine dress. Did I mention it looks like a rose petal?"

"Yes, thank you." It was the best of the dress compliments she had received tonight. Of course, St. Fell hadn't mentioned it once. Except for the way his eyes darkened when she smoothed down the front. Hell. She smacked her head with the heel of her hand. She ought to have dropped something on the floor in front of him and bent down to pick it up.

"Perhaps you would like to take off that blanket?" Lord Stonecroft suggested.

"It is not a blanket, it—" Good heavens! Arabella snapped her mouth shut. Lord Stonecroft was smiling at her with the kind of heat in his expression that would cause Papa to produce the stick. She looked around the library more carefully. Now the only light was from the candles flickering on the library table and the writing desks in the corners. The window seat where she and Lord Stonecroft sat was dappled in romantic shadows.

Arabella smiled. Lord Stonecroft was a rake.

Lord Stonecroft was a handsome and charming rake. Any woman would be happy to kiss him. He had very nice lips, always curved in a sincere smile. If she kissed him, she would finally be doing something with Lord Stonecroft first, something she had not already done with St. Fell.

Lord Stonecroft stretched his arm along the back of the window seat behind her. His smile deepened and so did his voice. "A man and a woman, alone in a dark corner. It is a tragic waste of an opportunity for kissing."

"Exactly!" she said. He flinched. Hell. She had to remember not to startle him. "I mean," she said more demurely, "truly?" A quiver of excitement went through her. She was going to be kissed! But she schooled herself. First, she had to take suitable precautions. She might be green, but she wasn't a fool. And while she couldn't very well ask the poor man if he was in love with her without seeming to fish for an affirmative answer, she did not want him to presume she was ready to marry him. She wasn't ready to marry anyone yet.

She cleared her throat. "In your opinion, as a sophisticated man about town, if a young woman of a certain mature age, say five-and-twenty, finds herself alone with a gentleman, on her birthday, do you think that if she kissed him, they would be obliged to marry?"

He laughed. "Certainly not! Did the Duke of St. Fell imply you were obliged to marry him if you kissed?"

"He did, actually!" Of course, he had not actually kissed her.

Lord Stonecroft reached over and patted her hand. "I can see why you are overset, my dear," he said comfortingly. "I assure you, in these modern times, one kiss between a man and a woman is not enough to require an offer of marriage."

She looked carefully into his eyes. His expression was steady, but she did not want to take any chances. "So you are quite certain that if I kissed a gentleman it would not mean I was agreeing to marry him?"

"Absolutely. It would be conceited to think so. Of course, the Duke of St. Fell is completely concei—"

"I am not speaking of the Duke of St. Fell! I do not know why you keep bringing his name up. This has nothing to do with him."

"Of course not, my dear. We shall not mention his name again."

"All right, then." She took a deep breath and closed her eyes. Her pulse began racing. She was going to kiss!

A few seconds later, she opened her eyes. Lord Stonecroft was looking at her with the same earnest expression.

"Are you not going to kiss me?" she asked.

He blinked. "Me? I thought we were speaking of the Duke of St. Fell!"

"Of course we are not! I do not think of the Duke of St. Fell when I am with you! That would be rude and insensitive. Do you think I am insensitive?"

"Certainly not, my dear. You are very sensitive. Why one only has to look at your face during one of my poems to know how deeply moved you are by intellectual beauty." He reached into the pocket of his evening jacket. "In fact, I have taken the liberty of composing—"

"No poems!" Hell! It was completely ridiculous. Her sister was off getting kissed by that idiot Belcraven while she had two London rakes as suitors. The first was refusing to kiss her until he decided she was ready to choose him, of all things, and why should she choose him, when he was the one who needed to be transformed from a smug, arrogant, conceited know-everything into someone who loved her and was humbled by it. And now the second rake wanted to trot out one of his endless poems. As if hearing about nymph thrall would serve any purpose. Honestly, did the term *rake* actually meant skittish old maid? "I mean," she said, trying not to sound excessively sulky, "surely we are past the point of communicating with words?"

"But I hoped my poem would put you in the right frame of mind for our first kiss."

How much more in a right frame of mind did the man need her to be? "Why do we not save your poem for afterwards?" she said.

"Yes, I suppose we could do that. After all, I would have to relight one of the wall sconces." He placed the sheaf of papers back in his jacket pocket and looked deep into her eyes. "Are you truly ready to kiss me, Miss Swann?"

"Yes." Obviously.

He beamed and reached out and put his hands on her shoulders and slowly bent his head toward hers. Arabella's heart raced. She was going to be kissed! She closed her eyes and leaned toward him.

She jumped a little when his lips touched hers. She should have kept her eyes open until they were actually kissing. His lips were firmer than she had expected them to be. They were soft, but firm.

She was finally kissing! It was extremely exciting. A tingle went through her lips all the way to her fingers and stomach.

She opened her eyes. He had closed his. His face was very close to hers. She could see the hairs of his eyebrows. Actually, the hairs of his left eyebrow were quite unruly. Men did not likely groom their eyebrows. She could see why people closed their eyes whilst they were kissing. It was very unsettling being so close to another person's eyebrows.

Stonecroft's eyes fluttered. Arabella shut hers again. She didn't want him to catch her looking at him, because people kissed with their eyes closed, and only the greenest of girls would be staring. Although it was interesting, really, how their noses seemed to fit together, side by side. Where one's nose went had been one of the things she had worried about kissing, but clearly, it was a simple matter to put one's nose to the side in order to let one's mouth meet the gentleman's. She wondered whether people made a conscious decision to actually put their noses to one side or the other. It might very well be a measure of compatibility. Perhaps people had preferences for whether they placed their noses to the right or the left, like Papa and Mama had about their side of the bed in the room they had shared.

She didn't really want to think about Papa and Mama. She had to just think of Lord Stonecroft and kissing. After all, it was very thrilling, being so close to someone. Touching a gentleman for such long a time. It was a shame she hadn't looked at the clock on the mantel before they started kissing. She didn't have a watch, obviously, not in her ball dress. Stonecroft probably didn't have one either in his dress clothes. Some gentlemen wore watches and fobs with their evening clothes. Not St. Fell. Or Stonecroft. She was thinking of Stonecroft!

She wondered if she ought to do something with her hands. He had his hands on her shoulders, but hers were folded in her lap. She couldn't really raise them to clasp his shoulders, because his body was leaning toward her, and she couldn't lift her hands without knocking him. She didn't want to knock him. He seemed to be very preoccupied with the kissing.

She had never quite noticed how silent it was in the library. Particularly when there was a ball going on. In comparison, the lack of noise upstairs was deafening.

Hell! One of her nostrils was making a whistling sound. She knew it was her nostril because she made a little snort and the whistle was louder. It was very embarrassing, but Stonecroft didn't seem to notice, thank heavens. It would be completely humiliating to have the man one is kissing stop the kissing to ask one to blow one's nose. Although it would hardly be fair for him to complain about her nose whistling, not when he was having so much trouble breathing that he had to keep opening his mouth. A few times his tongue even touched her lips and she had not said anything.

Yes, now she knew that she ought to have blown her nose beforehand. She must remember to mention it to Diana. It was exactly the kind of wisdom an experienced older sister would impart.

In any event, kissing was very lovely. And she wasn't thinking of St. Fell in the least. She was concentrating on Stonecroft. All of her attention was on Stonecroft.

Lord Stonecroft lifted his head and looked at her with a proud expression.

"What did you think?" His voice was husky.

"It was very pleasant," she said warmly. And she had not been thinking about St. Fell at all!

"Pleasant?" He looked hurt.

"I mean wonderful!" she corrected. "Wonderfully pleasant!"

He blinked at her, and she saw the vein in his broad temple throb.

"Thank you very much." She clasped her hands together in an appreciative posture.

"My pleasure." He really did have a very fine baritone voice. He probably sang.

Then he bent his head toward hers again. Oh, for heaven's sake! He thought they were going to kiss again! She shot to her feet.

"I should really go back to the ball now," she said, looking down at him with what she hoped was a smile and not just bared teeth, because suddenly, for absolutely no reason, she found herself desperately wishing Lord Stonecroft would turn into a puff of smoke and disappear off the face of the earth.

His brow furrowed. "But now that we have kissed, I think we should discuss our feelings for each other."

"But I thought we agreed that a kiss did not commit us to marry!"

He stood up and reached for her hands. "Just because we have kissed does not mean we cannot marry."

Hell. She snatched her hands away and hid them behind her back. She had not thought of it from that perspective! She paced to the table. And even though she was green, she knew perfectly well one did not dash off after kissing if the other person wanted to discuss their feelings. It was completely insensitive.

He walked over to her. "You see, my dear Miss Swann, you are so sweet and innocent and the way you look at me makes me feel as though I owned the moon and the sun and the—"

"I am not very nice, you know! I have many opinions and I can be quite sarcastic."

"Oh, no, my dear Miss Swann. You are perfectly wonderful. I have heard the way the Duke of St. Fell speaks to you, and you must not let his complete lack of appreciation influence—"

"I curse!"

Lord Stonecroft chuckled. "I have never heard you say anything the least bit improper."

"I curse all the time." Hell, she was cursing now. She lowered her voice. "I think the word *hell*, my lord. Constantly." She tilted up her chin. "I may very well be thinking it right now."

He gave her a look of fond amusement. "I do not see that it is a problem, as long as you do not say it aloud. Not everyone is as understanding. It is a shame, really, because it is quite endearing, just as your other delightful habits of speech—"

"Your poem!"

He blinked at her.

"You promised me you would read me your poem!"

He brightened and reached into his pocket and extracted his sheaf of papers. Unfortunately, it looked like one of his shorter efforts, only ten or so pages. But still, it had to be good for at least fifteen minutes while she tried to think of a way to leave without hurting him. He was going to tell her he loved her. Arabella could see it in his earnest blue eyes and the way he squared his broad shoulders. He was going to tell her he loved her and then he was going to cry.

And he was going to cry even more when she told him she didn't love him in return.

He took a candle to light the wall sconce and Arabella

closed her eyes and prayed for an earthquake. Or an attack by a lion. She could pretend to swoon, but then he would catch her, and if he touched her again she would scream.

She smiled at him encouragingly when he had finished lighting the lamp. Thank heavens for nymph thrall.

He cleared his throat. "It is called, 'My Darling Arabella.'" He smiled shyly. "Thanks to you, I have found a new inspiration. You are my muse now, my dear Miss Swann."

Hell. Arabella blenched. There was nothing for it. She was going to have to bolt out of the library like a great insensitive idiot. She braced one slipper against the carpet and grasped each side of the skirt of her gown.

There was a loud knock on the library door.

"Arabella! Your Grace! We have returned!" Aunt Ophelia called out. "And we are coming in right—" Her voice was cut off by the sound of a scuffle.

"We are not opening the door right away!" the duchess called out. She must have won the scuffle. "We are counting to three, then we are opening the door!"

Arabella walked back to the window seat and sank back down in relief. The duchess was even better than a lion. She hated poor Stonecroft. She'd chase him out in no time.

Chapter 12

Aunt Ophelia wobbled in a woebegone circle around the library as though she expected to find St. Fell filed away on one of the bookshelves while the duchess raised her lorgnette and looked right through Lord Stonecroft.

"Where is St. Fell, Arabella?" she demanded.

"He has gone down to the card room to see Papa," Arabella answered.

The duchess nodded. "Even so, he should not have left you alone in the library."

Arabella gave Lord Stonecroft a helpless smile, which she hoped showed she would have liked to continue their heartfelt discussion, but unfortunately she had no control over her ridiculous chaperones. Which was true, at least the part about her chaperones.

"Would you like me to go find the duke?" Lord Stonecroft asked, and even though Aunt Ophelia immediately declared that would be most wonderful, his eyes stayed fixed on Arabella's, and it was clear he was asking her the question.

Arabella nodded and bent her head over her hands in her lap. Tears pricked her eyelids. Not everything about acquiring experience and making one's own decisions was pleasant. This most certainly was not. She had used an innocent rake for her own pleasure, and when he tried to declare his affections, she sent him away to fetch her another man. She was completely insensitive. She didn't look up until she heard his footsteps retreat down the hallway. She might very well be completely insensitive, but she certainly wasn't marrying Lord Stonecroft.

Aunt Ophelia dropped into the window seat next to her and patted her knee. "Now that he is gone, I want to hear everything that happened with you and the duke! It was very dark in the conservatory."

The duchess wedged herself on Arabella's other side. "About time he left! What the devil was he doing in here alone with you? St. Fell will have his head for it."

"I kissed him." Arabella wiped away the tear that rolled down her cheek.

"My stars, Arabella!" Aunt Ophelia pulled the handkerchief out of her sleeve and handed it over. "I never expected to see you cry over having kissed a man. I always thought you were quite looking forward to it."

"Panting," the duchess muttered.

Arabella dabbed at her eyes with the handkerchief. "But he is in love with me. St. Fell told me and I said I thought it was ridiculous, but in my heart, I knew perfectly well it might be true." She sniffled a little harder at the thought of the poem. "St. Fell was right and now I feel very guilty."

The duchess snorted. "You should feel guilty! Only a deaf, blind, and stupid woman would not know he is in love with you. Frankly, I have no idea why St. Fell insists you are clever. I am afraid you are one of those people who thinks they know everything."

Arabella wadded the handkerchief into a ball. Honestly. The old bat did not have the slightest feminine feeling.

"In any event, there is no reason to feel guilty, dearest." Aunt Ophelia squeezed Arabella's shoulder. "You have the rest of your life to make it up to him once you are married."

Married? Arabella felt the blood drain from her head. She looked at her aunt over the handkerchief. "I am not going to marry him," she croaked. Hell! Marry Stonecroft?

"Not marry him? After he has kissed you?" The duchess's shoulders twitched so wildly the lorgnette on its ribbon snapped in the air. "On behalf of all of the dukes and the duchesses of St. Fell, I have never been so insulted!"

The nerve! Arabella leapt to her feet and turned around to glare at her. The woman had seven sons who were rakes. "I do not see why I should be obliged to marry after one little kiss! St. Fell has kissed"—and more—"hundreds of women! It is completely unfair!"

"Yes, it is!" Aunt Ophelia jabbed the air with the index finger of her right hand and held her plumes steady with her left. "Women should be allowed to be rakes too!"

"What rubbish!" the duchess barked. "You were left alone with a notorious rake and you admit he kissed you. You are going to marry him. That is all there is to it!"

Aunt Ophelia's face crumpled. "The old bat is right! You will have to get married. Women cannot be rakes. Their fathers take away their dowries!" She snatched back her handkerchief from Arabella's hand and wept into the clean corner.

"This is completely ridiculous!" Arabella tried not to sound desperate. "You are both foxed!"

The duchess pushed back her turban. "We are not foxed—well, we are foxed, but that has nothing to do with it. You are the one who is being completely ridiculous." She tried to look down her nose at Arabella, which was impossible because she was sitting down. She was reduced to lifting her lorgnette and glowering. "St.

Fell has accommodated your every whim and you have done nothing but be impertinent and unfeeling in return. This is the last straw!" Her voice cracked, and she bent her head over her lorgnette. "I am glad you will not be marrying into our family. You are going to break my poor darling son's heart, you ungrateful, smug, selfish . . ." she trailed off in wheezing snuffles.

Good heavens! The duchess was crying? Arabella felt ill. She fell back onto the window seat. She hated London. She hated meeting stupid London gentlemen. They were all deadly dull or overwrought pests like Stonecroft or arrogant, lying, manipulative, smirking beasts like St. Fell. And now she was going to have to marry Stonecroft and not St. Fell.

She had ruined her life for one stupid kiss.

She buried her head in her hands and burst into tears.

"I do not believe you have the cheek to be crying!" The duchess's voice broke through her sobs. "You are the one refusing to marry St. Fell after you kissed him!"

"No." Arabella wiped her nose on the duchess's shawl which was still around her shoulders. "I am refusing to marry Lord Stonecroft, after I kissed him."

Aunt Ophelia peeped over the edge of her handkerchief. "You kissed Lord Stonecroft?" Her damp eyes glowed with admiration. "Was it as fine as kissing the duke?"

"I do not know." Arabella choked back a self-pitying sob. "I did not kiss St. Fell. But kissing Lord Stonecroft was quite pleasant."

"Oh." Aunt Ophelia sighed. "That is disappointing to hear."

Arabella snuffled into the shawl. Not nearly as disappointing as having to actually do it.

"We left you alone with St. Fell and you managed to

kiss that dolt Stonecroft?" The duchess didn't even bother saying *ninny*.

"I keep saying we ought not to leave them alone," Aunt Ophelia said. "But no one listens to me. I am merely the spinster who knows nothing."

"Do you think I have to marry Lord Stonecroft?" Arabella asked, her heart in her mouth.

"Good Lord, certainly not!" the duchess barked. "Your papa has snagged himself a duke. He is not going to give that up over one dull kiss with a baron." She stiffened. "Unless you want to trade St. Fell for him?"

Arabella's heart nearly stopped. "Good heavens! Of course not!"

Aunt Ophelia gave her a bewildered frown. "But, dearest, why did you kiss Lord Stonecroft if you want to marry the duke?"

Arabella didn't know where to begin. "It seemed like a sensible idea at the time," she offered. Of course, now it was obviously completely stupid. But still, she couldn't help but feel cheerful. She didn't have to marry Stonecroft! She could marry St. Fell.

She stood up and smoothed down her dress. She ought to get back to the dancing. And to St. Fell. And see if Diana was ever going to speak to her again.

"Does St. Fell know you kissed Stonecroft?" the duchess asked.

Good heavens! Arabella's heart sank. "Not unless Lord Stonecroft told him." She peered into the duchess's face. "You do not think Lord Stonecroft will mention it to him, do you?"

The duchess shook her head and her lips curled in a smirk worthy of the name of St. Fell. "Stonecroft looked utterly miserable when he left here. Men do not share tender moments of commiseration with each other about their failures with women."

Wonderful. Arabella's heart soared.

"However," the duchess continued, "men usually manage to convince themselves that their disasters were
actually conquests, so you should probably tell St. Fell
yourself, just in case. He is not the kind of man who likes
to not know everything."

Hell. Arabella dropped back down onto the window
seat. She hadn't thought of having to tell St. Fell. But
he probably wouldn't mind. "He is a rake," she said
hopefully.

"Men have different standards for themselves than
they do for women," Aunt Ophelia said. "Although, from
what we know of the duke, I do not think he would
mind. Overmuch." She dabbed at her nose with her
handkerchief. "Probably."

"Oh, St. Fell will not care!" the duchess declared.

"Truly?" Arabella's spirits rose.

"Well, I cannot vouch for it beyond any shade of a
doubt, of course. He is a man and you are the first woman
he has ever decided to marry. I am sure he would be very
sensitive . . ." she trailed off, then shook herself and
righted her turban. "No, I know my son. He will not mind.
He dotes on you. Just explain it to him nicely." She
reached over and peeled her shawl off Arabella's shoulders. "Cry and try to drop something on the floor, if you
think of it. Everything will be fine."

Arabella nodded. Of course, the duchess thought St.
Fell would kiss her every time they were alone, and he
never did. But she was probably right. He wouldn't
mind. Probably. It wasn't as if he hadn't done much
worse considerably more often. Except that ever since he
had met her, he hadn't looked at another woman. He
only hitched for her. Even this evening, when he had
come back after his afternoon of raking, she knew in her
heart he hadn't been unfaithful, and not just because he

had said so. It was in his eyes, in the way he teased her. He hadn't thought of anyone else since he had met her.

She tried to imagine how she would feel if he told her he had gone and kissed someone else tonight. Perhaps she wouldn't mind. She pressed her hands to her stomach. No, she wouldn't mind in the least. Right after she killed him. Of course, first she would need to shout and throw things and kick him.

And she might very well not want to marry him.

Hell.

The duchess and Aunt Ophelia patted her shoulders.

"I would very much like another brandy right now," Aunt Ophelia said.

The duchess sighed. "St. Fell made us take it away."

Arabella smothered a moan. St. Fell didn't leave the brandy in the library in case she was tempted to drink some and rashly kiss Lord Stonecroft. Just like he had lit all the lights and kept the room cold and draped his mother's shawl over her bosom. And he had told her he wouldn't kiss her because once they kissed they would have to be married.

She pulled off her gloves. Her hands were damp and shaking. There was a distinct possibility St. Fell was going to mind that she had kissed Lord Stonecroft. She didn't have the slightest fear he would strike her, but he might very well decide he didn't want to marry her, and once she told him, she could not take it back. She ought to think of a metaphor for it and tell him that way, and then if he objected, she could deny it had anything to do with her kissing Lord Stonecroft.

"What is taking so long up here?" St. Fell strode through the library doors. "You are missing all the fun about Belcraven and Diana."

St. Fell! Arabella's heart pounded so fiercely she thought it might leap from her chest. He was here, with his shoulders hitching, and his long legs and his lean hips and hard chest and huge hands and firm jaw and thick straight brown hair with golden lights glinting in the candlelight and laughing gray eyes and his smirk. His adorable smirk on his sensitive lips that she would never get to kiss if he no longer wanted to marry her.

"Good God." His jaw dropped. "What the devil is wrong?"

"Nothing is wrong, Your Grace!" Aunt Ophelia said brightly, but her bottom lip trembled even more than her plumes. She held her handkerchief up to her lips and unsuccessfully smothered her sob.

The duchess stood up and jutted out her chin. "Yes, really, St. Fell, nothing is wrong. There is no reason to be so judgmental!" She grabbed Aunt Ophelia's arm and pulled her to her feet. "We were just on our way to go get a nice glass of brandy."

Aunt Ophelia pulled her arm free. "I think we should stay! Arabella may need our supp—Ow!" She rubbed the small of her back. The duchess had lorgnetted her. "I suppose we could leave you alone for a short while." She smiled down at Arabella and scurried out of the room after the duchess.

St. Fell shot Arabella a quick look, then grabbed a candle from the table and lit the sconce next to the window seat. She watched his long fingers cup the flame as he held it to the lamp. He was hers. All of him, even the smirk. But for the first time since she had met him, she didn't know if she still had him. She didn't know for certain he would marry her if she just said the word.

He belonged to her, but she might have lost him.

She laced her fingers together on her lap and took a deep breath. She was being perfectly ridiculous. It was not such a great matter. It was just one kiss. With his rival. Perhaps she should not even mention it until after they were married. She imagined St. Fell coming to their wedding bed, casually mentioning he had kissed Elvira Coulter. No. Arabella squared her shoulders. She had to tell him right now and get it over with. After all, her fortune hadn't changed. No matter how shocked he was, he might still marry her for her money.

On the other hand, maybe she shouldn't tell him. There was no real reason to tell him. After all, it was not as if the kiss had mattered.

He put the candle back and returned to stand in front of her. There was enough light for her to see the concern in his eyes. "Are you going to tell me what happened?"

"Nothing happened!" Not really. Nothing of importance.

"Did something go wrong between you and Stonecroft?"

"Certainly not! Why? Did he say something?" Hell! She tried for a nonchalant smile but she could feel her lips quivering.

His lips twisted into a ghost of his smirk. "At least you can still curse. And no, Stonecroft didn't say anything. He is too busy sobbing."

"He cries eas—"

"Yes, I know! He cries easily. But my mother does not. Ever. And your aunt just voluntarily left us alone, and as for you . . ." He ran his hands through his hair as though the words failed him. He knelt down in front of her and looked up into her eyes. "As for you, Arabella, you look like you have lost the most precious thing in world—Good God!" His face turned as white as his cravat. "Forgive me, sweetheart, I am completely insensitive. I understand perfectly."

He did? Was her face so transparent? Arabella's confidence that everything would be easily resolved plummeted along with her stomach. St. Fell looked very serious. She felt the tears well up in her eyes.

"Don't cry, sweetheart, please." He pulled out his handkerchief and gently dabbed her cheeks. "It is not the end of the world, honestly. I don't care what my mother and your aunt told you. It is not such a big deal at all. I am only sorry the circumstances were such that you are overset by it. I promise you, you will not even think of it once we are married."

She had the oddest feeling the conversation had got away from her like a runaway carriage, but the look in his eyes was so sweet and so touching she was having a hard time thinking. And breathing, because he was on his knees before her and his fingers were stroking her face. But she had the firm impression she needed to actually tell him she had kissed Lord Stonecroft. She took another steadying breath. "Lord Stonecroft and—"

"You don't have to tell me anything, truly." He put his hands over hers, where they were folded in her lap. "The only thing I need to know is whether or not you want to marry him."

Arabella looked into his eyes and tried not to pant. Did he know his hands were covering hers in her lap and she wasn't wearing gloves?

"Well?" He smiled tenderly, his eyes never leaving hers.

She swallowed. His hands were so much larger than hers that she was completely enveloped in him and his arms were resting along the top of her thighs, and the sides of his fingers were actually pushing down on the silk of her dress on her lap, and she could feel the heat all the way through to her—

"Do you want to marry him?" he repeated.

"Who?" she asked.

"Stonecroft," he said.

For heaven's sake. She blinked at him. Why was he talking about Stonecroft?

"Do you want to marry Stonecroft?" His voice was insistent.

"No, of course not!"

"Do you want to marry me?"

"Yes!" Now.

He squeezed her hands a little more tightly and she moaned and leaned forward, but instead of kissing her, he rose to his feet and ran his hands through his hair again. She slumped back in the window seat.

"Then everything is fine," he said, heedless of the fact that she might very well be dissolving. "I will speak to your father. You and I will be married. I will kill that clod Stonecroft. I don't give a damn if he is a war hero—"

"No!" Good heavens! Poor Lord Stonecroft. "It is all my fault! He wanted to bring me back to the ballroom right away. I feel guilty enough as it is—"

"You have nothing to feel guilty about! I told you, there is no reason to make such a fuss about it. And furthermore, it is always the responsibility of the more experienced party. You are completely green, he is a rake. Even though he is obviously incompetent." He dropped down in the seat next to her and took her hand in his. "If it's anyone's fault, it's mine. I completely misjudged Stonecroft. I thought he was harmless and that you could easily handle him. I mean, I expected him to try for a kiss—"

"You did?" But if he thought she would kiss Lord Stonecroft, then what was he in such a state about? Good heavens! She ducked her head down as a blush burned all the way through her. He thought that she and Lord Stonecroft had gone beyond kissing. Far beyond kissing!

"Of course I thought he would try to kiss you." She

caught a glimpse of his shrug out of the corner of her eye. "I thought you might want to kiss someone besides me."

Why, the manipulative wretch! He had set her up with Stonecroft so she could kiss him if she wanted to. It was so typical of him, so presumptuous, as if he knew exactly the way her mind worked. Which happened to be true, but still. It was smug.

On the other hand, he had offered to marry her when he thought she had been with another man. Without the slightest hesitation, tenderly telling her it was of no importance. It was the sweetest, most romantic thing a man could possibly do.

The poor darling was head over heels in love with her.

He squeezed her fingers. "I never thought anything would happen that would cause you the least distress, or I never would have left you alone with him." He bent his head, and his lips brushed the back of her hand. "My dear, can you ever forgive me?"

"Of course," she whispered. She peeped up at him quickly, then lowered her eyes again. All that running his hands through his hair had made it fall down over his forehead, and his eyes were shadowed with concern. His expression was not the slightest bit smug, but all heart-felt tenderness. And suffering. He looked completely adorable.

"You haven't fallen asleep down there, have you, darling?" he asked.

The silkiness of his tone made her glance up sharply, but the expression on his face was still wide-eyed and sweet. He had no notion he had completely misunderstood the situation. She looked down again. It was almost a shame for her to pop her head up and declare it was all a misunderstanding. Not that she was going to let him believe it for very much longer, certainly not. But he was so deliciously vulnerable. She doubted he was going to be as tormented about her having kissed Stonecroft. In fact, he was going to gloat about it, since he had set it all up. The minute she told him, he was going to careen from touching concern to gloating. And the longer she waited, the greater the gloating. Never mind how overset he might be if he knew she had let the misunderstanding continue.

She suddenly felt a keen pang of longing for carriage-accident amnesia.

"You aren't going to swoon, are you, darling?" St. Fell asked.

"I am merely still a touch overcome." Arabella kept her head down. Perhaps if Aunt Ophelia and the duchess came back they could help her tell him. No. She swallowed. They never actually managed to help.

He sighed. "I do not blame you for being overset, darling. This changes everything."

"It does?" she squeaked. He had just finished telling her it didn't matter!

"Certainly," he said. "You see, I am afraid everyone will assume our firstborn is really Stonecroft's. So if it is not too late already, I think we should avoid consummating our marriage for the first year. We certainly do not want there to be any gossip."

"I beg your pardon?" A year? That seemed like an excessively long time.

He sighed. "Oh, you are right. One year is hardly going to make everything better. I suppose we must resign ourselves to having a completely loveless marriage. In any event, I do not know if I will be able to perform, knowing you are dreaming of Stonecroft the entire time."

She looked up at him.

Hell. He was smirking.

She snatched her hand back.

"You aren't going to try to curse your way out of it, are you?" he drawled. "Because I am thinking of charging your father an extra ten thousand for that little performance alone. It was worthy of a Minerva Press novel."

She snorted. "I didn't do anything! You were the one who jumped on the horse and rode it halfway to Scotland!"

"And I suppose the minute you realized my mistake, you rushed to tell me."

This was the kind of discussion that might benefit from the application of books. Arabella leapt to her feet.

He followed on her heels. "You basked in it," he said. "Your face is completely transparent."

She rounded on him. "If my face is so transparent, then you did not need me to tell you anything!"

"You are right. I should have known perfectly well you had not done anything except kiss the poor clod. You are not the slightest bit rumpled."

He was so smug! "Perhaps I took my dress off!"

"Perhaps? My goodness, Arabella! Was it so exciting that you have no clear recollection?"

Smug and snide! She planted her hands on her hips and glared up at him. "Do you know why I didn't tell you right away when I realized you had misunderstood? Because for once in your conceited existence, you actually looked like you didn't know everything! You were suffering!"

He shrugged in his best gloating manner. "Why the devil should I suffer? You are suffering enough for the both of us."

"You see? It is exactly that kind of arrogant comment that makes me not want to marry you. You are impossibly smug!"

"Of course I am smug. I am handsome and charming

and a duke and I walked into this house and you took one look at me and fell head over heels in love. How could I possibly not be smug?"

"And you grow more smug by the hour!" She lunged for the bookcase.

He stepped in front of her. "Because you keep proving you would do anything to have me."

"You take me completely for granted!"

"Certainly not. That is the significance of the smug look."

"You are blaming me for your smirk?" She goggled at him, the blood roaring in her ears. "You are so . . . so . . . so smug!"

"What on earth is going on in here?" The duchess appeared at the doorway, cradling a bottle of brandy to her chest.

Aunt Ophelia and her plumes stood quivering next to her, her worried gaze shifting from Arabella to St. Fell.

"We can hear you shouting all the way from the staircase!" the duchess said. She jabbed her bottle in St. Fell's direction. "It had better not be about the girl kissing that clod Stonecroft."

"Your Grace!" Aunt Ophelia squeaked. "What if Arabella had not told him?"

The duchess thrust out her chin. "Well, he knows now."

Aunt Ophelia blinked anxiously at St. Fell. "Arabella was quite overcome with remorse about it, Your Grace. I had hoped you would be understanding. After all, I am sure you have done much worse." She smiled hopefully. "Haven't you?"

"Just say you forgive her and kiss her and be quick about it." The duchess took a swig of her bottle. "Her father has nearly done with Belcraven and he will be hunting for you two next. I know it is a shock, since

Stonecroft is completely insignificant, but you will jus
have to get over it."

Arabella folded her arms across her chest. "He knew
perfectly well that I kissed Lord Stonecroft. He engineered
the whole thing."

"Oh." Aunt Ophelia's smile became fixed. She
reached for the duchess's bottle and took a long draw
before she passed the bottle back. "You know," she said
in a conversational tone, "I am quite foxed. Yet, I find i
is not helping."

St. Fell leaned against the library table and crossed hi
long legs at the ankles. "Yes, I can see why Arabella i
overset that I manipulated her into making sure she did
not spend the rest of our married life thinking she had
missed something." He shot Arabella an evil smile. "Tha
is so much worse than letting me believe that I arranged
for her deflowerment at the hands of my rival."

"Oh, my God!" The duchess slumped against the
doorframe.

"I always think it will get better, but it never does,"
Aunt Ophelia moaned. She and the duchess wrestled
over the bottle.

Arabella marched to the library table and planted herself in front of St. Fell. "Oh, he is just being a grea
cabbagehead because he is head over heels in love with
me. He is prepared to marry me even if it means making
Lord Stonecroft's by-blow the next Duke of St. Fell."

The duchess shrieked, and the bottle slipped from her
fingers and fell to the floor. Brandy gurgled over the
Aubusson carpet.

"Do not worry, Mother. I was lying," St. Fell said. "I
would have left her at the altar, forced to raise the world's
dullest brat alone in disgrace."

Aunt Ophelia burst into tears. "I cannot take any
more!" she sobbed. "You win, both of you! You are both

horrible! I am not living with you!" She grabbed the duchess's arm and dragged her toward the door.

"We cannot go!" The duchess clung to the doorframe. "Every time we leave them alone it gets worse!"

"Yes, but at least if we go we do not have to watch it!" Aunt Ophelia pried the duchess's hands loose and dragged her out the door. "I do not want to be a chaperone anymore," she wailed as they went down the hallway. "I want to be a companion to an old lady. Not you!"

"Well, that was pleasant." St. Fell smiled at Arabella as the sound of the women's footsteps grew fainter. Then his eyes darkened, and his smile faded, and Arabella didn't bother to try to hide the fact that she was panting. Because she wasn't the only one panting. He wanted her just as desperately as she wanted him, she knew it. Just as she knew that she would surely burst into flame the instant he touched her.

But he didn't touch her. Instead, he swayed backwards, away from her, and he kept his arms at his sides and clenched his hands into fists.

"Have you made up your mind?" he demanded, his voice a barely audible rasp.

She nodded.

The line of his jaw tightened. "Then tell me."

She tilted her head all the way back and looked into his face. "St. Fell?" she whispered. She waited until he met her gaze, the pleading light in his eyes making her burn even hotter. Then she took a deep breath and told him what she had been waiting to say ever since the first time she saw him.

"Hell," she said.

He jerked like a fish on a hook and his hands shot out and he wrenched her toward him, and finally, she was kissing the Duke of St. Fell.

Chapter 13

He was finally kissing Arabella Swann.

And so help him, it was better than he had ever imagined, and God knew he had spent a great deal of time imagining it. The taste of her, the feel of her, her moan when his hand cradled the nape of her neck and the way she shivered and pressed herself to him when their tongues met. It was better. Wherever he touched her she was hot, and soft, and wanting.

Wanting him.

"Damnation! What the devil do you think you are doing!" A walking stick slammed down on the table right next to his and Arabella's heads.

Damn. St. Fell looked up. Damn again. Swann, red-faced and glowering, held the other end of the stick.

He looked vexed.

"I just passed your mother and my sister on the staircase!" he shouted. "You couldn't have been alone for longer than one minute!"

St. Fell blinked down at Arabella. She was lying flat on her back beneath him on the library table. Her eyes were glazed, she was flushed pink all over, and, of course, she was panting. He felt a surge of elation. And pride. All that in one minute.

Swann rattled the stick. "And you left the blasted door open!"

The door. St. Fell frowned. He hadn't thought of the door. Not that it would have stopped Swann, but he should have known better. Next time, they'd close the door.

"Well?" Swann snarled. "Would you like me to give you both a few more minutes in private or would you rather I sold tickets!"

St. Fell sighed. Even though he was having a bit of difficulty thinking clearly, he knew that Swann was just quizzing about leaving them alone. "Sweetheart"—he bent his head to whisper in Arabella's ear—"you have to let go of my hair now."

She swallowed and nodded, but she didn't. He propped himself up and took a few moments to gently pry open her fingers, which was just as well, given that he would have to turn around and face her father. He stood up and helped her off the library table.

She clung to his arm and looked up at him with her big brandy eyes. "Make Papa go away," she whispered.

St. Fell glanced at Swann. He was swinging the stick like a pendulum on a clock that had run out of time. He wasn't going to go away until after they were married.

"I can make Papa go away for the rest of your life if you just give me a few moments alone with him," St. Fell whispered back at her. He started to lead her to the door, but she lunged for the stick.

"Don't worry, Arabella," Swann bellowed, "I will horse-whip him for you!"

St. Fell tried to pull the stick out of her hands.

Arabella slumped against the library door. She didn't care what St. Fell and Papa said, she couldn't possibly go upstairs and wait for them to send for her. In the first place, she needed to go back into the library and finish kissing St. Fell. And in the second place, there was something very wrong with her legs.

The library door opened, and St. Fell caught her before she fell into the room. She looked up at him hopefully, but he shook his head and smiled, even though there was nothing the least bit amusing about it.

He steered her back outside. "I know, sweetheart, I know. But you cannot linger at the door. The sound of your panting is oversetting your father."

She nodded up at him. "Do not vex Papa." He had explained that to her several times, when he wasn't letting her chase Papa away with the stick.

"Exactly." He kissed the tip of her nose and put his hands on her shoulders and spun her around toward the staircase. "If I can do it, so can you." He gave her a little push.

Then he ducked back into the library and closed the door again.

She sighed and started mournfully down the hallway, holding on to the wall with her hand to steady herself.

By the time she entered her bedchamber, she still wasn't sure exactly how she and St. Fell had ended up on the library table. She remembered the beginning quite clearly. He had held the back of her head steady with his hand while he opened her mouth with his tongue. After that, it was somewhat hazy. There was his tongue . . . and her tongue . . . and his hands . . . and her hands . . . and she might have tried to climb inside of him. All she knew was that whenever she thought of it, her heart pounded and she panted and her knees weakened and her entire body felt like it was on fire.

It was exactly the way she felt every time she saw him. Only more so.

She sank down on the end of her bed and stared at her door.

A considerable time later, there was a knock, and Diana entered. "Papa wants to see you in his study," she said brightly. "It is your turn to be shouted at."

Good heavens! She had forgotten all about how she and St. Fell had set Aunt Ophelia and the duchess on her sister and Belcraven. "I am so sorry!" she cried. "Are you very angry with me?" She had not even been there to hold Diana's hand during Papa's lambasting.

"We were at first. But when Papa was done he agreed we can have the banns read starting this Sunday. We do not have to wait for you." Diana grinned. "Although I see you have kissed St. Fell."

Arabella looked down at her dress. She was rumpled.

Diana opened the wardrobe. "And Henry thinks he is quite the rake too, now." She shot Arabella a smug look over her shoulder. "He has been strutting around the ballroom trying to look casual. It is really quite adorable."

Arabella gasped. "The ball! I completely forgot about it!"

"I am not surprised. The only reason you had the ball in the first place was so you could get St. Fell."

Arabella sighed. She was not only completely transparent, she was utterly ridiculous. "But what about all those people? I have caused a great scandal." She tried not to sound pleased.

Diana pulled the blue damask gown from the wardrobe. "Oh, we were not the only ones. The countesses caught Mr. Carr and Lady Nola in the music room, although they are being married in two weeks, so it hardly counts. Everyone found it very diverting, which I think is the standard for London *ton* parties." Diana straightened her back. "In any event, we will be a duchess and a countess, and both extremely wealthy so I do not see that we are obliged to give a fig one way or the other."

After her sister had helped her change, they both walked down to Papa's study and Arabella accepted Diana's offer to stay with her. Diana promised to signal when he was getting close to the end, so Arabella could time her tears for the appropriate moment.

Papa was sitting at his desk, scowling fiercely. He wasn't alone. Aunt Ophelia and the Duchess of St. Fell sat in the chairs opposite his desk, and Belcraven and Lord Toby occupied the sofa against the back wall.

Diana went to sit next to Belcraven on the sofa. Papa growled. They moved apart a few inches.

Arabella squared her shoulders and remained standing. It didn't seem very fair for her to be scolded in front of St. Fell's family, and Belcraven. Although she supposed they were her family now. But still. And St. Fell wasn't there.

Papa cleared his throat importantly. "Arabella, it has come to my attention that the duke wasn't the only man with whom you were in the library tonight. Apparently you and Lord Stonecroft may have had—"

"One little kiss!" she protested.

Papa shook his head. "I don't want to hear—"

"For heaven's sake, Papa! I mean an ordinary kiss. Not a St. Fell kiss, obviously. No tongues or—"

"Damnation!" His face turned Belcraven red. "I mean I don't want to hear the details! You're my daughter. In any event, it doesn't matter what you and Lord Stonecroft did—"

"Did not do," she said in the interest of accuracy.

He mopped his forehead and muttered something about the wonders of brandy before taking a deep breath and trying again in a firmer tone. "What matters is that there was a rumor spread at the ball—"

"We were foxed!" the duchess shouted.

"Oh, it is our fault anyway," Arabella reassured her and

Aunt Ophelia. "We were just trying to chase you out of the library."

"That is all right, dearest," Aunt Ophelia said. "We understand you were in a hurry to be rid of chaperones."

"No details!" Papa shouted.

"I just never thought you would tell Papa," Arabella said.

"We did not tell your father!" Aunt Ophelia's plumes quivered.

"Certainly not!" The duchess looked equally indignant.

There was a moment of silence during which the duchess and Aunt Ophelia each looked down at her lap.

Aunt Ophelia spoke first. "We told Lord Stonecroft."

"He told your father," the duchess said.

Lord Toby grinned. "Apparently my mother gave Stonecroft her opinion of a man who takes advantage of a green girl who has come to London to make a good marriage."

"With her lorgnette!" Aunt Ophelia added.

"I thought kissing was a metaphor," the duchess grumbled.

The poor man. "Perhaps I ought to see Lord Stonecroft and apologize to him myself, Papa." It was the right thing to do, even though she never wanted to see him again.

"You will have to speak to him one way or another, Arabella," Papa said. "Because of the rumor, Lord Stonecroft has offered for you."

"Hell!" Arabella said out loud. Nobody even bothered pretending to look surprised. After all, she was going to be a duchess. She could use it with impunity in front of others when St. Fell wasn't present. She smiled to herself. And perhaps, on special occasions, in front of others when he was present.

"Arabella!" Papa shouted. "Get that look off your face

and attend to the matter! Lord Stonecroft has offered for you!"

"So?" she said. "Hasn't St. Fell offered for me as well?" Ages ago.

"He has, but . . ." Papa trailed off in a way that caused a knot to form in the middle of her stomach. He took a deep breath. "Lord Stonecroft has offered to marry you without your fortune."

Good heavens!

Papa nodded, then folded his hands over his stomach and glowered down at them for a minute, then he looked up and sighed. "But the Duke of St. Fell says he'll only take you if the fortune comes with you."

He shrugged and stared down at his stomach again, as if he were afraid to look her in the eye.

Arabella's throat tightened.

"Now that is a decent test of faith," Diana said.

"He said he knew you would understand," Papa muttered. "Although personally I think he's an idiot."

"Dash it!" Belcraven shouted. "No helping."

She pressed her hands to her fluttering stomach. St. Fell only wanted her for her fortune? Lord Stonecroft truly loved her for herself?

As soon as the library door finally opened, St. Fell put down his pen and stood up. Arabella stepped in, carefully shut the door behind her, and walked over to the table without speaking. Her lips were thinned in a straight line, and she kept her eyes down so he couldn't see into them. She chose the chair the farthest away from his.

He smothered his grin when he realized what she was doing. She obviously wanted to have one of those Minerva Press moments where he was not supposed to know that she loved him until she told him. She was absolutely delicious.

She folded her hands on the table as if she were praying and looked at him steadily. "Before we begin, you must promise that you will stay in your chair until we are done talking."

He looked at her suspiciously. How much talking did she think they would be doing? All they had to do was say they loved each other. That would take fifteen seconds. "Actually, I do not have much I need to say."

"I do," she said firmly.

God.

She folded her arms and leaned back in her chair. "Promise you will stay seated, or I will fetch my aunt and your mother."

"Fine! I promise." Anything but the chaperones.

She flashed him his favorite smile, the little smug one that went all the way through him. He had the sudden realization that promising to sit like a good little boy in his chair was going to be more difficult than he had considered. But he had promised. She was entitled to choose the game. He sat back and tried to look suitably worried.

"I have just met with Lord Stonecroft," she began. "I told him that as admirable as he was, I admired money more, so I unfortunately could not possibly marry him."

St. Fell nodded.

"Of course, he thinks I am completely insensitive," she said.

St. Fell smothered his snicker in a cough.

Her lips twitched, but she managed to keep a straight face. "He thinks you are completely insensitive too," she said, "but that is hardly newsworthy."

St. Fell lowered his eyes and studied the table. He didn't want to laugh too early and ruin the performance.

"In any event," she continued, "he wishes us a very happy marriage, as much as possible, given that we are clearly incapable of any true delicacy of feeling."

St. Fell snorted. "That must be poetic license for go to the devil."

She didn't smile. Apparently it wasn't over with. He lowered his eyes again.

"I have broken his heart, but not nearly as badly as I would have if you had also offered to marry me without my dowry and I had picked you." She paused importantly. "So thank you for insisting that you would only take me if I came with my dowry."

He looked up. She was beaming at him. It was over. He grinned back and stood up. "I lov—"

"Sit down!" She banged her hand on the table.

"But it's over . . ." he trailed off at her scowl but remained on his feet. "Isn't it?"

"It most certainly is not over! There are a number of things I want to know." She gave him a warning look. "You promised!"

He sank back down in his chair and she nodded in satisfaction.

"So?" She leaned forward. She had changed dresses and the neckline on this one was pointless. "Were you worried I had come to tell you I was going to pick Stonecroft?"

"Certainly." He smiled back at her. "I had no idea what you were going to say. I was sitting here all aquiver that you might not choose me."

She laughed. "Liar!"

"No, truly." He patted his lap. "Come over here and I will prove it to you."

Her eyes sparkled, but she wagged her finger. "Not yet. We have matters to discuss and I find when I touch you my thinking becomes slightly addled."

"Slightly?" It damned well was not slightly. She was already starting to pant.

"Must you be so smug?" she asked.

"Yes." How could he not be? He could make her pant just by looking at her. He gave her his best suggestive smile.

She rolled her eyes, but her cheeks pinkened, and her hand went to her bosom to try to steady her breathing. The neckline on this dress was so high that her hand was touching fabric. "You didn't just think of it as a test, did you?" she asked. "To see if I loved you even if I thought you only wanted me for my fortune?"

"I have always had faith that you loved me, Arabella. Besides, now I will never know if you love me for myself, or for your fortune."

She gave a little gasp. "You are right!"

He shifted in his chair. Of course he was right. He was always right. But she shouldn't be making gasping noises at him if she wanted him to just sit and chat. And damn it, why did she have to change dresses? It was not nearly so pleasant to watch her little hand resting on damned fabric. Especially this fabric. It looked like a tablecloth. And it was not half as good for her either. Touching herself through the tablecloth had barely sped up her panting at all. Why was she wearing such an ugly dress? This was the kind of dress more suitable for visiting vicarages with broth than to make love declarations in the library at midnight. God only knows how you got the damned thing off too, it didn't have any buttons—

"Are you listening to me?"

He blinked at her. Her brows were lowered in a scowl and her lips were pursed. Her lips should be on his lips, not pursing at him across the table. What the devil was she thinking of?

"Can we not have this heartfelt discussion after we are married?" he asked.

"For heaven's sake, St. Fell! We are not going to be wasting our time talking after we are married!"

True. He shook himself, took a deep breath, and sat up straight in his chair. "I beg your pardon. Please continue."

"I was explaining that if I had to choose between having you and no dowry or Stonecroft and the dowry, that would be a true test of whether or not I loved you."

"Oh, you know it would not be. You would just choose me and find a way to get your hands on the money. Wait!" He narrowed his eyes. "Did you say that you loved me?"

"Of course I did! Were you not listening?"

Damn! He had missed it. "Of course I was listening. I would merely find it easier to hear what you are saying if you would just come over here." He patted his lap again and let his eyes rove over her body.

"Certainly not!" she squeaked. "I have given a great deal of thought to what I am going to say and you are going to sit there and listen." She sniffed indignantly. "Unless you are only interested in me for one reason?"

"Of course not. You know I love your fine mind." Just as much as her fine bosom. He gripped the edge of the table. "Please talk. I am fascinated by the talk."

She shot him an exasperated look. "You know perfectly well it is just as hard—difficult," she amended. He must have smirked. "—for me as it is for you."

He was struck by the memory of her chasing her father around the table with the stick. He grinned.

"Exactly," she said. "In any event, I still feel very guilty about poor Stonecroft. I used him terribly."

St. Fell snorted. "What kind of a dolt comes between two people so obviously head over heels in love with each other? The clod is completely conceited."

"I suppose you are right. If anyone knows about conceit, it is you."

He sighed. "More silver-tongued flattery from Miss Arabella Swann." She said she had loved him, and he had missed it.

She blinked at him. "You know, you are right! I do not think I have ever said anything nice to you aloud!"

"Do not worry yourself about it. I know perfectly well you appreciate me." He put his hands on the table and drummed his fingers. She stared at them and a fine pink flush crept up her cheeks. And she panted. Five more minutes of this talking gammon, and they'd be on the library table.

She swallowed. "Just how transparent am I?"

He leaned forward. "Do you know how obvious I am?"

Her cheeks turned pinker.

"You are more so," he said.

"That is impossible!"

He shrugged.

"Although I suppose it might be true." She sighed. "You missed the big scene in Papa's study where everyone gloated. Diana, of course. And Papa said he had told me so from the very beginning."

"Your father is not living with us," he reminded her. Not that it was necessary to insist. Not after the stick.

"Your mother said that just because men were idiots didn't mean a woman could not be a fool!" She quivered in outrage.

"Annoying." And completely predictable.

"Yes! Especially since she had already told me so the first day she met me. She wrote it down on a slip of paper and has been carrying it around with her just waiting for the occasion to say it again! She is not living with us!"

How much more talking could she possibly do?

"Oh! And I told your brother Toby to shut up."

He nodded encouragingly. It might speed matters up if he didn't speak.

She sniffed. "I think your brother and Belcraven actually made a wager on how long it would take me to choose you."

Which he had easily won because neither idiot had the brains to pick under a minute.

"And Aunt Ophelia cried and said it was just like *Love's Heartsick Longing,* except I was that cabbagehead Raphael!"

Good God! St. Fell shot upright in his chair. "That would make me that insipid Lady Delfinia!"

Arabella narrowed her eyes. "I thought you said you had not read it?"

"Have you?"

"No," she lied. She always looked down to the left when she lied. She was a terrible liar.

"Then I certainly have not read it either," he lied.

"You are a terrible liar," she said.

"We understand each other perfectly."

She nodded. "Anyway, sweet Lady Delfinia wasn't nearly as annoying as that dimwitted Raphael. He was a complete idiot. Refusing to kiss the ground Lady Delfinia walked on when it was obvious that she loved him. And that he loved her."

Was that as close as she was going to come to saying she loved him? He smiled. "But I can see how it all seemed very reasonable to him at the time. Because poor Raphael had absolutely no experience, you see, and—"

"You did see," she said, and her smile softened. "You made Papa let us go to the Carrs' party and then you managed to convince him to stay foxed while I was horrible to poor Stonecroft. Why didn't you just tell me?"

"Yes, I forgot how much you dearly love being manipulated."

"Perhaps you are somewhat of a better sport about it than I." She gave him the smug smile, and he swallowed his moan. Why the devil weren't they kissing?

"It is good that you do not mind being manipulated," she continued, her voice suddenly silky, "because I must warn you, I am planning a judicious program for the use of the word—" She thought the word *hell* and her eyes danced at the way he twitched in the chair although she hadn't said it aloud. He swallowed. He wouldn't put it past her to think about using it in public. God, she was perfect.

"After all," she said, "I would not want to cheapen its value."

"Arabella, darling, why are we still talking?" he croaked.

She gave him a knowing smile, and for a moment he thought she was going to relent, but she shook herself, and her expression became serious. "Actually, I do have one thing that I wanted to discuss with you. Something we might not want to discuss again." She paused as though she were choosing her words carefully. "It occurred to me that you did not leave all the lamps and candles blazing and the room cold and send away the brandy because you were afraid I would kiss Stonecroft. You expected me to kiss Stonecroft."

Damn.

She nodded. "I thought of the strangest theory while I was in my room waiting to be called down—" She stopped abruptly and scowled. "It took forever by the way! I thought you and Papa had agreed we were to be married ages ago!"

He shrugged. "Stonecroft."

"Oh. All right then." Her frown faded. "As I was saying, while I was waiting—forever—to be called down, the strangest theory occurred to me. I realized you were not actually overset that I had"—she looked down and her cheeks turned pink—"been," she said meaningfully, "with Lord Stonecroft. You thought it might be a possibility. You were not happy about it, that is why you made the room bright and gave me the shawl and made that comment about being a saint. But what you were actually upset about was that it seemed to be an unpleasant experience for me." She looked up at him. "Good heavens, St. Fell! You are blushing!"

"I most certainly am not!" He folded his arms across his chest. God, he was completely pathetic. His brains eaten for breakfast with a spoon by Miss Arabella Swann. He cleared his throat. "You didn't happen to mention your strange theory to your father, did you?" Damn, did he just squeak? Wonderful. She had reduced him to Belcraven.

"Certainly not!" she cried. "Papa would kill you!"

St. Fell nodded grimly. The day after she delivered their first son.

"I do not think Lord Stonecroft would be too pleased either," she said. "Given how ill-used he felt about the kiss."

Oh yes. Stonecroft would shoot him. And even if he didn't kill him, it would put a definite crimp in their marriage, because he had a fairly good idea where the clod would be aiming.

"The thing is, Arabella"—he was pleased to see that he had stopped squeaking—"this strange theory of yours would only make sense if I had the ridiculous notion that you would have liked to have been a rake."

She flushed. "Well yes, I think I might very well have liked to have been a rake." She shot him a smoldering look. "Except the part that involves men other than you."

He shifted miserably in his chair. "Have I mentioned that you are perfect?" he rasped.

"No! Am I?" She bit her bottom lip and then let it go slowly.

"No! You are completely insufferable!" He clutched his head. "Why in God's name are we still talking! What possible romantic thing do we have left to say? I love you, you love me. You wouldn't have believed me no matter what I said. You were too ridiculous—"

"Green!"

"Whatever! You refused to recognize the obvious! And I would merrily do anything to have you, including vex your father and every other man who stands in my way! Oh! And you had to realize whether or not you love me has nothing to do with whether or not I love you! And so on and so on and so forth!" He leaned forward in his chair, panting.

"Have you finished?" she asked.

"I damned well hope so! And I might add, it is extremely unjust to take a man into the library at midnight and jaw him to death. You are missing the point of this game."

"Is it really taking so long?" she purred, damn her. She purred!

"Good God, Arabella, you know perfectly well this is taking forever!"

"Really?" She gave him an evil smile. "Because I feel that it is taking less time than, say, a Drury Lane performance of *Richard III*."

Good God. He lay his head on the table and moaned.

"Did you actually forget my birthday?" she asked, in the conversational tone of a woman who had made a list. "Or were you just being horrid?"

He didn't bother lifting his head. "Of course I forgot."

"How could you possibly be so unromantic!"

Easily. "I promise I will hire someone to buy you a present on your birthday."

"But your mother wrote you!"

"Just because I am in love with you does not mean I am

going to start reading my mother's letters. Toby wrote me about Stonecroft, and that was the only thing that mattered." He looked up without lifting his head. "And I am not going to start writing rubbishy poetry or buy you flowers or perfume, either. You have too many damned opinions for anyone but yourself to keep track of."

She sniffed. "At least you remembered my favorite bonbon."

He looked up at her blankly.

"The apricot nougat! You ate it from Lord Stonecroft's box of bonbons."

"Of course." He nodded. "Apricot nougat." The only damned flavor of bonbon worth the bother of eating.

She flung her hands in the air. "Oh, don't say it, I can see it on your face. Honestly, you are hopeless! You could not be more unromantic!"

"It is a flaw in my character. Otherwise I would be insufferably perfect."

"Instead you are perfectly insufferable!"

He looked down his nose at her. "I believe I have already mentioned that you are perfectly insufferable." He sighed. "Can we not agree that it means we are perfectly suited and be done talking?"

"Isn't there anything else you would like to say?" she asked.

"Certainly not!" Except that he was not making stupid promises again to sit in a chair. And that Minerva Press romances were a blight on humanity.

She looked disappointed. "I thought you might have written a speech."

He pinched the bridge of his nose. "Of course I have not written a speech! I did not think we would be speaking. It is worse than being in Parliament!"

"If you do not have a speech for me, then what is

that?" She pointed at the sheet of paper on the table before him.

He ground his teeth. "I was counting hats for you. Since you seem to be so overset about it."

"Really?" Her eyes brightened. "How many?"

He shrugged. "Thirty-seven other women besides you." Give or take a couple of hundred.

"Thirty-seven!" She burst into laughter. "Good heavens! You are either the world's worst liar or the world's worst rake!"

Damn. "You aren't going to make a fuss about it, are you? Because there is nothing I can do about it. It is over."

"Oh, do not worry." She waved her hand dismissively. "I have decided that it is not your fault that it took me so long to get to London." She smiled grimly. "But no other women."

"Certainly not." He had understood that from the beginning.

"And no other men either," he added.

"Certainly not. It was boring enough kissing poor Lord Stonecroft."

So it had been boring. He had known it, of course. But it was nice to have her admit it.

"Stop gloating," she said. "Honestly, do you ever stop being smug?" Her voice softened to the purr again. "Although, I am noticing the oddest thing. The longer you stay in that chair, the more your smirk seems to be fading. Why do you think that is?" She leaned back in her chair and gave him the full doe-eyed look.

He gripped the arms of his chair. "I beg your pardon? I cannot hear you. Why do you not come here and tell me."

"Very amusing. I still have a number of things to say, so unless you want to waste the entire half hour that Papa has given us—"

"Half an hour?" The blood drained from his head. He leaped to his feet, grabbed his chair and ran to the library door. The promise of a game was one thing, but this was an emergency. "Why the devil didn't you tell me that right away? How long have we been talking?" He wedged the chair under the handle of the library door. "Ten minutes?"

"Twelve?" she offered hesitantly, her eyes wide.

"Better say fifteen, just to be on the safe side." He fetched another chair for the second door. His blasted soon to-be father-in-law. "I hate your papa, you know," he said over his shoulder as he tested the effectiveness of the barrier. Swann must have been one devil of a rake. "Trust me, this is the last fifteen minutes we're going to get until we say our vows. Three weeks to read the banns. We'll have to wait a month to be married."

"What?" she gasped.

He turned around. She was standing up, clutching her hands to her stomach, her eyes bright with tears and her lush little bottom lip quivering.

"But I thought we would just get a special license and be married tomorrow!" she wailed.

Well, that explained the mystery of all the talking. He hurried across the room and drew her into his arms. "We cannot marry by special license, sweetheart." He kissed the top of her head. "We will have to have our banns read. And probably wait a month after that, just to avoid any rumors of Stonecroft."

She collapsed into sobs and buried her face into his neckcloth. He ran his hands soothingly along the sweet curve of her back.

He took out his handkerchief and lifted her chin and dabbed at her wet cheeks. "You don't want to marry by special license, anyway," he said comfortingly. "Everyone would just think we had anticipated our wedding vows."

She shot a yearning look at the top of the table. "But I thought we were going to anticipate our wedding vows."

He snorted. "Our first time in seven minutes on the library table? I should think not, Arabella! This is not some Minerva Press romance! What the devil are you thinking of?"

She bristled. "Well, nothing, obviously, since I know nothing! Perhaps I should go ask Lord Stonecroft to educate my opinion."

"All right, you have made your point. I beg your pardon."

She inclined her head in gracious forgiveness. "There is another thing I—"

He goggled at her. "We are not done with the talking?"

"There are only the important things left," she said. She gave him a pleading look. He melted.

He took a step back and pinched the bridge of his nose. He could last. It would kill him, but he'd do it. "Go ahead," he ground out. "Talk."

"Is it always like this?" she asked. "The way it is between us?"

"No." He smiled. "You know that yourself, don't you?"

"Oh." Her lips curved in satisfaction. "That's true. I have experience." Her smile faded, and she looked up at him with an uncharacteristically hesitant expression. She glanced over at the sheet of paper on the table. "Has it been like this before, for you?"

He shook his head. "No, never." Never.

Her little smug smirk returned.

"You do know I love you, don't you?" he said. She belonged to him.

"From that first day in the north reception room?" she asked.

He nodded. "From the moment that I knew it was you."

She threw herself at him and sniffled into his neck-cloth again. "And who says that you are not romantic?" she cried.

"You do!"

She scrubbed the tears from her face with the back of her hand. "Well, I obviously know nothing!"

He sighed. Well, if they were going to be Minerva Press stupid, then why not finish the matter completely? It wasn't as if she didn't already know he was completely pathetic. He took her arms and held her so he could see into her bright brandy eyes. He cleared his throat. "I wonder if you would mind telling me that you love me again?"

Her eyes sparked. "I knew you were not listening!"

"I was listening—oh, all right, I wasn't listening. You can throw a book at me later to make up for it. Now say it."

She turned up her nose. "I don't know if I should say it. I think you shall have to persuade me that you would appreciate it if I did."

His jaw dropped. "My God, Arabella! We have been talking forever and I have been waiting since the very first day for you to admit—"

She pressed her finger against his lips. "Not that kind of persuasion." She blushed pink from the tip of her snub nose all the way down to where the tablecloth started. "I mean, I should like to be persuaded the way Belcraven persuades Diana."

Oh. St. Fell grinned down at her. Thank God. They were finally done with the talking. He wrapped his hands around her waist and lifted her up onto the table.

And he proceeded to persuade her.

A multiple number of times.

AUTHOR'S NOTE

In the late eighteenth century, William Lane set up a printing press in Leadenhall Street in London and began publishing Minerva Press novels, melodramatic tales of adventure and romance, written mostly by female authors. By the Regency, Minerva Press novels were wildly popular with a wide range of women readers, from middle-class mothers and daughters to fashionable aristocratic ladies and their hard-working maids, not to mention many men. Of course, Minerva Press novels were also abhorred as vulgar indulgences by a number of other people, none of whom would ever admit to reading one. Or a dozen. In fact, it has been noted that Minerva Press novels were much like romance novels of today in authorship, readership, and the way they are dismissed as inferior by those who don't read them. (But that's all right, because we don't want stupid people reading romance, right?)

Oh dear. Sorry. Anyway, I confess that I don't know if Minerva Press heroes got into carriage accidents and had amnesia. I do know that they swooned and cried. But I thought that no one would believe me if I wrote about romantic heroes crying, because we never see that nowadays. Well, all right, we see that all the time nowadays. But I thought it might be nice not to see it or write it for a change. Furthermore, any poking fun at a certain other monolithic producer of romances that is not my publisher may be on purpose. Because they're not my publisher, so there.

More Regency Romance
From Zebra